Praise for
The Mother Who Loved Halloween

"John Juettner has written a strong book that will keep you reading late into the night. *The Mother Who Loved Halloween* covered several genres not usually all mixed together as one."
– Trudy LoPreto – Readers' Favorite

"*The Mother Who Loved Halloween* is a quick, exciting and interesting page turner. It has a little bit of everything - murder, missing persons, inept police work, mystery, dark psychic forces, revenge, adventure, struggles between good and evil, and even fishing."
- Mark A. LaRose - Justinian Society of Lawyers Newsletter

The Mother Who Loved Halloween

A Novel

John Juettner

Cover designed by: Collin Koetz and Alyssa Low

www.johnjuettner.com

ISBN: 978-0-692-32595-7
e-ISBN: 978-1-483-52117-6

To Hannah,
Without you, I never would have finished this.

And to Professor Nicky Beer,
Without your class, I never would have started this.

Table of Contents

Part IV – Cheyenne, Wyoming

Epilogue – The Bait and Tackle Shop

"Let it be noted that ectoplasm proper is more than a secretion or extrusion of material: if genuine, it has powers of operating, it can exert force, and exhibit forms."

- Oliver Lodge -

Prologue
The Immediate Aftermath

October 31, 11:44 p.m.

Alicia Martin stood up from the kitchen chair she was seated in and walked over to the large, lower cabinet under her junk drawer. From it she pulled a bottle of vodka that was slightly over half full. Alicia did not drink much anymore, but tonight she needed it.

She poured the vodka into the largest glass she could find; a few cubes of ice had already been placed at the bottom. She set the bottle on her kitchen counter – it was now slightly more than a quarter full – and walked back to her chair.

This one glass might be enough, but the bottle would tempt her. Alicia sat back down in the same seat she was in when the officer had told her what happened. She looked straight ahead into nothingness, as if trying to stare into the past, and took a large gulp from the glass in front of her. It did not taste good. She choked it down and brought the glass to her lips again. This time she only took a sip.

The following morning would be a nightmare. She would have to go down to the police station and seek out that officer.

What was his name?

Wallace? No. No. Wynner? No, that wasn't it either. Wait...Warner. It was Warner.

She had to find Officer Warner. He seemed so calm and caring when he broke the news to her, even if he unsettled her at first. In hindsight, it was probably just her nerves and his nerves reacting to one another, like some kind of cosmic magnet where the negative ends were being forced together.

She took another sip of the drink in front of her, and began to think of Josh.

Part I
The Chase is On

November 1, 6:23 a.m.

Tears were still falling from Alicia Martin's eyes when she heard movement from the hallway where her children's rooms were. Alicia did not sleep in her bed the previous night. She only dozed at the kitchen table in a few half-hour spurts. Her hair was out of place. Her eyes were bleary, and bloodshot, and heavy as all hell. She was not sure if she could explain what had happened the night before to the child walking down the hall – whichever one it was. She tried to gather herself, and, for the first time in seven hours, moved from the chair she was sitting in. The muscles in her back ached, and her legs were no better. Alicia ignored these feelings to the best of her ability.

She heard footsteps now, growing ever closer down the hardwood-floored hallway. *Who would it be?*

Angel walked around the corner and into the kitchen – her darling Angel. She was five years old, the youngest of Alicia's four children.

Alicia broke down again when she saw Angel walk into the kitchen. She walked over, bent down and gave her daughter the biggest hug she could. Tears rolled down Alicia's face.

Angel knew something was not right. She may have been young, but she was already keen to the emotions of others. She knew tears were bad.

"Mommy? What is wrong with you?"

"Nothing, baby. I'm just so happy to see you this morning."

8:12 a.m.

Alicia walked through the Vanguard police station doors. They were made of mostly glass, and had a brown trim. Inside the glass, wire intersected itself several times in an X pattern to prevent someone from getting inside if the glass was broken. Alicia did not notice these details as she passed through the doors. Her mind was focused on Josh. Once inside, Alicia looked in every direction, and was stunned by the calmness that surrounded her. These people caught criminals for a living, and they seemed completely relaxed. To them, it was just another day.

"Excuse me," Alicia said to an officer as he passed by. "I'm looking for Officer Warner."

"Oh, sure," the officer said. "Follow this hallway and you will hit a big open room on your left. That is where most of the other officers have their desks. Warner's desk is in there somewhere, just ask someone and they'll point him out to you."

Alicia followed the nameless officer's directions and arrived at a large room filled with desks that faced each other. She stopped the first person she saw.

"I'm looking for Officer Warner, do you know where his desk is?"

"Oh, I know Jim Warner," the man said. He was wearing a suit and tie instead of a uniform. "I'll show you to his desk. What do you need Jim for?"

Alicia thought it best to talk with Officer Warner before telling anyone else why she was at the station.

"He delivered some news to me last night and told me to come by this morning to finish up with it."

Alicia was trying to remain calm, although she was not sure if her tone was giving away the panic she felt. She exhaled deeply in an attempt to bolster her composure.

"My name is Jack Fuller," the man said to her. "I'm a detective here. I've known Jim for a little while now. Good guy."

Fuller thought something was amuck. This woman seemed a

little panicked. And she had a look of despair deep in her eyes; there was sadness in there. Nothing but sadness. Fuller had learned over the years that the eyes usually betrayed the act. Only the truly gifted could bury their emotions so far below the surface they could not be detected.

"Here we are," Fuller said as they approached Officer Warner from behind.

Alicia thought the man in the chair looked shorter and stockier than the man who came to her house last night. When Officer Warner turned around, Alicia's suspicion became reality. Confusion rushed over her like a cold shower.

"Jim," Fuller said, "this woman is looking for you."

Officer Warner and Alicia stared into each other's eyes for longer than Fuller thought they should have. There was no recognition on either side.

"You're not Officer Warner," Alicia said nervously.

"Um…yes I am, ma'am."

"You came to my house last night?" Alicia asked.

"No, I was home by six-fifteen and did not go anywhere," Warner said slowly while glancing at Fuller. "Those trick-or-treaters kept ringing the bell."

Horror came over Alicia. She felt her legs start to bend against her will. Alicia did not fall all the way to the ground. Her butt was able to catch enough of a chair that was next to Officer Warner's desk to prevent that. Fuller stepped beside her.

"What's going on?" Fuller said.

Alicia's head dropped into her hands, much like it had the night before when a man came to her house, a man who apparently was not Officer Jim Warner of the Vanguard Police Department.

"Is there another Officer Warner at this police station?" she mumbled.

"No, there is not. Just Jim Warner," Fuller said.

Alicia began to cry harder than she had last night. Her body shook with each sob, and she wheezed as she gasped for air in an attempt to control herself.

Suddenly, Alicia lashed out.

"Is this some kind of joke?" she yelled to Fuller as she lifted her head up and shot out of the seat. She was like a cobra snapping at its prey. "Is somebody screwing with me? Trick-or-treat? Is this a damn trick?"

"Whoa," Officer Warner said. "What's going on ma'am? I don't understand."

Fuller was intrigued instead of startled. A dark curiosity had grabbed him. He felt something physically pulling at him. He could not turn away, and it was as though his emotions had been turned off by the flip of some unseen switch. He stood there, feeling numb inside, as Alicia sat down in the chair again. He wanted to feel empathy, but he could not.

Alicia took a few short breaths to gather herself.

"A man came to my house last night," she said. "A man wearing a police officer's uniform. He said he was Officer Warner; the nametag on his uniform said Warner." Alicia's speech was slow and deliberate, but her voice was quivering. Officer Warner and Detective Fuller looked at each other. They knew that with any kind of provocation she would lose control again.

"This man, he…," she broke off for a moment. Alicia was trying to hold back her tears and control her emotions. "He told me my son was dead. He told me my son, Josh, had been murdered last night and that they found the body."

Detective Fuller and Officer Warner looked at each other again. Officer Warner's mouth was agape.

"This man said I could come down here this morning because of how shocking it was last night," Alicia continued. "I was crying. I was upset. I didn't want to leave my house. Plus it was late and my kids were asleep. They only have me to take care of them. I'm a single mother, and the kids are young. I know it probably seems foolish to you for me to stay at home last night, but he was so convincing. So here I am. And you are not the man who came to my house."

She was looking at Warner as she said this.

"So where is my son?"

Tears were streaming down Alicia's face now. Detective Fuller and Officer Warner each grabbed a chair and sat near Alicia. The trio formed a triangle next to Officer Warner's desk.

"What time was this at, ma'am?" Fuller asked.

"I don't know for sure, after eleven."

"What is your name?" Officer Warner asked.

"I'm Alicia Martin. My son is Josh Martin. Do you think he is dead? Do you think he really is dead?"

Fuller had been thinking about that question since she mentioned what happened. Finding the answer would require time and effort from many at the Vanguard Police Department. Maybe her boy was still alive. Maybe.

"Alicia, we need you to call your son's cell phone," Fuller said. "Call his friends' cell phones. Call their houses. Call anyone who could have seen him last night. We need to track him down."

Fuller was being cautious with his words. Hope is powerful. He did not want to raise Alicia's hopes of her son being alive too high, but he did not want to crush them either. The police needed her help, and a glimmer of hope – just the right dosage – would be a great asset.

8:50 a.m.

Alicia sat at Officer Jim Warner's desk with her cell phone in hand. She had been dialing every name in her contacts list. Old friends, relatives, neighbors, anyone.

Find Josh.

She kept dialing, and her voice became shakier with each call. She was on the merry-go-round from hell, and there was no jumping off.

"Hi, Jamie, it's Alicia. Have you by any chance heard from Josh?"

5

Alicia could barely say her son's name without breaking down. She was holding herself together by a thread of hope.

"No, Alicia, I haven't heard from Josh. Is something wrong?"

Holding back her emotions in the moments when her friends explained they had not heard from Josh took great effort. Somehow Alicia did it. Her emotions remained buried beneath her demeanor.

"Maybe," Alicia said with a slight quiver, a little hoarseness, no air in her lungs. "I don't know. I haven't heard from him. I'm starting to panic."

Her conversations were becoming a blur; one seemed to merge with the next. She could not remember whom she had called and who remained. And with each call, her heart sank a little farther. Josh was slowly disappearing.

The thread of hope holding her together was beginning to fray.

9:20 a.m.

There were a few spots in the police station to get coffee. Two pots lived in the area of desks that beat cops like Jim Warner called home. This area was termed the bullpen, and the coffee brewed by the bullpen coffee makers was usually stronger than Detective Jack Fuller liked. He preferred the coffee that was brewed in the kitchen. Fuller never knew what made the difference, he seldom made a pot himself, but the coffee from the kitchen always tasted better to him.

Fuller walked back to Warner's desk with a cup of coffee from the kitchen in hand, and found Alicia with her head smashed between her folded arms on top of the desk. It did not look like a comfortable way to sit, like she was hurting herself. Her phone was on the desk next to her. She was quietly sobbing. Officer Warner was sitting next to Alicia with his hand on her back in an attempt to console her. He looked lost. Warner glanced over his shoulder and saw Detective Fuller approaching. An expression of relief passed over the officer's face.

Fuller walked over to Alicia calmly. "Ms. Martin?" he said while placing his hand where Jim Warner's hand just resided.

"He's gone," she mumbled into her arms. It was far too muffled to be heard.

"What did you say, Ms. Martin?"

Alicia picked her head up and stood up from her seat. She stared into Fuller's eyes, and screamed, "My son is gone!" at maximum volume.

The room went silent. Everyone looked at the trio. Fuller put his arms around Alicia. She accepted the hug, burrowing her head into his shoulder. There was no animosity in her voice when she yelled. It was frustration. Fuller waited two full minutes before saying anything.

"Ms. Martin," Fuller said. "I need you to sit down. I have to ask you some questions."

Alicia complied with Fuller's request, taking the seat nearest to him.

"How do you know that your son is gone?"

"Nobody has heard from him. Nobody saw him since he left Tommy Basil's house yesterday."

"That isn't the end of it," Fuller said. "Josh could still be…"

"That bastard killed him. That bastard who came to my house killed him. I know it. I can feel it. He did it, or he helped or something, but my son is gone."

"Ms. Martin, calm down, I can't imagine what you are going through right now. Mentally, it just has to be…"

"A wreck. A goddamn wreck," she said, completing Fuller's sentence. With that the tears really began to fall. Fuller reached across the desk and touched Alicia's left hand. To Alicia, the hug he had given her felt empty, like it was done out of duty. Now, feeling his hand on hers was able to calm her down a bit. She began to

7

breathe normally again. Her hand was twitching slightly under Fuller's, but with each passing moment, he could feel her gaining control.

"Now, Ms. Martin," Fuller said. "What can you tell me about Josh?"

*   *   *   *   *

He woke. The alarm clock was buzzing. It seemed like the clock was calling from a distant realm, and that it had been echoing in his room for a while before the sound roused him. That would make sense. He did not sleep well last night. Nightmares with dark imagery kept destroying his sleep cycle.

He stumbled out of his bedroom and toward the bathroom. As he did, the large hockey bag in the living room caught his eye. He noticed his equipment was strewn about, but the bag still appeared to be full. He pondered what to do about the mess as he removed his sweatpants and entered the shower.

*   *   *   *   *

"Josh is a typical teenager," Alicia said, beginning to calm a bit. "He has a core group of friends and the girls are starting to catch his eye. He's fifteen, about five-foot-eight, and a hundred and thirty pounds. He has brown hair and brown eyes. He's a good older brother. He's into sports, but not very athletic. He tries hard, though."

"What about scars? Something we can use to identify him further?" Fuller said.

"No scars on his face or arms. He has light freckles. On his left cheek there is a mole. I have a picture of him with me in my purse."

Fuller was taking notes of her description. He stopped to take the picture from Alicia.

8

"Can we keep this?" Fuller asked. "And do you have any more we can use? We've got to get Josh's face out there. I'm hesitant to use the media at this point, and I'm not sure if you want that kind of attention during this difficult time, but our officers need to see Josh."

Alicia nodded. She was hesitant about the media too.

"You can have that picture, and if you need more, I can give you more."

"Thank you," Fuller said. "Now, we've called our sketch artist. He's coming in from Boston as we speak because we don't have one here in Vanguard. When he gets here, which is hopefully soon, you're going to describe the man who came to your house."

Alicia nodded. She did not want to think about those moments in her kitchen just before midnight. It was the lowest she had ever felt.

"So try to remember every little detail you can," Fuller said while sliding a notepad in front of Alicia and handing her a pen. "Write the details down, sketch his face, whatever you need to do."

The face of "Not Officer Warner" came into view in Alicia's mind. She began to jot details on the notepad Detective Fuller gave her.

"We're going to find him," Fuller said.

"My son? Or this man?" Alicia asked.

"Both. We're going to find them both."

10:15 a.m.

"He had a square jaw and short hair. A buzz cut, it looked like. He didn't take his hat off so I can't really be sure, but it was pretty short on the sides," Alicia Martin said to the sketch artist. "His hair looked sandy blonde. I can't remember his eye color; they were dull. Maybe they were blue or gray. He was pretty young – younger than thirty, I would guess. No freckles or marks on his face that I can remember. He was fit. I'd say six-feet even and maybe one hundred seventy pounds."

Robert Coughlin, the sketch artist from Boston, was drawing Alicia's description of "Not Officer Warner," also known as the man who came to her house on Halloween night to inform her that her son was dead.

"What about his ears?" Coughlin said. "Big? Small?"

Alicia considered this for a moment. She had not noticed anything extraordinary about the man's ears.

"I'd say regular," Alicia said tentatively. "I don't remember his ears. That probably means they weren't overly small or overly big, right?"

Coughlin nodded as he sketched, "Probably," he said. "His nose?"

Again, Alicia considered it. There were so many details to a face. It was incredible what she realized she had missed now that she was forced to think about it.

"It was rounded, not pointy, and it turned up a little bit at the end."

Coughlin put some final details on the sketch and turned his paper to show Alicia. When she saw it, she recognized it as the man who came to her house, but something was missing. She could not pinpoint what was off.

"That's the man, more or less," Alicia said. "It's the best I can remember."

Detective Fuller, who was quietly standing behind Coughlin and looking over the sketch artist's shoulder during Alicia's description, took the sketch in his hands to get a better look.

"Are you sure this is the best you can offer?" Fuller asked Alicia.

"Yes, Detective. I am sure."

Fuller nodded.

"Alright," he said. "I'm going to go talk to McAvoy."

Ronald McAvoy was the Captain at the Vanguard Police Department – the highest-ranking officer at the station. Fuller felt he had enough information to bring McAvoy up to speed on the case, and perhaps enough details for an AMBER alert, which would be ultimately McAvoy's decision.

Detective Fuller rapped his knuckles on the doorframe of McAvoy's office.

"Hey, Ronald," Fuller said as he did so. "Do you have a second?"

McAvoy wanted to be called Ronald. He hated being called Ron or Ronnie when he was a kid. His mother had always called him Ronald, and he loved that.

"Sure, Jack," McAvoy said. "Come on in."

McAvoy had a large office with very little clutter. He always had three pens and two pencils in the coffee cup that read, "Daddy's the Best" on his desk. There was a legal pad in the middle of the desk, and his files were neatly tucked away in their appropriate places in the file cabinets that sat along the office's far wall. These things were the constants of Ronald McAvoy's office.

Fuller elected to stand instead of taking one of the open chairs in front of the Captain's desk as he brought McAvoy up to speed on what Alicia Martin had told him and Warner.

"I see," McAvoy said when Fuller was done. "And the sketch? How does that look?"

Fuller handed over Coughlin's drawing for McAvoy to study. Fuller knew what his boss would think of the sketch.

"Looks a little generic, don't you think?" McAvoy said.

"We didn't catch many breaks there," Fuller said. "Facial hair, a scar, something like that would have helped. She said it was the best she could do."

McAvoy nodded while still looking at the sketch. He handed it back to Fuller and took a sip of his coffee. The cup he was using had a picture of his wife and two children on it. "We love you, Daddy" was printed beneath the picture. McAvoy liked to rotate the drinking cup and the pen-holding cup every so often. The rotation was probably on some kind of schedule only known to McAvoy, but Detective Fuller would notice when one was serving as the pen and pencil holder and the other was being used as a vessel to bring the department's above-average coffee to McAvoy's lips. Maybe next time Fuller would track the amount of days in between rotations for amusement. It would come in handy as a conversation starter the next time Fuller was at the bar with other members of the Vanguard PD.

"What about his vehicle? Do we have any description on that?" McAvoy asked.

"No, sir. She did not get a look at his car. It was nearly midnight, and very dark as a result," Detective Fuller said. "Do you think it is enough for an AMBER alert?"

McAvoy folded his hands and brought them to his lips in thought.

"No," McAvoy said. "I don't. We just don't have enough of a description to warrant sending out an alert. I don't think it would help us."

Fuller hoped McAvoy would approve sending out an alert despite knowing the information was spotty at best.

"It's right on the line," Fuller said. "If we had the car, I think we could do it."

"I agree," McAvoy said. "But we just don't have enough, Jack. I'm sorry. Do you want me to inform the mother?"

"No," Fuller said without hesitation. "I'll let her know."

2:51 p.m.

Alicia Martin sat in her living room. She had been in the kitchen for enough hours over the last day to become tired of it. The walls in there looked dreary, and the sight of the table made her want to cry. She made a promise not to cry again on this day, and to this point she had kept her vow. No more tears.

The room around her was quiet. The children were in their

rooms. As she sat on her couch a sparkling blue stream appeared before Alicia's eyes, replacing the floor of her living room. She walked toward the stream and dipped her toes in the water, even though her body remained seated on the couch. The water felt good. Peace rolled over Alicia's body.

A raft made of bamboo slowly drifted by. Alicia extended her left leg and stopped it with her foot. She climbed aboard, and sat on the raft cross-legged as the raft gently made its way down the stream. Alicia could see images from her life – her memories – appear on the stream's surface. The memories stretched for miles, much farther than she could see. Alicia wanted to let everything in. She thought it could only make her feel better.

As the stream weaved around a bend, Alicia spotted the lake house of the Bosher family on shore. Brittany Bosher was a friend of Alicia's from high school and Alicia would find a way to get to her lake house once every summer. Brittany had a son named Robert who was only a year younger than Josh. As she drew near the Bosher family home, Alicia saw Josh and Robert running along the shoreline, chasing after the raft. They appeared to be waving at her. Alicia called out for Josh. He did not respond. He only continued to wave.

The current of the stream picked up a bit beneath Alicia's raft. She instinctively looked forward down the stream to see if any danger was lurking. There was none that she could see. When she turned her attention back to the shore, Josh and Robert had vanished.

Alicia looked up at the ceiling in her living room, but instead of drywall she saw a darkening sky. The raft veered to the left at a point where the stream forked. The room darkened further for Alicia. She saw an image of when she was only five years old. It was a memory she did not like visiting, and one she was not sure she still had with her until this moment. She assumed this stream would not lead anywhere dark or sinister. Quickly she was realized this was not the case.

The image Alicia saw was of her standing near the pool of

her childhood neighbors. It rose up from the stream and hovered in front of her as the raft continued to gain speed. Alicia saw herself fall into the pool as she was chasing one of her childhood neighbors around the pool deck. When she tumbled into the pool, for some reason Alicia did not swim to the top, instead sinking to the bottom. She sat there, eyes wide, staring at the sun and its distorted reflection from the water. Alicia remembered feeling a slight burning in her lungs and the sun becoming brighter with each passing moment. At the time she had no idea what was happening, but now Alicia realized that she was dying. The air was slowly leaving her lungs. While drifting on the raft the image floating in front of her had switched to her own view from that day. She saw the distorted light again, and felt the burning in her lungs.

Alicia could not help but wonder if that was the same feeling Josh experienced when he died. The tears began to flow again. She could not keep her vow. She felt like she was wrapped in a blanket of darkness, and the room continued to grow dark around her. For the next hour she sat frozen on the couch as the room around her transformed from a lovely stream to a raging rapids, and then to a vast, dark ocean of nightmares. It was all of her worst memories and worst fears at once, and yet she could not stop the images from appearing before her. She could not even move. At one point, Angel came into the room to sit with her mom. Alicia did not even realize the child was there. Her gaze was transfixed straight ahead at the empty fireplace. The tears would not stop. Her soul was in agony.

2

November 2, 1:15 a.m.

There were no lights on in Detective Jack Fuller's apartment when he opened the door. He had gone out to the bar after work and was now returning. A taxi had dropped him off. Having ridden to the bar with a few other policemen, Fuller's car was still at the police station. He missed the light switch by his front door as he stumbled toward the kitchen. Fuller pulled a bag of pretzels from a cabinet and a beer from the fridge. The light from the fridge allowed him to see clearly for a brief moment. With the fridge door closed, he turned around to find his apartment in complete darkness once again. As he began to walk through the living room toward his bedroom, his left shin collided with his coffee table. He fell; the bottle of beer shattered on his hardwood floor.

None of the pain registered. He was too drunk for that. He also had no motivation to get up. Fuller slept on the floor with a puddle of beer inching its way toward his torso. He did not dream that night. It would be the last time he slept soundly for the next year.

9:35 a.m.

The previous afternoon and evening were quite strange for Alicia Martin. She had not felt like herself. As much as she tried to shake the thoughts of her worst memories and deepest fears, she could not do it. Eventually she pushed herself to a point where she could get off the couch and take care of her children. This seemingly simple task came with much effort.

Currently, she lay awake in her bed. She had dreamed of Josh the night before, and had woke feeling the same dark despair she had felt the previous day. Alicia considered calling her mother to tell her what happened to Josh, but something inside told her it was not a good idea. In time, perhaps, but not now.

10:15 a.m.

When Fuller opened his eyes he had no idea where he was. Immediately he felt pain in his head and queasiness in his stomach. He pressed his hands to the floor, and pushed himself to his knees, realizing only then that he was in his apartment. That was the good part. The bad part was, in addition to feeling awful, his midsection was soaking wet. He saw the shattered bottle to his right sitting in a waning puddle of beer.

"Jesus, Jack," he said aloud.

He fought his way to the nearby couch, removed his beer-soaked shirt, and stared at the ceiling for a few minutes as he gathered his thoughts. Flashes of memories from the previous night passed through his head. He remembered being out with some of the guys from work, and apparently drinking a lot. They started out by talking about Alicia Martin. There were several gaps, though. Winding up on the floor was a mystery. There was a dull pain coming from his left shin, which was something else his mind could not account for this morning.

It had been quite a while since Fuller drank as heavily as he did the previous night. He was usually able to maintain his faculties, and, most importantly, make it into his own bed at the end of the night. He sighed loudly, and gingerly walked toward his bedroom.

Fuller showered, and then made coffee and toast. The thought of food made his stomach turn a little, but he forced it down knowing it would help with the hangover. He was wearing black sweatpants and a gray Vanguard PD T-shirt. He gathered his things, and headed out of the apartment to his car.

It was only then he realized he did not drive it home from the bar last night. In the light of the morning he was proud of himself for at least being a little smart the night before.

10:50 a.m.

Alicia had still not left her room. She was sitting on a loveseat, and looking out the window at nothing in particular. She wore the same shirt and sweats she had worn to bed the night before. Her hair was disheveled, as she had not yet showered. There was a knock at her door.

"Come in," she said.

The door opened, and Macy walked in. Macy was thirteen years old. Alicia saw a little sorrow in Macy's face, but the child hid it well. Alicia could tell her daughter was being strong or at least trying her best.

"What is it, Macy?"

Macy walked over and sat next to Alicia on the loveseat.

"You didn't come out of your room," Macy said.

"I know. Not yet."

"Sam and Angel were hungry. I made them cereal."

"Thank you."

"Are you going to come out for lunch?" Macy asked, trying to get her mother to think about something else.

"I'm not sure. Maybe."

Macy looked at her mom. She did not see what she normally saw in her mother's face. Macy felt her mother had not heard what she had said. She did not want to get up and leave her mother alone in the room, nor did she want to be there with her mother in this state. Macy felt scared sitting there with her mom. The normal spark from Alicia Martin was missing. Macy hid her fear well. She had grown adept at disguising her emotions.

Without saying anything more, Macy walked out of Alicia's room and closed the door behind her. Alicia did not move or look at her daughter as she left.

11:30 a.m.

Alicia Martin's story from the day before had rattled Detective Jack Fuller. Fuller was usually able to compartmentalize his feelings from his reasoning. He was good at building walls in his brain. This was different. His mind was a vast, open space and at the moment his emotions were running the show. His senses were dulled, almost as if he was under some kind of spell.

Alicia had taken the previous days' news about not sending out an AMBER alert well. She understood that the department needed certain criteria to be met in order to send out such an alert. During their talk, Fuller felt small rushes of normalcy returning to him. To the Detective it felt like he was splashing water on his face in the morning to help wake up.

Fuller reasoned that Alicia Martin's story about her son was the cause for these abnormal feelings. In one sense this was true. Detective Jack Fuller would never have started to feel strange if Alicia Martin had not walked through the doors of the Vanguard Police Department hoping to find her son. That was not the sole explanation for the uneasiness he felt. Alicia's story roused something in Fuller's soul. Something he might not have known was there.

Alicia's story had brought something else out of Jack Fuller, in addition to abnormal feelings. Alicia talking about her son going missing made Fuller think of his own son, Daniel, and Heidi, his ex-wife, from whom he had been divorced for three years. Fuller realized after the divorce was final that he never loved Heidi. He loved the way she looked, loved her personality, at times, but he simply did not love her on a daily basis. The feeling would come and go, and eventually the inconsistency wore on both of them. Fights became more explosive and more frequent. Their sex life became non-existent. Fuller spent the last two months of their marriage sleeping on a couch in the den. Eventually, staying together for the sake of Daniel, something they had wanted to do, no longer made sense. Heidi had found someone else during those final two months of marriage, and even though the relationship did not last, it was a signal that the time had come for Mr. and Mrs. Fuller to part ways and move on with their lives.

Fuller and Heidi decided that sole custody would be easier for Daniel, especially since Heidi wanted to move to a city where it was warm all year long. She had a great body and to be able to show it off for twelve months would significantly increase her odds of meeting someone new. She always hated the winters in the northeast anyway, even though she had grown up there.

Daniel was allowed to pick whom he wished to live with. He was already settled in at his school and had always enjoyed spending time with his father, so Daniel chose to live with Fuller. It was a situation that would only last for six months after the divorce. Fuller became tied up in a murder investigation and did a very poor job of making time for Daniel. Daniel decided to head to Florida to live with Heidi once the school year concluded. Fuller had only seen him twice since then, even though he technically still had full custody of his son.

The last time Fuller had any contact with Daniel was a year and a half ago when Fuller was on a summer vacation in Naples. During the trip, Fuller drove down to Miami to see his son. His first impression was amazement at how much Daniel had changed. He no longer looked like a child. The then-fourteen-year-old Daniel looked much more like a man than a boy. He might have already shaved for the first time. He had probably kissed his first girl. He might have even tried a cigarette or alcohol or weed.

On their first day together, which would turn out to be their only day together, the two went out for a late lunch of burgers and fries at a place called the Burger Shack near Heidi's townhome. Once there, things quickly went downhill between father and son.

"How are things going down here?" Fuller asked.

"Okay," Daniel had said. "The first little bit of school was kind of tough. Next year I'm going into the high school, so that will be good. Easier to blend in."

"That's good, Dan. I'm happy you're finding your way down here. I can imagine it is so tough with what your mom and I went through."

"It's not tough because of you and mom. It's tough because of you. You're the reason I had to come down here."

"I'm the reason?" Fuller instinctively raised his voice at the accusation. He did not want to, but it happened. He could not calm himself before the next sentence either. "What do you mean I'm the reason?"

Daniel was a little startled, but the boy held his ground. He had never stood up to his father before, and it had taken courage to say what he said.

"You didn't take care of me. I was constantly fending for myself for food. I had to walk to the store and buy stuff all the time – with my own money. You barely even talked to me."

Fuller was on the defensive at that point. When looking back on it, he knew he should have calmed down and had a discussion with his son. Instead Fuller began shouting at Daniel in the restaurant.

"I was busy doing my job, Daniel! I'm sorry there were bad things going on in the world. I did everything I could to take care of you and provide for you. Everything in my power. I worked long hours so you could have what you wanted."

It was a low moment for Fuller. He knew it when it was happening, but he could not contain his emotion. Fuller's stomach began to tighten as he currently sat at his desk in the Vanguard Police Department thinking about the awful final meal he had with Daniel. Yet he could not stop thinking about it.

"You're a liar. You did nothing for me. I was on my own since the day mom left for Florida. I had to come down here to be with her just to survive. When I told her how things were with you, she wouldn't have it any other way than me coming down here. She is the one who cares about me. Not you."

They did not say anything to each other for the rest of the meal. There was a baseball game on the TV at the bar, and that is where they turned their attention while they finished their burgers.

Fuller broke the silence when they walked to the parking lot towards his rental car.

"I'll take you home," he said.

Daniel looked at him, right in the eye, and said, "I can walk. It's not far."

Those were the last words Fuller had heard his son say. It was the last time he had seen his face other than in photographs. Fuller spent the rest of his time in Florida drinking heavily.

Fuller heard a voice from the bullpen. It shook his thoughts and returned his focus to the present.

"Hey, Jack. What are you doing here on a Saturday?" Officer Jim Warner said to Fuller as he was walked towards Fuller's open door.

"Just reviewing the Martin case a little bit, seeing if anything stands out. What are you doing here?"

"I'm covering for Michaels," Warner said. "I didn't expect you to be in here. Find anything so far?"

Fuller shook his head. "Not really. We don't have much to go on other than her statement."

"That's for sure. Our preliminary canvass didn't turn up much. The neighbors near the Basil house didn't see anything. Same goes for the neighbors around the Martins. From what they tell us, Alicia Martin doesn't interact too much with the neighbors. She's big into Halloween, though. She always has the house decked out. McAvoy was telling me that you are going to interview the kids' friends on Monday."

21

Fuller nodded. "I think you're going to be helping with that too."

Both men were quiet for a moment, then Fuller said, "Hey, Jim. Do you think the kid is dead?"

Warner scratched his head with his right hand. His eyes turned up toward the ceiling. "I don't know for sure, but my gut is telling me yes. He's only fifteen years old. He'd have turned up by now. He doesn't seem like someone who would run away from what Alicia told us. I think we have to assume he is dead since the guy showed up and told her as much."

Fuller sighed, and nodded his head. "That's what my gut is telling me too."

"McAvoy's had patrol out looking. Looking for any sign of him. I'm sure they would have found something by now. It's like some sort of cosmic vacuum scooped him up. He's gone without a trace."

Fuller nodded again. "It's just, I don't know how to describe it. It's like I have this little voice in my head telling me maybe the kid isn't dead. Maybe he ran off somewhere. Or maybe it was a kidnapping. But it's like this little whisper saying he's still alive, even though all of my reasoning says he's gone. Does that sound crazy?"

"No. No. I hope your whisper is right, Jack," Warner said. "I'd love nothing more than to bring that kid back to his mom."

"I'd have to say, when Alicia looked at you, that was the strangest thing I've encountered on the job," Fuller said.

"Most definitely. It was sheer panic in her eyes when she looked at me. I've never seen that kind of look on anyone's face before."

Fuller was tapping his pen on the notepad in front of him now. Consciously he did not notice he was doing it. Warner noticed though, and took it as a sign of impatience on Fuller's part. Warner's impression was the opposite of the truth. Fuller was actually enjoying their conversation.

"Well, I'll let you have at it," Warner said as he stood up from his chair.

"Okay, I'll be seeing you, Jim."

Warner nodded and headed back toward the bullpen.

"Hey, Jim," Fuller called.

Warner eagerly turned around.

"Did you check on your uniforms? Alicia Martin said the guy at her door had a nametag that said Warner. Are you missing one?"

Warner put his head down to think. He began to speak as he pulled his head back up. "You know, I haven't checked. I've been tied up going door to door with the other officers," he said. "I'll get on that right away."

"Let me know," Fuller said. "I'm going to be leaving in an hour or so. It'd be great if you could let me know by then."

Warner nodded, and headed off toward the locker where he stored an extra uniform. If everything he kept in that locker was in its place, he would drive home to check his closet. If he needed to drive home his wife would question him. He never went to his house while he was on duty. The thought of a nagging wife made him resist the idea of driving back to his house. And while this aversion was strong, he felt even more strongly that did not want to find that something was missing from his locker at the station.

12:02 p.m.

There was a lot of noise in the kitchen, but it turned quiet when the children heard their mother's door open from down the hall. It was not a distinct sound, but they all knew it must be her door. The home was a sprawling ranch. The kitchen, living room, and dining room all flowed into each other on one end of the house, while the bedrooms were on the other end. A long, wood-floored hallway ran from the kitchen to the bedroom wing. The children could hear footsteps coming down the hall.

Macy had made peanut butter and jelly sandwiches, and dumped a pile of shoestring potatoes on each plate. She had taken charge. Being the oldest child to wake up in the Martin house that morning, she needed to take charge. The children eagerly looked at the opening where the hallway met the kitchen; waiting for their mother to appear. But she did not turn the corner and enter the kitchen. Instead, they heard her footsteps cease, and another door open.

Alicia was standing in Josh's room. It was the first time she had opened his door since Halloween night. The room was messy, but not cataclysmic. Josh was pretty good about picking up his clothes, and there were none on the floor at this time. His desk was another story – filled with different stacks of papers. Josh's bed was not made either, something Alicia always tried to get him to do. She wanted desperately to make the bed right then, but also wanted to preserve the room as though it was Josh's farewell letter to the family. These two urges wrestled in her mind. She decided to leave the room how it was.

The comforter was strewn on the left side of the bed while the right side was uncovered. Alicia sat down on the uncovered side, and looked out the window. Gray clouds filled the sky. Rain did not appear imminent. Alicia lay down in Josh's bed and rolled over to grab the comforter. She held it as tight as she could in her arms. She never wanted to let it go.

12:15 p.m.

The lockers in the Vanguard police station were tucked away near the loading dock in an obscure corner of the building. Warner had not been to his designated locker in a week. There was nothing he needed out of it. He kept spare items there because his memory failed him at times. One day, in his first year on the job, Warner had come in early to exercise in the small weight room at the station. He had forgotten his uniform, though, and had to drive back to his house to retrieve one. After more forgetful moments, he came up with the idea of keeping a spare set of everything at the station. The system had worked so far.

He reached his locker, and was a little unsettled when he saw an open padlock hanging from the handle. He pushed the locker door open to find absolutely nothing inside.

"Shit," he said.

He looked in disbelief at the locker anyway, even though he could see everything was gone.

"It was cleaned out," Warner said. He was back in Fuller's office, and sitting in the same chair he had occupied on the last visit.

"Was the lock broken?" Fuller said.

"No. It was just undone. I could have left it like that. I've done it from time to time. Just forgotten about it. But I haven't gone to my locker in a week or so. I haven't needed to."

"That means the uniform came from here. It means whoever went to Alicia Martin's house that night was in the station at some point."

"You think it was a cop?"

Fuller shook his head.

"No. I don't think a cop would have taken your entire uniform. People come and go in this place. It could have been anyone. It could have been a suspect that wandered down the wrong hall."

Since there was not a lot of major crime in the town, sometimes the policies at the police station got a little lax. The station mostly dealt with people filing complaints about their neighbors or reporting that their car was broken into at the grocery store. Detective Fuller himself could not be excluded from taking a lax approach at times. He routinely did not question an unfamiliar face walking by him in plain clothes. He assumed every person was headed where they were supposed to be.

Fuller's mind rattled through some possibilities of who could have been around to steal Jim Warner's uniform. In a matter of seconds the mental list had too many names on it to be considered a productive start. There were also no internal cameras at the station, something that popped into Fuller's head rather quickly. A few years ago word had been that security cameras were coming soon, but the station was still waiting. Fuller silently cursed the bureaucratic process.

"I've got to head back out on patrol," Warner said while looking at his watch.

"Go ahead," Fuller said. "And Jim, keep quiet about the uniform for a little while. I think it would be best if nobody knew for now."

"Not a problem, Jack."

3

November 3, 8:14 a.m.

Fuller's eyes felt heavy. A dull pain swelled from behind them. He had been awake for hours, but had yet to get out of bed. Sleep tempted him during the night. Instead of drifting off peacefully, two terrible dreams haunted Fuller, keeping him from sleeping through the night. He did not wish to return to the places his dreams brought him. Both dreams involved him being unable to run away from a dark entity. He had not seen what he was running from in either dream, but he knew it was there, and he could not outrun it. Twice he had woken in a sweat, with the same thought hammering in his head.

The kid could have just run away.

There was no evidence to support a murder other than Alicia's statement about a uniformed cop telling her so. One of Jim Warner's uniforms was missing, but that did not mean a murder took place. Fuller's gut told him it was Jim Warner's uniform on the back of the mystery guest at Alicia Martin's door on Halloween night. What his gut was currently undecided on was whether that man murdered Josh Martin.

Fuller attempted to sit up from his bed only to be met with resistance. He had felt chained to his bed in the night despite being woken up by his nightmares. Now his body was responding as if a one hundred pound weight was tethered to his back. After a moment of much more effort than he had ever spent getting out of bed, Fuller let his feet touch the ground for the first time since the night before. He sat there for a moment on the edge of the bed. Only boxers covered his body. He glanced out the window, then down at his feet. A deep breath followed, and Fuller looked up at the ceiling.

The kid could have just run away.

9:15 a.m.

He woke up groggy, and slogged to the bathroom still in a haze from his slumber. Despite a fifteen-minute shower, he felt no more awake. It was not until his feet toed the carpet outside of his bedroom after toweling off that he felt alertness creep into his mind. It came like a cat stalking a bird. He had a towel around his waist and another draped over his shoulders. His chest was still a little wet. He sat on his bed and gazed about the room. There was not much there. Nothing new, at least. His gaze settled on his hockey bag, and flashes of memories slowly returned to him. He shuddered at the thought of what had happened. It was alarming to him how distant it all seemed. How much it felt like a dream.

Was he still dreaming?

After getting dressed he grabbed his keys, wallet and the hockey bag and headed out the door. The bag was much heavier than he thought it would be. With some effort, he tossed the bag in the trunk of his car and drove toward work. He was fed up with thinking about what he had done. It was a mistake.

He knew no one would ever see it his way. He would be unable to convince anyone of what he felt really occurred. They would think he was crazy.

9:57 a.m.

The sweet aroma of fresh pastries filled Jack Fuller's nose as he approached the Farnelli Bakery and Pastry Shop. The shop was only a ten-minute walk from his apartment, and with it being a beautiful morning Fuller thought the walk would be a remedy to unclutter his mind. A bell jingled when he pushed the front door open, and the smell of freshly baked goods multiplied by ten.

Fuller frequented the Farnelli Bakery and Pastry Shop, but he was not there enough to be called a regular or be known by name. He had been in several times when Gloria Farnelli, the store's 65-year-old proprietor was behind the counter. Gloria would politely chat with every customer. If she knew who you were, she would call you by name. Gloria was working the counter on this morning, and greeted Fuller with a smile. She did not call him by name.

"What would you like?" she asked.

Fuller scanned the display case filled with cookies and cannolis. He wanted a cannoli very much, even though he knew it was too early in the day for one.

"I'll have a coffee and one of your Italian breakfast sandwiches."

"I love those sandwiches," she said. "Anything else?"

"I'll take a dozen cannolis to go."

He paid, and sat in a corner booth with the box of cannolis and his coffee. He opened the paper he brought with him while he waited for his breakfast sandwich. There was no news pertaining to Josh Martin, which pleased Fuller. He did not want any information out for public consumption, and he also wanted to get away from the case for the day. He already felt a physical effect from it. His body was sore, and, in addition to the nightmares, his head was currently pounding with pain. Fuller scanned a couple of headlines before settling on a story about the success of a fishing boat called *Catiana*. The boat was about to begin its twentieth lobster season, and the first with Charlie McGuffey in full command as Captain. Charlie was taking over for his father, Vince, who was still the sole owner of the boat. Vince would be along on the voyage as a Co-Captain to help mentor Charlie during his first voyage in the wheelhouse. It was a pleasant story. The local boy had done good.

As Fuller finished up reading about Charlie and Vince, his breakfast sandwich arrived. It consisted of two Italian sausage patties, scrambled egg, and a large juicy tomato served on lightly toasted bread with a tasty herb seasoning on it. Fuller took a large bite, and looked out the window. He felt better being outside his stuffy apartment. The fresh air had done him good. The feeling of darkness was not inside of him as it had been the night before.

10:32 a.m.

Alicia Martin was making omelets in her kitchen. She had not eaten the day before, and had not fed her children. Macy had done all the motherly work. Alicia spent a good portion of the day lying in Josh's bed, holding his comforter tight to her chest. She did not feel remorse for her actions. She had been consumed with her own pain, and could not recall thinking about her other children. When the omelets were done, she placed them on Macy, Sam, and Angel's plates, and set the plates in front of each child. Then she put one on a plate for herself, and sat down with a Bloody Mary that was pink in color. It was as though yesterday never happened.

"Are we going to school tomorrow?" Sam asked.

Alicia took a bite of her veggie omelet and a sip of her drink. She had dropped the children with her next-door neighbor, Karen Lawrence, on Friday when she went to the police station. She had not given much thought to what to do about tomorrow.

"Yes," Alicia answered. "You are going to school tomorrow. So get your homework done."

"We didn't go on Friday. We have no homework," Macy said.

Another thought that had not crossed Alicia's mind. She felt in a haze the past few days. Josh's death was having more than an emotional effect on her. She could barely think about her other children. They did not seem real to Alicia, even while sitting with them in the kitchen. It felt like a dream.

Alicia took another bite of her meal, got up and walked to her room without saying a word. Half of her omelet was still on her plate.

"What the hell?" Sam, who was nine years old, said.

"That's a bad word, Sam," Angel said.

The trio finished their meal in silence. Macy cleaned up afterward. Then all three went to their rooms, afraid to make a sound.

4

November 4, 1:34 a.m.

Sirens scream bloody murder in the distance. They yell like a lost child. Always growing closer, always growing louder. He can hear the urgency in their tone, as he lies sleepless. He knows they are coming for him. And then they stop.

Silence.

He waits for a knock at the door, a knock that never comes. He smiles. A state of peace rolls over him as he falls into sleep.

*   *   *   *   *

Jack Fuller is sleepless on the same night. It is fear that keeps him awake. He tried to take a break from the Josh Martin case. He wanted so badly to sleep soundly and head into work refreshed in the morning. Instead, a terror haunts his dreams – the darkness. He fears this shadowy entity as it chases him around his inner thoughts. The darkness wants him to embrace it. To allow it access to his mind. Fuller cannot help but resist. His fear is greater than his wont to know.

5:30 a.m.

Detective Fuller startles awake to a song on his radio alarm clock. In his daze he cannot be sure what the song is before he presses the button to silence it. He stumbles toward his bathroom to gain some clarity.

Has it really been four days?

5:37 a.m.

Four days.

Alicia Martin wonders how she made it through them. Lying awake on her bed she can barely remember the last few days. They blur together like the trees of a forest when viewed from a distance. She cannot remember the small details that make each day different from the last. For Alicia, Halloween had lost its frightening ability long ago. Not since she was a child had October 31st sent a chill down her spine. Instead it became a day of wicked pranks with girlfriends in elementary school, and basement make-out sessions with boyfriends in high school. It had evolved from *Nightmare on Elm Street* scares to the thrill of sipping jungle juice in Ricky Fredrick's basement, when she was dressed up as Marilyn Monroe.

As a mother, Alicia made sure Halloween was a big part of her kids' lives. She made sure that each one had the best costume at class parties in elementary school. She also served as class mom for each of her children. Volunteering without hesitation to run the annual classroom Halloween party.

"Too bad Mom doesn't get this jazzed about Christmas," her children would say to one another.

"I bet I could get ten video games if Christmas was her favorite holiday."

The disguise of Halloween always pulled at Alicia's soul. The ability to be someone else for a day was something she embraced. She wanted to be someone else on most days, but on Halloween it was acceptable. On Halloween she could always put on some makeup, get drunk and not be held accountable for her actions. She could step outside of her everyday life and run away into a fantasy world for one night a year. For one night she could be Marilyn Monroe or a catholic schoolgirl in a tight mini skirt. For one night she felt confident enough to grab James Walker by the hand, lead him upstairs at Ricky Fredrick's house and have her way with him.

On Halloween night, fantasy was able to take over.

Now Halloween is where reality set in. A reality that felt dark, cold, and horribly foreign. Perhaps it was a reality from which she would never be able to escape.

The fear from her childhood had returned. A dark omen would hang over the date in her mind. She would never be able to associate Halloween with anything other than the death of her son.

5:53 a.m.

He awakes with a start. A bang at the door of the apartment next to his is the cause. As he sees the clock on his bedside table he calculates that the extra twenty-two minutes of sleep will not be worth it.

When his feet hit the carpet, he thinks of how uncomfortable it is.

The thin layer of carpet provides no cushion. He wishes he could have some kind of lush, fluffy carpeting. Wealth is truly measured by your carpet. Just about anyone could lay down four hundred dollars a month to lease a Porsche, but when you can throw down forty grand for a finely woven carpet, then you have really hit the big time. This is a harsh reminder that always hits him on his way to the bathroom in the morning.

He smiles as he closes his bathroom door. He could be a successful businessman; he had breezed through his two years of college. But when he sat down to think about his junior year, he decided he did not want to go back. He knew that it would be another pointless year of monotony in which nothing was really learned. He attempted to break into the business world, but every company was looking for a college degree. While he impressed in all his interviews, explaining how it was just a document, and that the degree was not a measure of his ability, he was still turned away each time. His patience grew thin after about five months of interviews, and he gave up his quest.

He was still out to prove that he could succeed without a college degree, but as it always was for Houston West, his intentions were misguided.

He was smart – borderline brilliant. But Houston felt a dark sensation growing inside of him. He was calm. He welcomed it. His calmness assured him it was a good thing, even though he was alarmed on his first journey into the dark.

6:02 a.m.

While stopped at a stoplight on his drive to work, Detective Fuller looks at himself in the rearview mirror. His dark brown hair is still full, but he notices it is turning gray in some spots, particularly near his ears. His eyes look heavy, and they have bags underneath them. Sleep had been difficult over the weekend. He made a mental note to get to bed early tonight, hoping it would help his looks.

6:17 a.m.

The kids will be up soon.

While Alicia Martin was toweling off from her shower all she could think about was her children. The hardest part was explaining what happened - telling her other children their big brother was not coming home anymore. The children and Alicia had cried together. It crushed her to see any of them hurt.

It had to be the oldest that died, she thought. He was their leader, he was the one the other three looked up to. *Why did it have to be Josh?* It was a dark thought that had been thrust upon her during the previous days. She felt sickened thinking about how Josh could help her with the death of another one of her children.

Alicia bent down and vomited into the toilet. Somehow it helped clear her mind.

In a time like this the others could lean on Josh in a way they could not lean on Alicia. It was now up to Macy to help Sam and Angel deal with death. Alicia could still remember Macy plopping on the floor to watch cartoons. She was not sure if her oldest daughter was ready for this.

Alicia saw herself in Macy. Macy was smart yet reserved. She had a keen sense of what she wanted, and the drive to obtain her desires. It was almost as though Macy had no father at all. As though she had been created from a piece of Alicia, a clone perhaps.

Alicia laughed when she thought of Macy like that. Even in this time of grief, a giggle was able to escape as she put on her shirt.

For the first time since Josh's death, Alicia felt normal again for just an instant.

7:48 a.m.

Fuller reached his desk at the Vanguard police station, and set down the box full of files he was carrying. It was Monday morning, and Fuller was hoping a fresh week would bring him some needed energy. After his restless night's sleep, his hopes were not being answered promptly. He walked toward the kitchen, and poured himself a cup of coffee. It was his second of the morning. He needed to shake his sluggish feeling.

McAvoy, the Captain, walked over to Fuller's desk.

"Jack, can I talk to you in my office?"

"Of course, Ronald."

As usual, McAvoy's office was immaculate. Detective Fuller made a mental note that the "Daddy's the Best" coffee cup was still serving as a pen holder.

"Jack, as you probably are aware, our weekend canvassing

did not turn up a whole lot of new information. We learned that Alicia Martin was not very involved in the neighborhood. She's been to some of the neighborhood parties, but it's infrequent. There seems to be a little bit of a neighborhood clique and Alicia is not a part of it. We received nothing but rave reviews on the children. They are all well behaved according to everyone we spoke with. We knocked on doors around the Basil house, where Josh was last seen. Nobody saw anything suspicious on Halloween night."

Even though Fuller had received a brief update from Officer Jim Warner on Saturday it was good to hear this information again from McAvoy's mouth.

"I think word is going to get out on this thing this week," McAvoy said. "The press has been pretty quiet so far. They weren't going to get any news out of this office on Friday. That was a certainty. But with the days piling up a little now, I think they'll get something this week."

"I've been reading the papers, and I haven't seen anything yet. Maybe we have more time. We made it clear to Alicia that we don't want her talking to the press at this time, and I think she's going to listen," Detective Fuller said.

"How sure are you about that?" McAvoy said.

"I'd say eighty percent," Detective Fuller said. "You said yourself that she isn't that involved in the community. I feel like she is a very private person."

"The press will find out somehow," McAvoy said. "And the Commissioner wants to make sure we are on top of things when the press starts throwing questions our way. That's why he's coming here for a meeting at one this afternoon."

Fuller thought a meeting with the Commissioner could be possible on this case, but only if the case dragged on for a bit.

"Why now?" Fuller said. "I figured maybe down the line. But now?"

"Commissioner Drake thinks this thing is going to be front page news," McAvoy said.

"Why? It's just a murder," Fuller said. "Well, we think it's a murder. The big papers in Boston don't put every murder on the front page. Drake thinks it is going to be front page from the start?"

"Yes," McAvoy said. "The whole single mother aspect of it, losing her first-born…"

"She's not a single mother," Fuller interrupted. "She's a widow."

"Even more so then. The press is going to see the human element in this soon enough. Plus, the theatrics that happened late Halloween night are going to make them drool."

"Those theatrics aren't going to hit the papers," Fuller said. "We are not going to release that information."

"Think about it, Jack. This place has its leaks. Who knows about what happened at Alicia Martin's house Halloween night?"

"Me. Warner. You. Maybe a couple other guys."

"Everyone knows, Jack," McAvoy said. "Those couple other guys you are talking about means you don't know where it ends. That's why Commissioner Drake is coming here. He knows about it too. And he wants to keep a lid on it."

"I get it, Captain. So what is the meeting with the Commissioner about specifically?"

"Commissioner Drake wants to be certain, beyond any doubt in his mind, that what happened Halloween night at Alicia Martin's house never makes it to the public forum."

Fuller nodded. He knew that if that information ever got out, it would send the press into a frenzy, and it would make the Vanguard PD look very, very bad.

8:22 a.m.

The route Alicia Martin was driving was a familiar one. While everything looked the same as always, the feeling was far different. She was driving Macy, Sam and Angel to school. The police were not officially calling Josh's disappearance a death yet, but that is what Alicia felt it was. She knew it. Deep inside. She had told her children as much.

"Josh is gone, and we have to be strong without him," she had said.

The children were confused, but Alicia thought Macy realized what was going on. She picked up on people's moods and their emotions. Macy saw what was going on in her mother's eyes and sensed what was going on in her mother's heart. Even at her age, Macy knew she had to help her mom.

Dread was washing over Alicia. She felt so normal when she woke up, but now all she could think about was Josh. He was consuming her as she drove; each little boy on the street walking to Benjamin Franklin Elementary and Junior High, a kindergarten through eighth grade facility, became Josh as he was bouncing his way toward the very same building. Every adult that was standing beside a child became a killer in Alicia's mind. A shiver rushed over her. The hair on her arms stood on end.

As she pulled up to the school, Alicia did not want the children to go. She could not let them out of her sight.

"We are going back home, guys," she said.

"Why?" asked little Angel, just in kindergarten.

"We need more time at home. We aren't ready for school. Mommy isn't ready for this."

Macy, who was sitting in the passenger seat looked over at her mom.

"It's going to be okay, Mom. It's going to be okay."

A tear fell down Alicia's cheek as she pulled away from the school and began to drive back home.

9:50 a.m.

Detective Fuller was staring at the files on top of his desk. The interview process with Josh Martin's friends – the last people who saw him – was about to get moving. He was going over his notes from interviewing Alicia Martin.

The five friends of Josh's who were at Tommy Basil's house on Halloween were going to be coming into the station after they got out of school – it was a half day for the school district. Fuller had their names written down and had already checked to see if they had any kind of record. Sure they were young, but even young kids do things that earn them a manila folder and a computer file with the Vanguard PD.

Fuller headed towards Officer Jim Warner's desk in the bullpen, where Warner sat shuffling papers.

"Jim, you got some time for a quick meeting to go over some key points for the interviews?" Fuller said.

"You bet," Warner said.

Fuller did not think Warner could ever be a detective, and he was not sure if Warner wanted the added responsibility. All Fuller could do was hope Warner was up for the challenge today.

"The biggest thing is trying to nail down some kind of timeline for Josh Martin on that night," Fuller said. "We've got to find out where he was at what times. The more specific the better. The other important thing is to make sure the stories the kids are telling match up."

"Right, right," Warner said.

Fuller could see Warner's mind ticking back to his days at the Academy, and what was said about how to question a potential witness. Detective Fuller also suspected Warner was thinking about all the *Law & Order* episodes he had seen.

"Now, there are five kids coming down here today," Fuller said. "I'm going to be interviewing three and you'll take the other two. The interviews don't have to be too long; if something comes up later we can always track the kids down again. Take notes though, Warner, don't rely on your memory."

"I will," Warner said. "Got an extra legal pad? I only have my small pocket notebook."

"We'll get you a legal pad. Make sure the kids' stories line up, and if they don't, be sure to call them out on it. We'll compare notes at the end."

"Sounds good, Jack."

"Also, have you kept your mouth shut about your uniform disappearing?"

Warner looked away, embarrassed. After a moment he turned back to Fuller and said, "I heard the Commissioner is coming down here today."

"You heard correctly, Jim."

"You think I'm in deep shit?" Warner said.

"Maybe. Maybe not."

Warner exhaled deeply. Fuller did not think Warner was in deep shit. There was not going to be any disciplinary action. Fuller knew that for sure. The department wanted to keep this whole thing quiet.

"Just keep your mouth shut about it. Okay, Jim?" Fuller said.

Officer Warner nodded.

10:35 a.m.

The house looked the same, but it felt very different for Alicia.

She was standing in her kitchen, looking into her backyard. Only a few leaves still clung to the trees – the final holdouts. The kids were in their rooms. The house was quiet.

Alicia was standing there, staring into nothingness, when the phone rang. It did not startle her. She was too numb.

"Hello."

"Alicia," it was her mother, Cynthia, on the other end. "How are you today?"

Alicia ran a home furnishing business from her house. It was completely common for her to be around the house on a Monday morning.

"I'm fine. Everything is fine."

The words came out slowly, as if Alicia was under some kind of spell. Immediately, Cynthia was concerned.

"You don't sound fine. You sound tired."

"It's just work. It's been busy. Plus it was Halloween, and you know how busy that makes me."

Cynthia thought this last sentence was a little better even though her daughter still did not sound like her normal self.

"Okay. Your father and I had a lovely weekend. We took a trip up the coast to San Francisco. The weather was beautiful. It reminded me a little of back home. Nice and cool."

Alicia did not say anything.

"Are you there? Alicia?"

It was quiet for another ten seconds.

"Alicia?"

"I have to go, mother. Goodbye."

Cynthia heard the click of a disconnection. She felt a rush of fear. Her daughter never called her "mother", and she never hung up the phone in the middle of a conversation.

12:30 p.m.

Thirty minutes ago Detective Fuller finished the egg salad sandwich he bought for lunch, and he was now sitting at his desk blankly staring at paperwork. Josh Martin's friends were going to be at the police station soon. Each of them had been with Josh on Halloween. Fuller was going to start by questioning Tommy Basil. The other boys – Ritchie McGill, Frank Saunders, Johnny Vincent, and Nick Abbottello did not seem as important as Tommy Basil. Officer Warner could handle any one of them.

Fuller was blankly staring at one record. Of the five kids coming in for questioning, only Tommy Basil had a police report with his name on it. Fuller did not think what Basil had done linked him in any way to what happened to Josh, but it gave him pause.

Fuller's phone rang; it was Lucy, the receptionist. All of his guests had arrived. They were early. Fuller thanked her, hung up the phone, and went looking for Warner.

*   *   *   *   *

Tommy Basil was seated at a wooden table in a small interview room inside the police station. There was double-sided glass along the wall he faced. There was one chair next to him, and one chair across the table from him. A desk, like one he would have seen at school, was in one corner of the room, with an extra chair stacked on top of it. Tommy had been in one of these rooms once before at the Vanguard police station. It was not this exact room, but it looked very similar.

Jack Fuller opened the door to the room, and stepped halfway through the doorway.

"Would you like something to drink, Tommy?"

"A Coke. Thank you."

"We'll get that right for you," Fuller said. "Hey Chuck," Fuller yelled to someone Tommy could not see. "Could we get a Coke down here in room five?"

"Yeah, I'll grab one," Tommy heard this unseen man who must be Chuck holler back to Fuller.

"Okay, Tommy. That Coke will be right in. I'm Detective Jack Fuller. Thank you for coming down here today. You understand why you are here, right?"

Fuller couldn't believe how young the kid looked. He was fifteen, but looked even younger. Maybe thirteen. Maybe twelve. Tommy was little. He had not hit his growth spurt yet. Fuller guessed he was maybe 5-foot-3. He could not be sure because the kid was sitting down. Tommy's brown hair was buzzed very short,

44

and as he looked at Fuller with his green eyes, Fuller could see a little bit of fear in them. And why not? The kid was sitting here in the police station, and one of his friends was missing.

"Yes," Tommy said. "I'm here to answer questions about Josh."

"That's right. Are you comfortable doing that?"

The boy looked out the doorway. Fuller had left the door open because he was waiting for Chuck to bring the Coke. He did not want Tommy to be distracted by anything that was going on out there, so he stood up and closed the door.

"Yes," Tommy said after a moment or two.

"Tommy, did your mother bring you here?"

"No," the boy answered. "Johnny's mom drove all of us down here."

"Did you want me to get your mother? Or would you like Johnny's mother to be in here with you?"

Tommy hesitated for a moment as he thought this over.

"No. I'll be okay," he said.

There was a knock at the door, and Chuck entered with the Coke for Tommy. Tommy popped the tab immediately and downed a quarter of the can.

"Halloween night, you were having friends over to your house, is that right?" Fuller asked.

"Yeah. It was going to be a few people. Nick, Ritchie, Johnny, and Frank were there. Josh was there. There were going to be more people coming. We were going to try to get some girls to come over."

Fuller remembered those days. Getting girls to hang out with him and his buddies was all he focused on. Like the summer of 1977, when Danielle Sabatelli developed breasts. He tried the entire summer to get Danielle over to his buddy John Lawrence's house, because the Lawrences had a swimming pool. He finally achieved his goal when a squelching heat wave ran through his hometown of Hazleton, Pennsylvania in late July. It was in the 90s for eleven straight days. On the fourth day of the heat wave Danielle finally said yes to him. She brought her friends Michelle Avara and Lizzy Sorin with her. Which made John, and their friend Mike Pansul very happy. Fuller was smiling as he looked at Tommy Basil.

"It was just the six of you at first, right?" Fuller asked.

"Yes. Just me, Nick, Johnny, Ritchie, Frank and Josh."

"What time did everyone start showing up?"

"I don't really know. The sun was still up, that's for sure. It wasn't setting or anything. So it had to be before five. We had school that day, so it was after three-fifteen, that's for sure. Maybe four o'clock?"

Fuller began making notes on his legal pad, and Tommy had another sip of his Coke.

"What were you guys doing?"

Tommy scratched his ear before answering. "We were just hanging out in my basement. We played some video games. Watched some TV. I got an air hockey table down there. I think Josh and Nick were playing that for a little bit."

"Did everything seem okay?"

The question seemed to befuddle Tommy. He turned his head slightly to the right, and looked at Fuller out of only his left eye.

"What do you mean, okay?" Tommy said.

"I mean there was nothing strange going on? Nobody was mad at each other or anything?"

Tommy shook his head. "Nothing like that, man. It was a normal day."

Fuller jotted down more notes, and scratched the side of his face.

"Did everyone get along? Nobody had problems with any of the other guys, right?"

"No. Nothing like that," Tommy said. "We are all cool. Ritchie and Frank used to not get along. It was for no real reason. They just always seemed to be battling. Be it over sports, girls, whatever. But that was back in elementary school. Now they are, like, inseparable."

"Did you eventually get these other people to show up?"

"Yeah. Later on we got some girls to come by and a couple of our other buddies too. But Josh wasn't there when everyone else showed up."

"Where was Josh?"

"He had to leave. He said he forgot his cell phone and was going to run home to get it. He never came back. I called him once to see where he was, but he didn't pick up. I figured he was just at his house. His mom is big on Halloween. I figured he was just hanging with her. It wasn't until Josh didn't turn up at school the next day that I thought something was wrong."

Fuller wrote this down, and realized that his previous notes were actually doodles. His mind had been wandering.

"What time did Josh leave?"

"It had to be like six or seven. I'm not really sure."

Fuller felt satisfied in what Tommy Basil was saying. But he still had another question for him.

"What about your knife, Tommy?"

Tommy flinched at the word "knife." His eyes were no longer looking at Fuller. He was looking at the table now.

"What...what do you mean?"

Detective Fuller continued with a stern look on his face.

"Well, Tommy, I checked all you guys out before you got down here to see if any of you had a record. It seemed like it might have been a waste of time, since you guys are so young. The first names I searched came up empty. But then your name hit."

Tommy was looking everywhere in the room except at Fuller. Maybe it was nothing, but maybe it was everything.

"That was a misunderstanding."

"Tommy," Fuller said. "You brought an eight-inch blade to school with you. You were caught pulling it on another boy in the bathroom by one of your teachers."

Tommy looked at Fuller now.

"You don't get it, man. Doesn't it say that everything was dropped in that? Doesn't it say I didn't do anything wrong?"

Fuller shifted in his chair. He looked at the file again, like a poker player re-checking his hand to be certain the cards match his memory.

"It says all charges were dropped, and that they confiscated the knife."

"Well good, because that's what happened."

"I still want to know about it, Tommy."

Fuller noticed Tommy was antsy. He could tell the boy did not want to discuss what happened, but after mulling it over for a moment Tommy blurted everything out.

"The kid was bullying me. Jim Thomas. Every day he would either cram me in my locker, or take my money or my jacket. I'd had enough, man. I grabbed a knife that my pops had and when he tried to jump me in the bathroom, I pulled it on him. Scared the shit out of him. I told him if he came near me again, I'd use the knife. He screamed for help. I got busted."

Fuller set his pen down. He wished all that was in the file. Lazy police work had left it out. He was not positive Tommy was being truthful, but the kid was very convincing. Tommy's story lined up with the charges being dropped. Fuller had originally thought maybe the other kid was too scared of Tommy to do anything.

"He left me alone, though," Tommy said. "He never came up to me again."

Fuller closed Tommy Basil's file.

"I'm sorry, Tommy," he said. "I'm sorry I put you through that again. I just had to ask."

Tommy was holding back some tears. "It was wrong. I knew it was," he said. "I just needed to scare him."

Tommy took another sip of his Coke, and held out the empty can.

"You got a trashcan in here?"

Fuller took the can, and stood up.

"We're done, Tommy. You can go back out there and find your friends. I still need to speak with a few of them, but you can wait with the others."

Tommy stood up and grabbed his jacket off the back of the chair.

"Did you want another Coke or something to eat?" Fuller asked.

Tommy shook his head.

Fuller tossed the empty Coke can in the trashcan that was on the other side of the door and led Tommy back to his friends.

12:35 p.m.

Cynthia dialed Alicia's number again. It was the fourth time she tried since the brief phone conversation with her daughter ended this morning. Once again, the phone only rang twice before going to voicemail. Cynthia decided not to leave another message. She had already left two of them.

"Nothing again?" Herbert, her husband, asked as she set the phone in its cradle.

Cynthia shook her head.

"Maybe she ran out?" Herbert said.

Cynthia said nothing. She shrugged her shoulders instead. Herbert put his hand on hers.

"I'm sure everything is ok," he said.

*   *   *   *   *

Alicia was seated at her kitchen table. The phone was in her left hand. She had listened to her mother's voicemails. Cynthia was obviously concerned, and deep inside Alicia felt the need to alleviate those concerns. But she could not bring herself to do it.

Something was stopping her. Alicia could not tell her mother the truth. No matter how hard she tried, she could not do it. Alicia felt like it was something beyond her control. She was terrified that her actions were not matching up with her intentions.

2:45 p.m.

The interviews with Tommy Basil, Ritchie McGill, Frank Saunders, Johnny Vincent and Nick Abbottello had gone smoothly. Their stories all matched up. Josh Martin left Tommy's house sometime between six and seven to walk back home for his cell phone. None of them realized something was wrong until Josh did not show up at school the next day. The last time any of them had seen their friend was right before he walked up Tommy's basement stairs and headed for the door. Nobody had heard from him since then.

Now Detective Fuller and Officer Warner were standing next to each other at the back of the bullpen. Commissioner Andrew Drake was in McAvoy's office having a brief discussion with the Captain. Any moment Commissioner Drake would address the Vanguard Police Department as a whole. There was a murmur throughout the bullpen – quiet small talk amongst the sheep. Fuller and Warner said nothing to each other. They looked out over the flock, waiting for the shepherd to appear.

The shepherd – Andrew Drake, Suffolk County Police Commissioner – emerged from Ronald McAvoy's office with a neutral look on his face. The sheep stopped their bah-ing and looked up attentively, awaiting instructions. Fuller sensed there would be no yelling and screaming in this address. It would only scare the flock.

"Good afternoon," Drake began. "I am here to talk about the Josh Martin case and lay out some ground rules."

His voice was stern, and held the attention of his flock.

"As you know, this case has the potential to be front page news. A young, white child vanished from his middle-class neighborhood. The press eats that up as it is. Throw in the fact that someone came knocking on the mother's door the very same night – Halloween night – dressed as a Vanguard police officer, and the headlines nearly write themselves."

He paused for a moment to make sure he still had everyone's attention. He wanted to be sure what he said next stuck in deep in everyone's heads.

"You will not talk to the press about any of this. No leaks. No exceptions. If this hits the papers before we want it to, I will launch a massive internal affairs investigation. I know I'll have to explain that cost at a review at the end of the year, but it doesn't matter to me. Leaks will not be tolerated. Is that understood?"

The sheep bah-ed.

"Good. Keeping Alicia Martin, the mother, from talking is a different story. We can't very well silence her. She's a private citizen, and a taxpayer. But, if we do our job she should have no reason to run to the press. I have been told she has already been informed to keep quiet about this whole situation, and that she has agreed to do so. If you work hard and find her son, or find the person who impersonated a police officer, then we won't have to worry about her going to the press. We can have a wonderful press conference on our own terms stating another case has been closed by the Vanguard police department, and that justice will be done in the courts. Is everyone clear on this?"

The sheep bah-ed again.

"Good. If anyone has any questions, feel free to speak up."

No one had anything to say. Commissioner Drake had been crystal clear in his speech. The shepherd nodded his head, and walked toward the door. The sheep scattered about the room – going back to their everyday business.

5

November 8, 4:28 p.m.

The clock on the wall was spinning faster than Fuller realized. He was chatting with Warner about the case, and was totally unaware of the time. Fuller's plan of attack was to examine the route Josh Martin would have walked on his way home from Tommy Basil's house on Halloween night. Fuller wanted to walk the path yesterday, but was pulled into a meeting led by McAvoy that discussed the final stages of the neighborhood canvasses. There was no news to report at the meeting. Nothing of use had turned up as a result of the canvassing. A similar meeting had taken place earlier on this day; only it was regarding the newspaper article that appeared in the morning paper about Josh Martin being a missing person. It was obvious one of the neighbors had talked, and not a member of the department or Alicia. There was no mention in the article of the man who came to Alicia Martin's door dressed as a Vanguard police officer. As a result of this previously unscheduled meeting, Detective Fuller was now killing time that he did not need to kill. He caught a glimpse of the clock on the wall in between jokes with Officer Warner.

"Oh shit," Fuller said. "I've got to get out of here. It's getting late."

"What do you have to do? Isn't it nearly quitting time?"

"I wanted to walk the route Josh Martin walked Halloween night. Shit. I'm so late."

"Well do it tomorrow," Warner said.

"That's what I said yesterday. I've got to go."

Fuller grabbed the last of the Italian sandwich he had been eating for his lunch, and headed for the door. As he was rushing out of the station he bumped into a janitor who was on his way in to start his shift.

"Sorry," Fuller said, as he continued to hustle out the door.

The janitor rubbed his shoulder. "I'll be all right," he said back. Detective Fuller was opening the door to his car when the janitor, Houston West, was walking into the Vanguard police station to start another shift of cleaning toilets and mopping floors.

5:01 p.m.

Fuller parked his car in the driveway of the Martin house and exhaled.

As he climbed the steps to ring the doorbell, he could see the outside of the house had been a little neglected. The Halloween decorations had not come down yet, and four now rotting jack-o-lanterns sat on the front porch.

Fuller rang the bell.

It took a minute or two for Alicia Martin to answer. She was dressed, and clean. For some reason Fuller expected her to be in a bathrobe looking disheveled.

"Detective Fuller," Alicia said in a flat tone. "What are you doing here?"

"I'm sorry to just drop by like this, Ms. Martin," Fuller said. "But I need to know Tommy Basil's address. It isn't in the report I have."

This was a lie. Detective Fuller had Tommy Basil's address. He was at the Martin house because he wanted to see Alicia. Even though he wanted to examine where Josh might have taken his last steps, he felt it was important to check in on Alicia. He knew no one else had done so.

She paused for a moment before answering.

"Tommy and Josh have been friends for so long," she said. "But for the life of me I can't remember his address right now. I just know the house. It isn't far."

"Could you tell me how to get there?"

"Go left out of my driveway on Dunwoody here. When you hit Ivy Hall, which is the third or fourth street, go right. Then turn on the second street, you can only go right there. It's Orchard Street. The Basil's live in the fourth house on the left."

Fuller nodded as he jotted the directions on his notepad.

"Thank you, Ms. Martin," Detective Fuller said without looking up.

"When are you going to start calling me Alicia?"

"Maybe when this is over, Ms. Martin."

Fuller paused for a moment to finish writing.

"Are you holding up okay?" he asked as looked up from his notepad.

"I'm trying to be strong. Trying to be there for my kids."

"Have you looked for any help?"

"Help with the children? No. No. I couldn't."

Fuller shook his head. "No, Ms. Martin. Help for you."

She did not speak for nearly thirty seconds. She was looking past Fuller. Her gaze was on the house across the street, but she was staring right through it.

"No," she finally said. "I haven't looked into any of that."

"Well, I could try to find someone. The department has several good resources."

"Thanks," she said with a slight smile. "I will call you if I need anything."

"Don't hesitate," Detective Fuller said. "Did you see the newspaper article this morning?"

Alicia slowly nodded her head.

"I did," she said. "It wasn't me who said anything."

Detective Fuller put his hands up in an "I come in peace" gesture.

"Of course not," he said, then dropped his hands, and slid them into his pants pockets. "I know that. It seems like one of the neighbors who was questioned as part of our canvass said something, which is fine. The parts we want to keep secret are still secret. That's what matters. I don't think the article is going to help us find Josh. We'll probably get some folks calling in with tips. Most of those don't pan out, and might slow us down a little. I promise that we're going to do our best to find him."

Again, Alicia slowly nodded her head.

"I know that."

Alicia looked into Detective Fuller's eyes. There was conviction there. Despite the early roadblocks she had been informed of, she saw belief in Fuller's eyes that he would find out what happened to Josh. Alicia was happy to have a man like Fuller working on the case. She bought his sales pitch.

"You give a call if you need something or if you think of anything else," Detective Fuller said.

"Thank you, I will do that. Anything else?"

Fuller shook his head.

"Just that. Thank you for your help."

"You're welcome," Alicia said. "Goodnight, Detective."

"Goodnight."

Fuller walked back to his car. Alicia closed the door and stood behind it to watch through the door's small window as Fuller climbed in his car. Her kids were sitting at the kitchen table. A dinner of hot dogs and mac and cheese was on their plates. On the counter behind them were sympathy cards and Tupperware containers of baked goods that people from the neighborhood had dropped off after reading the story about Josh in the newspaper. Alicia never felt much of a connection with her neighbors. Nonetheless, she appreciated their gestures of sympathy at this time. Alicia's plate, which had been placed in front of the same chair she sat in when "Not Officer Warner" told her of Josh's death, had a small helping of mac and cheese on it. Next to it sat a large glass of wine. She took a generous gulp from the glass before settling back into her chair.

"Who was that, mommy?" Angel said.

"That was the detective who is trying to figure out what happened to Josh."

"Is he going to find Josh?"

"He says he is," Alicia said. "And I believe him."

Alicia's two other children sat quietly eating their dinner.

*   *   *   *   *

There was a small park across the street from the Basil house. Detective Fuller noticed it as he turned his car onto Orchard Street. The park had a parking lot with ten spots in it, two of which were taken. Fuller pulled his car into the lot, parked, and got out.

Detective Fuller looked at the Basil house. He decided on the drive over that he was not going to knock on their door.

How would Josh Martin have gone home? He would not have gone back to Ivy Hall, would he? It seemed like the long way to go. Josh probably would have headed through the park, and cut across a back yard or two to get back home. Fuller headed into the park, walking past a low-standing, yet large sign stenciled with the words Orchard Park. The sun was nearly all the way down. It was difficult to see the park's landscaping. The houses surrounding Orchard Park were still clear to Fuller. Darkness was settling in.

*   *   *   *   *

Sam was washing the dishes. Macy and Angel were in the room they shared. Alicia still sat at the kitchen table. More than half the bottle of wine in front of her was gone. She had opened it just before sitting down to dinner.

"Mom," Sam said.

"Yes, Sam."

"How can we keep doing this?"

"Doing what?"

Sam shut the water off and turned around to face his mother.

"Pretending that everything is okay. Pretending that Josh isn't gone."

57

"No one is pretending, Sam," Alicia said as she took a sip of wine.

"You are pretending, Mom. You haven't even told anyone in the family yet. Nobody's been here except for the neighbor ladies who came today, and you didn't even let them in the house."

Alicia wasn't looking at her son. She was looking at a magazine in front of her.

"Are we going to have a service or something?" Sam said.

The words shook Alicia inside, but she did not show it on the exterior. She took another sip of wine, and turned the page in her magazine.

"We should have some kind of memorial, Mom."

Alicia just sat there.

"He's gone," Sam said. "He should be remembered."

A single tear trickled down Alicia's face. She wiped it away, turned the page, and took another sip of wine.

*   *   *   *   *

Fuller walked through Orchard Park along a paved bike path. A jungle gym and two baseball fields with their backstops backed up against each other occupied most of the park. The path cut between the two backstops, behind which sat two small sections of bleachers for parents and relatives eager to cheer on the little leaguers, and led out of the other end of the park between two houses.

Fuller was standing in the area between the backstops. The last flickers of sunlight were vanishing quickly. The ever-growing darkness masked his vision. Detective Fuller spun in a slow circle, looking into the lit windows of the houses with their backs to Orchard Park as he turned. When Fuller had turned all the way around he stood still for a moment, and closed his eyes.

When he opened his eyes, standing in front of him was what looked to be a man, but he had no face. Fuller stumbled back a step or two, and reached for his gun.

"Hello?"

The man did not move.

As Fuller looked him, or perhaps it, up and down he noticed that in addition to having no face, this thing in front of him had no feet. It was hovering there in the fading twilight. What hovered in front of Fuller was the darkest dark. Completely black. There was no skin showing. Fuller could very clearly make out a necklace dangling off what would be described as shoulders. The necklace was silver with a red heart dangling off the center of it. Fuller's spine locked in fear as he saw the heart dim to black then slowly turn red again. He took two steps toward the thing, and in a flash, it was gone. No more red heart. No more anything.

The path Fuller was standing on started up a slight hill and cut between two white houses ahead. He spotted the dark mass again as his eyes moved up the hill. It was hovering about a quarter mile away. The red heart was glowing, and Fuller could spot it even from this distance. Fuller took off after the entity in a full sprint. Ten paces into his run, he thought of how he needed more exercise. His lungs inhaled the cold November air, and each breath stung more than the previous one. When he reached the top of the hill, Fuller tasted blood in his mouth. Detective Fuller was now standing on Roberts Road. To his left Roberts met up with Pine, which led back over to Dunwoody where the Martin's house was.

As Fuller glanced toward Pine, he saw the dark mass again not far in the distance. His chase resumed. This time the black, hovering mass did not move or disappear. Fuller caught up with it at the corner of Pine and Roberts, his legs feeling slightly better than after the first sprint.

The dark, half-formed body hovered above a bush, and as he moved closer to it, Fuller caught a phrase in his head. A group of words formed together in his head, and he could not shake them or their meaning. It was like the chorus of a song, stuck in his brain, playing on repeat.

Fuller closed his eyes, and listened to it play over and over in his head.

When you need me, you'll find me, but first you must wake from this dream.

When you need me, you'll find me, but first you must wake from this dream.

When you need me, you'll find me, but first you must wake from this dream.

When you need me, you'll find me, but first...

When Fuller opened his eyes again he was not standing in front of a bush on the corner of Pine and Roberts. He was back in Orchard Park, standing between the backstops, and staring into the night.

Fuller again – or was it for the first time? – started to run up the hill on the bike path that ran between the two white houses. When he reached the top of the rise his legs screamed for relief. They begged his brain to stop making them run. Standing on Roberts he looked toward Pine. Fuller saw nothing in that direction. No dark figure. No necklace. He jogged toward Pine. His legs were much happier with the pace.

The houses at the corner of Pine and Roberts were set back in their lots. There was a lot of space around the corner where the streets intersected. A row of bushes ran on an angle at the corner of each lot that touched the intersection of Pine and Roberts. It must have been something the developer or the city had put in, because Detective Fuller noticed the bushes were identical, well almost identical. The bushes for the house on the right side of the road looked as though someone had been pushed into them. It was in front of these bushes where Fuller had stood moments ago and heard those words dance in his head.

When you need me, you'll find me, but first you must wake from this dream.

Fuller saw something stuck in one of the bushes. He reached in and pulled out a New York Yankees baseball cap. On the underside of the brim of the hat, there was dried blood. Fuller took out his cell phone and called Alicia Martin. She picked up on the third ring.

"Ms. Martin, it's Jack Fuller."

"Yes, Detective?"

She sounded out of it, like she had been asleep.

"I'm sorry, did I interrupt anything?"

"Just my glass of wine," Alicia said.

Alicia had not been sleeping. She was drunk. But who could blame her?

"Ms. Martin, I'm sorry to bother you, but I have a quick question. Did Josh have a New York Yankees hat?"

There was silence.

"Ms. Martin?"

"Yes. He did. The kids up here teased him for being a Yankees fan, but he loved that team. I tried to take him down there for a game each year."

"Okay, Ms. Martin. That's all I needed. Thank you."

"Did you find his hat?" she asked.

Fuller briefly considered withholding the information to spare Alicia more worry. It was an instinct he quickly suppressed.

"Yes. Yes I did."

Alicia held the phone away from her mouth as she tried to hold back a fresh batch of tears. Detective Fuller patiently waited on the other end of the line for Alicia to gather herself.

"I'd like to have it whenever you are done with it," she said in a weak voice.

"Of course, Ms. Martin. I'll get it to you."

"Thank you," she said.

"It's no trouble."

"Thank you," she said again.

Fuller pictured Alicia Martin at her dining room table with a quarter of a bottle of wine left in front of her, and tears running down her face. She needed help. Fuller would make more of an effort to check in on her, and he would seek out a grief counselor or a therapist who had experience with mothers losing their children.

"Goodnight, Ms. Martin," Fuller said for lack of a better way to end the conversation.

He ended his call, took a breath, and dialed McAvoy.

"Hello?" McAvoy said.

"Ronald, it's Jack."

"What is it, Jack?"

"I found the abduction point. Or maybe the death point. I'm not sure. But I need a team over here."

"What did you find?" McAvoy said.

"I found the kid's hat. The mother said he had one like it. It's got blood on it. It looks like he got thrown into some bushes over here somehow. Maybe there was a struggle. Maybe there is some evidence."

"Okay, Jack. I'll send a team to you. Where are you?" McAvoy said anxiously.

"I'm at the corner of Roberts and Pine."

"Sounds good, Jack," McAvoy said. "Sit tight for a bit."

"Will do."

Both ended the call on their cell phones. Fuller looked up at the sky, which was completely black now. The stars were dim because of light pollution. His gaze turned to the houses around him. He counted twelve that could have had a clean view of the spot he was standing in. *How could no one have seen this happen?* His thoughts drifted back to the dark entity that had hovered before him, with a heart necklace dangling off its shoulders. Fuller did not believe in ghosts and goblins, but he believed in what he saw. It was no ghost. When Fuller saw the hovering black mass, it was as though he had been possessed. Fuller did not believe in that sort of thing either. He did believe in power, though, and whatever the dark form was it definitely had power.

When you need me, you'll find me, but first you must wake from this dream.

11:00 p.m.

Houston West spotted the night foreman, Mark Quill, while

making his rounds. Quill was polishing the floor with the large, circular floor-scrubbing machine. It was the task Quill most regularly performed.

"Mark, do you have a second?" Houston said.

Quill turned off the machine, and looked at Houston.

"What's up?"

"I'm quitting. Tonight's my last night."

The news did not impact Quill at all. He was surprised Houston was still working this job. It was not for him.

"I'm actually happy for you, Houston. You're better than this job."

"Thanks, Mark. It was nice working for you."

Houston did not mean that line. He did not like the way Mark did things, mainly because he felt Mark was an idiot.

"You can get out of here now if you want," Quill said.

"It's no bother. I can finish."

"No, no. You should leave."

Quill's tone had changed. He didn't seem as happy as he was moments ago. Houston saw pain in Quill's eyes.

"Okay," Houston said. "I'll go."

Houston was headed for the door when he heard Quill's voice call after him. He turned to face Quill for one final time.

"Don't let those ladies bother you," he said with a smile.

Houston smiled and put his head down.

"And always go back to the hole," Houston said.

"There you go," Quill said.

They were inside jokes between the two of them. Nobody else would really understand.

11:07 p.m.

Fuller was awake in his bed. He rose, and twirled his bare feet over the edge of the bed. As they hit the carpet, Fuller paused a moment to let out a sigh.

He switched on his bedside lamp, illuminating the area in front of his bed. The floor was covered with open files, thrown about in no particular order. Fuller sat down in front of them and began to page through the pile once more. There was nothing there. No crime scene with photos to search for a clue. The search at Pine and Roberts had not yielded anything other than Josh Martin's New York Yankees hat. McAvoy said they would come back in the morning when the sun was up in case the dark was hiding any evidence. The rush of finding something new had quickly worn off as Fuller stood in the background watching the techs search the scene with their flashlights. Now, with each file Fuller looked at, a new question would crop up and another screw would tighten in his mind. There was only going to be one way he could pump some life into this investigation.

We have to go public with the sketch. It's the only way.

6

November 16, 2:55 p.m.

Houston spent the last week mulling around his apartment. He watched TV and movies, read news online, and masturbated often. He had given himself a week to mentally relax after quitting his job. The planned relaxation did not go well. He read the story about Josh Martin going missing, which had strongly influenced him to quit his job at the Vanguard police station. During the past week he had seen updates on that story with a police sketch that was supposed to be of him. Frankly, Houston did not see the resemblance. It must have been the mother who described him, and she had done a poor job of remembering. After three days of worry, he started to avoid news about Josh Martin at all costs. Instead, Houston had become fascinated with an article he read about a fishing boat called the *Catiana*, and the passing of the torch from Vince McGuffey to his son Charlie.

Houston thought the idea of working on a lobster fishing boat provided a masculine romanticism from years gone by. It also might help him with a problem he was having with Josh Martin. He had called the port where the *Catiana* made its berth, and had gotten word of its planned return to shore.

Now, Houston West sat in a small restaurant at the Rounder's Point marina called The Dock, waiting for the boat to arrive. He had not thought through much of a plan of attack. The goal was to get aboard the *Catiana*, and Houston was going to use all of his will to achieve his goal.

Houston had been sitting at The Dock since a little after ten. The restaurant had not seen many patrons, and Houston's waitress, Betty, had checked in on him often in the first hour. He explained to her that he was waiting on a ship, and Betty had pretty much left him alone since. On two occasions Houston had waved her down to place a beer order. Otherwise he had remained in his seat and stared out the window at the harbor.

Around quarter after three a ship pulled up to the dock. It had a black hull with a white stripe down the side. Houston recognized it immediately from the picture that accompanied the story he had read. It was the *Catiana*.

As soon as the *Catiana* was docked, a man who looked to be in his thirties came running off the boat with a duffel bag and a backpack. Houston could see the men who were standing on the boat's deck, and they appeared to be shouting at the man who just left.

The *Catiana* was in port to unload its first batch of lobster, refuel, and head back out. From his seat in The Dock, Houston saw the men begin the work of offloading, without the help of their recently departed deckhand. He was looking for an opportunity to approach the boat. The offload did not take as long as Houston thought it would. Seeing that the crewmen were finishing up, Houston left the restaurant and headed toward the *Catiana*. His bill had been paid two hours ago.

"Hey there," Houston called up to one of the men on the deck.

"What's up?" the man responded.

"I was wondering if I could talk to the Captain about joining the crew."

"Well, this boat normally doesn't take newbies who just straggle in off the dock. But we got a new Captain this year. So maybe he does. You see the other guy just walk out of here?"

Houston nodded.

"I did," Houston said. "Maybe it's my lucky day."

"I'll grab the Captain."

Relief passed over Houston. It could not be too bad from here on out. At least the Captain would speak to him. As he waited, Houston thought the Captain might send the guy he had just talked to back to tell him there was no interest. The nervous feeling Houston had before rushed back over him. After a few minutes, the crewman Houston had been talking to returned.

"He said he'll be down to talk to you."

"Okay," Houston said. "Thanks."

Charlie McGuffey had the look of a fisherman – a barrel chest, bleary eyes, and a thick red beard. He smelled like a man who had been at sea for a while, too. It was a faint smell of body odor mixed with a strong stench of bait and fish. As the two stood on shore, Charlie McGuffey shook Houston's hand and won the battle of whose grip was stronger.

"You know, you're here at the right time," Charlie said.

"I saw that other guy bail out of here," Houston said. "But I was going to try to talk to you no matter what."

"Well, we need a guy, that's for sure. My dad had made some calls on the way back to port because we knew we were going to fire Mikey. But you're here now, so that gives you an advantage. We'd like to get back out to sea, and keep fishing."

Charlie stroked his beard with his left hand and tilted his head toward the bright blue sky.

"You ever worked on a boat before?"

"No," Houston said.

Charlie exhaled. He did not like taking on greenhorns, but his urge to begin fishing again was pulling at him. The first offload was not as big as Charlie expected. He needed to make up for the shortfall.

"You have your stuff with you?" Charlie said.

"Yes I do," Houston said with a smile.

"Get it. Welcome aboard. If you fuck up too much, though, we'll kick you right back out of here when we come back to port."

"Understood," Houston said.

Houston jogged back to his car and grabbed the large duffel bag he had shoved in the backseat. He popped open the trunk and grabbed his large hockey bag as well. It was quite heavy.

When he first set foot on the *Catiana* the crewman who he

spoke with earlier was there to greet him. The crewman was wearing a black stocking cap, and also sported a full beard.

"Welcome to the *Catiana*," he said. "I'm Ryan."

Houston shook Ryan's hand.

7:30 p.m.

Alicia Martin was in her kitchen making dinner for herself and her children. She had felt better in the last few days. The numb feeling that had enveloped her was slowly fading away. She missed Josh more than ever, but now she felt like her own soul had returned. Everything seemed brighter.

Seeing the police sketch on the news and in the paper had helped her shake her dark feelings. Even though Detective Fuller had not spoken with her since the night he found Josh's Yankees hat, Alicia felt things were moving forward with the case. She did not know that the efforts of the Vanguard police department had not unearthed any quality leads.

Macy, Sam and Angel were sitting at the kitchen table talking about school. Alicia had kept them home the week after Josh disappeared, and the trio had just finished their first week back. They seemed much happier, much more normal.

Alicia turned around from the stove, and saw Josh seated with her other children. Her knees buckled.

"Josh!" she yelled. "You're back! My god you're alive!"

Macy, Sam and Angel stopped talking and stared at their mother. There was a look of happiness on her face. Alicia walked over to the empty chair at the table where Josh always sat. She wrapped her arms around air as though she was hugging her son from behind.

"Mom, Josh isn't there," Macy said.

Alicia looked at her daughter. There was no joy left in her face. It was anger. Pure anger.

"He's right here, Macy, don't be silly." Alicia's tone was not that of anger. It was sweet, almost songful. Her mouth was in a scowl, though. Her eyebrows were angled downward toward her nose.

"There's nothing there, Mommy," Angel said.

Alicia unwrapped her arms from the empty space on the chair she thought her son occupied, and silently walked over to Angel. She squatted down so she could be eye level with her youngest child. Angel was scared. She had her head down. Her hands were clasped together.

"Look at Mommy," Alicia whispered.

Angel did as her mother told her. Tears began to fall down Angel's cheeks as she turned her head. Without another word, Alicia picked Angel up, but did not hug her. She held Angel away from her body like she was poisonous. Alicia turned and walked out of the kitchen and down the hall toward the room Macy and Angel shared. She set Angel down on her bed.

"You stay here, until Mommy says so," Alicia whispered.

Alicia returned to the kitchen. Sam and Macy were wide-eyed while looking at her.

"Go to your rooms," Alicia said in the same sweet tone as before. Her expression had not changed. Her eyebrows were slanted downward and her mouth was turned in a scowl.

Sam slowly stood up, but Macy sat still.

"We haven't eaten yet," Macy said.

Alicia's head snapped toward Macy like an animal that had spotted its prey. She slid a chair out of the way, took a step toward her oldest daughter, and crouched down to Macy's eye level. Macy's heart and brain were racing. She felt like she was not in control of her emotions. Her demeanor was controlled, though. Her mouth was closed tight, and her face was expressionless. Her eyes had a hint of defiance in them.

Alicia stared into those eyes. She did not say a word this time. She picked Macy up, and Macy began to struggle and scream, things Angel did not do. Macy pleaded for her mom to put her down. To stop. It was as though Alicia did not hear anything. She silently began walking toward the room Macy and Angel shared. Sam followed. He was grabbing at his mother, trying to physically stop her. Alicia did not react. She did not feel what Sam was doing.

"Mom, put her down. What are you doing?" he said.

Alicia appeared to hear nothing, and Sam's effort could not stop her from reaching his sisters' room. Alicia dropped Macy on the ground upon entering the room the way someone drops a heavy log they have been carrying for a lengthy distance. Macy shrieked in pain and began to cry. Alicia turned and pushed Sam away from the doorway. She closed the door to Macy and Angel's room.

"Do not come out," Alicia said in a voice just loud enough for them to hear inside. It was still light and songful.

She looked at Sam now. He was crying too, but Alicia did not notice.

"Do you want to eat dinner with your brother and me?" she said.

Sam looked at her in astonishment.

"He's home. Everyone should be happy. We should have a nice meal."

Sam nodded. Agreeing with his mother was the only way he was going to get dinner that night.

"Sure," Sam said.

"Good," Alicia said with a smile. "Come with me."

She took Sam's hand and walked down the hall toward the kitchen. Sam heard his sisters screaming and crying from inside their room. His mother did not seem to notice.

7

November 17, 3:25 a.m.

The *Catiana* steamed toward the fishing grounds with most of its crew asleep in their bunks. Captain Charlie McGuffey was behind the wheel. His eyes were heavy. The Captain needed sleep, but lit a cigarette instead. He did not trust anyone on the boat to drive while it was dark except Rooster, and Charlie knew he needed Rooster fresh for the day's work ahead. He had that new kid on board, and Rooster was going to be working double to cover up the kid's errors. It was just the way Rooster was.

Let him sleep.

Charlie did not know the new kid, Houston West, was not asleep. Houston was standing at the rear of the boat, out of sight from the wheelhouse. His hockey bag was beside him.

*   *   *   *   *

Houston opened the exterior door that lead to the rear of the ship and slipped below deck. The hockey bag was not with him anymore. The inside of the *Catiana* was very tight quarters. Houston already liked the openness of the deck better, even though he knew that was where he was going to be working himself to exhaustion. There was a small galley kitchen that no more than two men could stand in comfortably at the same time. Three short hallways led to the kitchen like prongs on a fork. The middle hallway led to a staircase that went up to the wheelhouse. Next to the staircase there was a door that opened to the Captain's bedroom. At seven feet by ten feet, it was the largest bedroom on this ship.

The two outer prongs also led to bedrooms. There were two down each hallway, each were six by eight and housed two bunks.

Despite being the current Captain, Charlie McGuffey slept in one of these smaller bedrooms by himself. Charlie's father, Vince, still occupied the Captain's bedroom. That left the other five members of the crew to pair up in the other three rooms. Veteran *Catiana* crewman Martavious Roost, known as Rooster to everyone on the boat, had his own room as well. Ryan Olsen, the deckhand who had greeted Houston, was Houston's bunkmate.

Houston turned the knob to his bedroom as quietly and carefully as he could. There was a slight creak when the door opened. It was not loud enough to wake Ryan, who was asleep in the bottom bunk. Houston had snuck out of his bed easily enough, but it was easier to quietly slip down the small ladder than it was to climb back up it. Each rung of the wooden ladder creaked as Houston climbed, and when he was almost in his bed he heard Ryan move beneath him.

"You awake, man?" Ryan whispered in a half asleep mumble.

"Yeah, I had to piss," Houston said.

"Get some sleep. Today's one of the few days we get a decent rest. You'll need it for the morning."

"Right. Thanks."

Houston expected Ryan to say something else, but he never did. It took Houston a little while to doze off. Eventually, sleep came strong and fast.

8:07 a.m.

It took Angel a long time to fall asleep the night before. She did not have any dinner, and her stomach kept her up with hunger pains, but she did not dare open the door.

She dozed off at about a quarter after one in the morning. Macy fell asleep long before that, and she was still sleeping now. Angel was roused by hunger. She stayed in her bed for a few minutes, listening for commotion coming from somewhere in the house.

She heard nothing.

Quietly, she slid the covers down her body and set her toes on the carpet. She opened her door, peeked around the corner, and seeing nothing, headed for the kitchen. Her heels never hit the floor.

Angel went for the snack drawer right away. She saw two unopened boxes of crackers first and a container full of cookies. She grabbed four cookies out of the container and gobbled them down. Then, Angel snatched the two boxes of crackers and headed back for her room. The house was still silent.

While she was walking down the hallway, Angel saw her mother coming out of her room. Angel froze. Her mother looked at her.

"What do you have there, sweetie?" Alicia asked.

8:17 a.m.

It had been a little over a week since Fuller saw that thing in the park – the giant dark form with no feet or arms. Since then his mind had been on overdrive. He had not been able to sleep for more than a few hours each night, and his appetite had vanished. He had lost five pounds, and had not shaved. What was stubble could now be classified as a beard.

He was at his kitchen counter, sitting on a stool with the shades to his apartment drawn to block the rising sun. He had a notebook in front of him and a pencil in his hand. He was sketching the black entity over and over again. It looked like a blob of dark gray on his notepad, and Fuller was growing frustrated with not being able to recreate it as he had seen it in Orchard Park. Fuller could tell there was a density to it. It had some kind of mass. It was more than a fog or a cloud. Despite not having any proof, Fuller was sure that if he tried to walk through the dark mass he would be unsuccessful.

8:32 a.m.

Alicia calmly made Angel breakfast. It was as though last night had not happened. Angel was not sure know how to act, so she quietly sat at the kitchen table while her mother made scrambled eggs. Angel's head rested on top of her folded arms.

"Is Josh here, Mommy?" Angel asked.

Alicia sighed, and looked down at the eggs she was making. Then, she turned to face Angel.

"Sweetie, Josh is gone. Don't you remember what I told you?"

Angel vividly remembered the night Alicia told her and her siblings that Josh was gone. She had never seen her mother as sad as she was that night. The image haunted the little girl. She was also troubled by what her mother did to her last night – sending her to her room without dinner. It was something Alicia had never done before.

"I remember," Angel said without lifting her head from her arms.

Alicia walked toward her youngest child and placed her hand on Angel's back.

"It'll be okay, Angel. It will be okay without Josh. We will never forget him, but eventually things will be okay."

Angel nodded; her head was still on her arms.

"Now sit up," Alicia said. "You won't be able to eat your breakfast with your head on the table."

8:51 a.m.

"Time to get up. You need some breakfast."

Houston had only recognized the word "breakfast" coming from Ryan's mouth.

"What?" Houston groggily said.

"It's time to get up," Ryan repeated. "You need to eat. We've got to get out on deck."

Houston nodded his head, and started to climb down from the top bunk. His legs wobbled when his feet touched the ground. He could tell the boat was pitching more than it was last night, and he immediately had trouble maintaining his balance. Ryan noticed Houston's struggles.

"You alright?"

Houston did not feel normal, but he knew he could not say that. He needed to act the part of a fisherman.

"I'm fine. I just have to get used to this."

Houston followed Ryan to the galley. Mario Diaz and Lou Abbott were sitting at the small table. Rooster was standing over a pan of eggs that was on the stove. Houston had met everyone in a blur of introductions yesterday, but he remembered their names despite the whirlwind. Still, he figured it would be best to keep quiet around the breakfast table this morning. While serving himself a plate of eggs and sausage, Houston silently marveled at Rooster's size. Houston was right around six feet tall, and considered himself of medium to lanky build. His eyes were at Rooster's shoulder level. The man must have been six foot seven or eight. Rooster had a large barrel chest, and biceps that looked like something out of a cartoon. Houston imagined Rooster was not very comfortable in the cramped quarters of the *Catiana*, but the big man was not complaining now. Rooster was wearing a short-sleeve shirt, and Houston thought his forearms resembled the lower leg of an average man.

"Hopefully this trip goes smoother," Lou Abbott said.

Diaz nodded in response. His mouth was full of food.

"All that matters is good fishing," Ryan said.

"We had solid fishing the last time, but that kid, Mikey, was a mess. He caused too many problems. Hopefully the new guy is better," Lou said.

"Definitely," Diaz said. "Too many issues last trip."

"What do you say, New Guy? Is it going to be a good trip?" Lou asked of Houston.

The *Catiana's* greenhorn nodded his head. "I'll help in every way I can. I'll work hard for you guys."

Lou rolled his eyes and smiled. "Yeah, yeah. That's what they all say."

An intercom speaker that was mounted on the wall near the table let out a low-pitched buzz and then a voice came on.

"About ten minutes guys. Better get dressed."

It was the voice of Charlie McGuffey. Everyone quickly finished their eggs, and hustled to a small room where every crewman's raincoat and pants were hanging. Houston struggled to get his gear on over his clothes. He noticed everyone else was dressed much quicker than he was.

Once dressed, the crew walked out onto deck. Rooster led the way. Houston brought up the rear. The cold air wrapped around Houston like a vine. He shivered, and questioned what he had gotten himself into. Earlier this morning Houston had been on the deck, but it felt much colder now. The *Catiana* was much further out at sea, and it felt like the temperature had dropped fifteen degrees.

The lobster traps were stacked neatly on the deck. The task at hand for the crew was baiting them and tossing them into the sea. Houston quickly found his job to be bait boy, and also the deck's gopher. Orders were barked at him in increasingly impatient tones by his fellow crewmembers. Houston did his best to keep his mouth shut and keep up with the work being sent his way. He knew complaining would not earn him any points. Rooster, the deck boss, said the least. His only words to Houston on this day were, "Faster. You need to go faster."

Houston tried to go as fast as he could, but found he could not keep up with the accelerated pace of the experienced crew. He was trying to make every task a sprint. This approach quickly wore down his strength and energy, and began leading to mistakes. He fell on deck a few times, fortunately avoiding major injury.

Carrying the plastic milk jugs filled with bait seemed like an easy task at first. As the day wore on, the five-pound jugs made his arms feel weak. Eventually it seemed like the jugs weighed ten times what they actually did. His body ached before the shift ended, and he wondered how it would feel after his adrenaline wore off.

His biggest spill came when he was hurrying across the deck with both hands holding bait. His foot nicked the edge of a board that was not flush with the others. The board was not outright dangerous. It was warped just enough to catch the edge of Houston's boot as he hurried by. The result was Houston tumbling forward at an alarmingly fast rate. He tried to put his hands out to brace for the fall, but he could not let go of the bait in time. He crashed to the deck in spectacular fashion. He barely got one of his arms extended in an attempt to cushion the fall. As hard as he tried to protect his head, his face collided with the deck without any cushion. Immediately after rolling onto his back he could feel a welt forming above his right eye. Luckily for Houston, no bones were broken.

It was Mario who helped Houston to his feet.

"You alright, kid?" Mario said.

Houston tried his best to shake it off. "Yeah. I'm fine."

"Your head ok? You need to go in?"

Houston was very tempted to say yes. His pride would not allow him to. He did not want everyone else viewing him as someone who had failed in his first shift. He wanted to show them that he had what it took to be a valuable member of the *Catiana*'s crew.

"No, I'm good," Houston said while rubbing the lump above his eye. "It doesn't hurt that bad. And it will heal."

A surprised look crossed Mario's eyes for a second. Houston caught it, even though it vanished quickly as Mario's eyes narrowed.

"Sounds good," Mario said, and then turned to the other crewmen who were looking on. "He's alright. He'll be fine."

Everyone went back to work. Houston felt better about

himself. Somehow the spill had given him confidence. Houston was confident he could handle any task he faced on the *Catiana*, and that he had earned some respect from his co-workers. For a few brief moments the *Catiana* was at his feet, and there was no task he could not conquer.

8

November 24, 4:47 a.m.

The crew of the *Catiana* was slogging through another long haul. They had hit the deck a little after eight the night before, and were still grinding away. The hope was this long grind would fill their tanks and they would be able to steam back to shore. From the wheelhouse, Charlie McGuffey could tell his boys needed rest. Part of him wanted to give them an hour or two of sleep right now. He suppressed the urge by telling himself it would be crueler to order them to sleep now when the job was not finished. In another few hours they would be done with this trip, and be able to get a full sleep in.

On deck, Houston was in a daze. He had downed a cup of black coffee almost two hours ago, and the jolt it had given him was evaporating. Houston had discovered a strong will to push through fatigue during his time on the *Catiana*, but now that will was fading. He craved sleep, and could not wait for Captain Charlie to send the crew in. Houston marveled at the abilities of the other men, especially Rooster. Rooster had not complained once on the entire trip, at least not that anyone had heard. The big man did not involve himself in the bickering of the other crewmen. He rose above it all, and in times of need, the crew looked to Rooster for guidance. Without a doubt, he was their leader.

Houston was sorting through one of the lobster pots when he caught a glimpse of Rooster out of the side of his eye. Rooster was standing in the middle of the deck looking out at the horizon; his broad shoulders took up more space than any one man should be able to. He was completely still; a man frozen in time. Lou noticed it too. He spoke before Houston did.

"Everything alright, Rooster?"

Rooster looked unfazed, as though the words had never been said. He then turned his head toward Lou and nodded.

"It's fine," Rooster said.

Rooster moved toward a stack of pots, and examined the mesh tied around the outside. Houston thought the move looked like a ruse. That Rooster was only doing it to appear to be working. Faking being busy was not Rooster's style.

Many years ago, Vince McGuffey had seen how the other crewmembers looked at Rooster. He broached the subject of Rooster becoming deck boss while the two sat in the wheelhouse early one morning about ten years ago. Rooster was hesitant at the time. He knew Charlie McGuffey, Vince's son, also worked on the boat and had his eye on becoming the deck boss. Vince had explained that Charlie only wanted one thing: the Captain's chair. Vince told Rooster in those daybreak hours that Charlie would get his wish some day.

Vince explained that if Rooster wanted to be a Captain, he should begin searching for a boat that afforded him the opportunity. The *Catiana* would not give him the chance. But if he didn't mind being a deck boss, he could have the job for as long as he wanted on the *Catiana*. As was his nature, Rooster said very little in his conversation with Vince. He spent most of his time staring at the ocean out of the window in front of him. His eyes barely met Vince's.

"Why?" Rooster had said after a long silence.

"Why?" Vince said. "Why you?"

Rooster nodded.

"Because everyone looks to you. You may not realize it, but I see it. Charlie sees it too. I asked Charlie who he viewed as the best crewman on the boat. Without hesitation he said your name. I'm not going to blow a bunch of praise up your ass, because that's not my nature, but you're made for this Rooster. You really are."

Rooster nodded his head, and was quiet for another minute.

"I'll take the job," Rooster said.

"Good," Vince said. "You'll start immediately."

At the time a man named Arthur Saunders was the deck boss, but he was going to be leaving the *Catiana* after the trip they were on. Saunders had secured steady work on land, and was leaving the fishing industry. His body was beaten, but not broken. Saunders figured it was a good time to try to lead a normal life. Vince informed Saunders of Rooster's promotion, and the retiring fisherman took it in stride. Saunders was a good man, and a fine deck boss. Vince was sorry to see him go. The excitement of seeing Rooster in his new role far outweighed Vince's sorrow over losing Saunders.

Since his promotion, Rooster had been nothing short of great every time he stepped on deck. He was not a vocal leader, and that had always worked for the *Catiana*. Because of his size, the other members of the crew feared what would happen if they did not match his effort. They knew he would not physically harm them, but men as big as Rooster are always intimidating.

For the past twenty minutes, though, Rooster's effort seemed to be dragging along with the rest of the crew.

The men on deck noticed it, and Charlie McGuffey spotted it from the wheelhouse as well. Every few minutes, Rooster would stop to look out at the sea. He was not looking up in the sky, instead staring straight ahead at the horizon. Charlie decided to raise him on the intercom.

"Hey, Rooster," he said. "Could you come up to the wheelhouse real quick?"

Charlie knew this would be his first wheelhouse meeting as Captain of the *Catiana*. He did not know it would be his only wheelhouse meeting as Captain.

5:25 a.m.

Alicia Martin was lying on her side in bed when her eyes fluttered open. Her vision was blurry, and she blinked a few times in an attempt to focus. She had little success. Alicia closed her eyes for a minute or two, then opened them again. This time the world around her was clear, even in her darkened room.

She rolled onto her other side to face the windows that lined her bedroom. There was the slightest glimmer of a sunrise beginning. The sky was bright red. Alicia felt more in control than she had in recent days. It was as though something sinister had left her. Her thoughts were clear, and already she could tell she could compartmentalize any feelings she had about Josh. Her emotions were no longer consuming her.

Goosebumps formed on her legs as she slipped her bare feet out from under the covers. She walked to the shower to get ready for the day, vowing to herself it would be a good one.

5:31 a.m.

Booming, methodical thuds on the stairs precluded Rooster's arrival in the wheelhouse. Charlie was not scared or intimidated by the big man. He never had been. Charlie respected Rooster. A Captain's biggest concern was how his crew was performing, and Charlie was confident in his abilities to coax his crew into working hard. The Captain figured this conversation would be nothing but routine. There was no door at the top of the steps that lead to the wheelhouse. Rooster knocked on the side of the wall to make his presence known.

"I could hear you from your first step on the stairs, Rooster," Charlie said. "Come on up."

Rooster had to hunch slightly in the wheelhouse. Otherwise his head might have grazed the ceiling.

"Take a seat real quick," Charlie said.

Rooster obliged.

"What's up today, Rooster?"

Rooster turned his head to look out the window. Then turned back toward Charlie.

"Nothing's up," Rooster said.

"I don't believe that for a second. You keep stopping your work to look out at the horizon. Do you miss home? I know this has been a long season, but we're getting close. We'll be back soon enough."

Again Rooster turned to look out the window before looking back at Charlie.

"It was a dream, Charlie."

A puzzled look crossed Charlie's face.

"A dream? What dream?"

"The last time we took a break. That quick one. I slept for an hour or two."

Charlie nodded for Rooster to continue. Rooster said no more.

"What happened in the dream?"

"I don't want to say. I fear it may be real."

"Real? How could it be real? You dreamed it up. Listen, Rooster, if all this is about some dream you had, I've got to say that you've got to get it together. You're slacking out there this morning and that isn't like you. I don't care how real the dream felt. It's still a dream."

"The sky is red," Rooster said while looking out the window in front of him.

"I see that. It probably means we are going to take on some shitty weather if you believe the old sailor's saying. And that means I need you at your best out there."

"The sky was red in my dream."

"So it's real then? You dreamed about today? Rooster, a red sky doesn't mean shit for your dream. You can go back on deck now. Just pick up the pace."

Rooster turned to look at Charlie. His eyes looked hollow and dull.

"We are all going to die."

5:48 a.m.

The nightmare Jack Fuller was having came to a screeching halt, like a train stopping at a station. The imagery of Josh Martin being captured by the same black figure Fuller had seen in Orchard Park faded away.

The blackest of night turned to the brightest blue of daytime sky. The color fell from the sky like someone had kicked buckets of paint from a scaffold – streaking its way downward. Physically, Fuller's heart rate slowed and his body relaxed. The rigid houses of the neighborhood around Orchard Park gave way to a rolling prairie. Tall prairie grass sprouted from the earth to surround Fuller, and he allowed his hands to graze the tops of the stalks while he walked.

Detective Fuller's mind found a peaceful sleep. He had been released for a few hours. Fuller's soul was no longer being tortured.

5:53 a.m.

"Say that again," Charlie said.

Rooster was still looking at Charlie. He did not speak

"We are all going to die?" Charlie said. "How do you know this? Because of a dream?"

"Yes," Rooster said. "We are all going to die."

"A fucking dream? Well, thanks for the tip. I'll be careful with the boat. C'mon Rooster, it is crazy enough on this boat. You'll spook everyone with this kind of talk. You know we are a superstitious lot."

Rooster did not wish to say any more. Charlie was not going to believe him. It was no use explaining how he felt, and what he had seen in his dream. There was no proof he could offer. His only conviction was the slight red shade of the sky above, and the blankness he had seen on the horizon line. In his dream, as was the same this morning, the atmosphere and lighting was so that you could not tell the difference between the ocean and the sky at a distance. The earth had become a black marble, and Rooster knew he would never see it blue again.

He had nothing to prepare for. If reality was about to match his dream, there would be nothing to stop the death of everyone on board. It felt like a supernatural act when Rooster had dreamed it the previous night. He knew, though, that it felt too sinister to be something God had intended.

"Can I go back to work?" Rooster said.

"You sure you don't want to tell me anything else, Rooster?" Charlie said with sarcasm dripping from the sides of his mouth like the juice after a bite of a fresh nectarine.

"I will go back to work."

Rooster left the wheelhouse. The stairs creaked as he walked down them.

"Unbelievable," Charlie mumbled while shaking his head. "Un-fucking-believable. I need to make sure these guys get more sleep."

Rooster stood in front of the door that led to the deck of the *Catiana*. He did not want to turn the handle and go back to work. He felt if he did, everything he dreamed would become real. Perhaps staying in the galley could change what was about to happen. Rooster chose not to go out on deck with the other members of the crew; sacrificing a tongue lashing from Charlie to perhaps save everyone on board. Rooster sat at the small table in the galley area, and silently prayed.

After ten minutes passed, Charlie noticed Rooster had not returned to deck. He cursed, and yelled for Rooster down the stairs. There was no response. He debated waking his father up to take the wheel, but decided against it. The intercom on deck crackled to life.

"Lou," Charlie said.

Lou Abbott was sorting lobster when he heard his name called.

"Yes, Captain?" he said.

"Rooster didn't come back on deck did he?"

"Haven't seen him. I figured he was still up with you."

"He's not," Charlie said.

"Well maybe he's taking a shit," Lou said.

Charlie thought it was possible, and his temper cooled a little bit. He wanted to know for sure, though.

"Can you check for me, Lou?" Charlie said.

"Will do."

Charlie put down his end of the intercom system while watching Lou walk off deck. He did not notice that the impending sunrise was seemingly fading back toward night.

Lou walked into the *Catiana*'s lower quarters and found Rooster sitting at the galley table.

"Rooster, what's up?" Lou said. "Charlie was wondering why you aren't back on deck."

Rooster said nothing. He didn't acknowledge Lou at all. From above in the wheelhouse, Charlie heard Lou talking to someone.

"Lou, is that Rooster you are talking to down there?" Charlie shouted down the stairs.

"Yeah. He's just sitting here at the galley table with his eyes closed. He's not asleep, though. His lips are moving."

"Motherfucker," Charlie said. "Lou, get up here and take the wheel."

Charlie was already trudging down the stairs. He passed Lou awkwardly in the narrow hallway that went from the galley to the staircase that led to the wheelhouse. The *Catiana* was temporarily without a driver, but she managed for a few moments on her own.

"Rooster," Charlie called as soon as the big man came into his vision. "Why aren't you back out on deck?"

Rooster gave Charlie the same treatment he gave Lou. He did not acknowledge him at all. Instead, he continued to pray in silence, his lips mouthed the words. Charlie slammed his hand down on the table in an effort to surprise Rooster. It did not work. The big man did not flinch.

"Rooster, look at me," Charlie said.

Again, there was no response.

"Rooster, if you do not look at me, you are fired. I will not allow you back on this ship. You can sit here all you want, but the next time we make port you are gone."

With this, Rooster opened his eyes and looked at Charlie.

"Now get your ass back out on deck," Charlie said.

6:00 a.m.

Alicia was seated on her bed, wrapped in a robe. She surveyed the room around her and noticed a thin layer of dust had collected on the surfaces of the furniture and picture frames in her room. She could not recall the last time she had cleaned the house. Clearly she had not done a good enough job.

She grabbed the notepad and pen she kept on her bedside table and wrote "CLEAN UP!" on the top line. Unknowingly, she touched the base of the pen to the right side of her head just above the ear as she looked at her handwriting. Alicia flipped the notepad to the next page, and jotted another note, this time not in all capital letters.

"What have the police done?"

6:06 a.m.

Houston was on the deck of the *Catiana* sorting lobster. He glanced at the wheelhouse and noticed Lou was behind the wheel instead of Charlie. He wondered where Charlie and Rooster were, and hoped there was nothing wrong mechanically with the ship. Ryan approached him.

"What do you think is going on in there?" Ryan said. "Rooster is never off deck for this long."

"Do you think it's something mechanical?" Houston said.

"I doubt it. Lou is the one who does the mechanical work. I see him up there in the wheelhouse."

"I didn't realize Lou was in charge of that," Houston said. He then changed the subject. "How much longer do you think we have before we sleep?"

"Can't be long now. The tanks are nearly full."

"I'm beat," Houston said.

"We all are. Just keep grinding."

Houston looked off the starboard side of the ship and saw a patch of the sky that was darker than the rest. The sun was not up yet, so the visibility was not great, but Houston could still spot a part of the sky that was blacker than the blackest of night. It was as if all light had been drained from that part of the world. Nothing could shine through it. It was pure darkness. The patch was growing larger, and seemed to be moving closer to the ship. Houston thought it was his eyes playing a trick. The lack of sleep must have been wearing on him.

"Do you see that?" Ryan said while pointing toward the sky.

Houston looked at Ryan. He felt a tingling sensation in his toes as he did.

"I see it," Houston said. His voice was slightly above a whisper.

"What the fuck is that?"

"I can't even guess."

Mario Diaz was working nearby. He had not stopped for any kind of break. He hauled some more lobster traps from over the rail, and found some full with the tasty crustacean. Fatigue seldom affected Mario. He always found a way to summon energy from somewhere inside. When he started on the *Catiana*, what he lacked in knowledge he made up for with effort. Even though he was now an established veteran, he still worked with that same effort.

"Hey, Mario," Ryan called out. "What is that?"

He pointed to the sky as he said the words.

Mario stopped for a moment and glanced up.

"I don't know," he said. "And neither do you. So get back to work."

"Is it a UFO?" Ryan said.

"I don't know," Mario said. "I've never seen a UFO."

Ryan shrugged, and took another look at the black patch in the sky. He was mesmerized. For some reason it looked beautiful to Ryan. It was the reverse of how a sunny, snow-filled morning looked so crisp and clean. This was the exact opposite, but no less beautiful. The blackness was complete. Ryan tried to go back to work, but found himself glancing skyward time and again to see if it was still there. Ryan did not know how often he stared at the sky that morning, but it felt like every thirty seconds.

In the wheelhouse, Lou Abbott did not notice anything in the sky. His focus was on the dark sea in front of him. The sky was clear and the light of the moon combined with the glimmer of a rising sun in the distance made Lou feel like he could see for miles. The actual distance was far less. He did not see the running lights of any other ships, but he knew from experience that did not always mean the boats were not out there.

A few years back, when Vince was still the Captain and Charlie was merely a deckhand, the *Catiana* came within mere feet of broadsiding an idling ship named *The Vixen*. *The Vixen*'s Captain was attempting to catch some shut-eye and had mistakenly turned off his ship's running lights when he turned off the spotlights on the deck. It made the boat nearly invisible, especially since it was a foggy night. Lou did not want a repeat of this incident while he was on watch. He methodically scanned the ocean in front of them for any sign of another ship.

Houston tried his best to ignore the deep black patch of sky. He felt drawn to it, though. It was a feeling he had felt before, and it made him shiver. The darkness, growing ever closer, was like a siren from an ancient tale calling out to him. He knew he should resist its beautiful song, for danger was on the horizon. But he could not. He continued to glance up, and the darkness continued to near the *Catiana*.

Despite summoning all his will to not look at the sky, Houston turned his head again. This time, the dark patch was so near it blocked his view of the few remaining stars above. He noticed there was a similar darkness in the water as well. He opened his mouth to call out to Ryan and Mario, but it was too late.

Suddenly, and without warning, it was upon the ship. It came from the sea and the sky at the same time, meeting at the *Catiana* like two lines crossing on a graph. The screech of metal being sheared and the firecracker-like sound of the wooden deck boards exploding merged together into a sound that Houston could only relate to a bolt of lightning cracking at his feet. He thought for a moment that perhaps it *was* lightning that struck the boat and not this dark mass. Then he saw the dark entity emerge from the crack in the ship's deck. Houston's cheeks, rosy red from the frosty conditions, drained of their color.

Houston looked around and saw Ryan in a heap amongst the lobster traps. Mario was nowhere to be found. He must have fallen through the ever-widening hole in the deck. Houston realized now that the boat had been sheared in half and the two parts were beginning to drift apart.

The dark mass slowly emerged from below, like steam rising above a shower basin. Houston bolted for the inside of the ship. He remembered being instructed that his survival suit – a large, orange wetsuit – would save his life if he ever went overboard. He now raced to find it.

Once he opened the door, he heard the distressed shouts of Charlie, Vince and Lou.

"What the fuck do you mean, Lou?" Charlie yelled.

"It just broke in half!" Lou yelled back.

"Help! Help! Help!" Vince was calling from his room.

After finding his survival suit, Houston raced to Vince's room and threw open the door. The old man was wedged between his bed and a wall. The floor was angled downward because the ship was sinking, and it had caused Vince to tumble off the bed. The bed had then slid forward and trapped him. Houston scampered over the top of the bed and grabbed Vince's hand.

"Help!" Vince repeated.

"I'm here, Vince," Houston said.

Houston struggled a little, but was able to pull Vince up to a point where he could place both of his arms on the bed. From there, Vince was able to free the rest of his body.

"I need a suit, kid," Vince said.

Houston nodded, and stumbled out of the former Captain's room toward what the crew called the wet room, where the gear hung. Upon entering the room, Houston noticed the door that led out to deck – the same door he had come in through moments ago – was still open. He went over to it to close it and felt his feet leave the ground. Houston was being pulled into the air by something. His head banged against the top of the doorframe as he was yanked out into the open air. A sharp, hot pain rushed through his head and trickled down the rest of his body. Immediately his head was throbbing. He touched his hand to the spot where the pain was greatest. There was no blood. Houston was suspended fifteen feet above the deck.

While hanging in the air, Houston could see the damage done to the *Catiana*. The gash in the deck cut through the entire ship. Even with his limited knowledge of boats, Houston knew the *Catiana* would not last long. Houston heard a voice come from nowhere.

You do not belong here. It said.

Houston looked down and saw what looked like a person standing on the rapidly sinking deck of the *Catiana*. The man had no arms or legs. The only discernable feature was a heart pendant dangling from a necklace off the phantom's shoulders, or at least what Houston assumed were shoulders. The pendant was a dark red, but Houston noticed it fade to complete black – as black as the patch of sky he had noticed before the ship exploded – and then return to its red color.

Inside the wheelhouse, Charlie and Lou stood with their mouths agape as they looked at Houston West suspended above the deck with no ropes or wires to be seen.

You do not belong here.

"What?" Houston shouted. "What do you mean?"

Charlie and Lou could hear Houston say something, but they were unsure of what it was.

You have endangered everything. You need to leave.

What Charlie and Lou saw next could not have been real. It must have been their imaginations. Houston West disappeared. He was dangling in front of their faces one moment, with his back to them, and the next, he was gone. Never to be seen again.

While looking for a sign of Houston, the top of the *Catiana* was sheared off by something neither Charlie or Lou ever saw. The metal screech was deafening. Both men dropped to the floor, and instinctively covered their ears. Lou's eyes were closed as shards of metal and glass crashed down around him. He heard Charlie scream and opened his eyes to look in that direction.

Charlie was writhing in pain on the floor. Lou figured something had fallen on the Captain. Then Lou felt a sharp pain in his back. He screamed, and began to slither along the floor as if being pulled by a strong force. It felt to both of them as though their spines were slowly being fed through a pepper grinder.

Rooster heard Charlie and Lou's screams while still sitting at the table in the galley. His eyes were still shut. He continued to pray. So far it had gone just as his dream had foretold. His prayers had not been answered.

"Rooster, Rooster. Get up, man. We've got to get off the ship."

It was Vince's voice. Rooster knew it well, but he also knew there was no leaving this ship alive. He tried his best to ignore Vince and focus on his prayer. Vince reached out and grabbed

Rooster's shoulder. It was a fatherly touch – one of comfort. Rooster opened his eyes and looked up at Vince.

A hole burst in the side of the ship. Neither Vince nor Rooster flinched. The cold Atlantic air rushed into the galley, but neither man seemed to notice.

"We are going to die," Rooster said.

Vince steadied himself by wrapping his free arm around a nearby post. He did not say anything to Rooster. He knew the big man was right. The ship was being destroyed around them. Vince knew that Rooster could probably survive in the water. The former Captain also knew that with his own advanced age, he would not last an hour. Rooster's hope of survival had long since gone. As big and strong as he was, he knew there was no way he would live past sunrise.

Vince nudged himself onto the bench Rooster was sitting on. The big man wrapped his arm around Vince's shoulders to ensure he would not tumble off. The pair each prayed silently as the ship around them continued to crumble. The dark force that was wreaking havoc on Charlie and Lou avoided Rooster and Vince. It decided to let them die in peace.

In the wheelhouse, Charlie's vision rapidly deteriorated. He thought his eyes were still open, but quickly all he could see was black. Across the floor from Charlie, Lou was experiencing the same sensation. Suddenly each man could not hear the screams of the other. Shortly after that they could not hear their own screams. Their breathing slowed. Soon they felt nothing at all. They were both gone. Their bodies remained, and those found their way to the ocean floor amidst the wreckage of the *Catiana*.

7:30 a.m.

He felt a warm sensation on the left side of his face. It forced him to open his eyes. His left eye opened cleanly, and he saw a blurry landscape of blue and tan. His right eye remained closed; buried in the sand. He lifted his head and immediately felt pain shoot through his skull. He touched the top of his head and felt a large welt. His eyes narrowed in pain.

Houston West's vision began to clear, and he could see he was sprawled out on a sandy beach. He could hear cars driving along a road somewhere behind him. He was shivering from the cold. Not a drop of water was on him. He rolled onto his backside and looked out at the ocean. There was only a vast seascape of blue.

In a rush he got to his feet. Thoughts of the *Catiana* danced through his head. He wanted to call out for Ryan. He realized quickly this would be of no use. He scanned the horizon line, looking for any sign of a ship.

He saw only blue ocean.

Houston sat down on the beach and crossed his legs. He crossed his arms over his chest in an attempt to warm himself. What he could remember from his final moments on the *Catiana* played on a loop in his head. A confusing, displaced feeling grew from Houston's belly. He had felt it once before, on the night his life changed forever. It felt like walking the line between consciousness and dreaming.

Houston stood up, and scanned the horizon line one last time. Having spotted nothing, he turned his back to the ocean and made his way toward the road. He spotted a restaurant a short distance into his journey. Once inside, he asked to use a phone. The hostess obliged him, and Houston dialed the first number he could think of.

The call went straight to Lauren Funst's voicemail. Houston did not leave a message. He asked the hostess if she knew the number of a cab company. She provided one to him, and twenty minutes later he was on his way to his apartment. He hoped he had some cash lying around to pay for the taxi ride.

9

March 22, 10:11 a.m.

"What the fuck is this, Jack?"

Fuller was standing in Ronald McAvoy's office. He had arrived at the station at ten and was immediately summoned by the Captain. McAvoy had a bunch of files strewn across his desk. It had been over four months since the disappearance of Josh Martin.

"It looks like a bunch of files to me," Fuller said.

"They are files, you wise-ass," McAvoy said. "They are your files on the Martin case."

"So what?"

"I told you that you two weeks ago were off the case. On to another assignment. I told you the case of Josh Martin is still open, but we aren't actively pursuing it. There are crimes to be solved, Jack. Crimes with victims we can identify. We aren't sure what happened to Josh Martin. We don't even know if he was killed."

"Fuck you, Ronald. This is a murder and you know it."

McAvoy never admitted to believing Josh Martin had been murdered. Part of him always thought the kid was alive somewhere. It was a small part, but a part nonetheless.

"Jack, I have to see to it that you stop with the Martin case. It has you too wound up. You are too emotionally invested. You're slipping away. You don't look good."

"Isn't that what a good detective should be? Emotionally invested?" Fuller asked.

"Not when it's affecting your work, Jack. There is a case log filled with other cases. It's been four months, and we haven't caught a break with Martin. Hell, we haven't even found a body. It's gone cold. And you've become obsessed."

There was a part of Fuller that knew McAvoy was right, but

he did not want to give up. He had become obsessed with this case. His police instincts told him it was time to move on and forget about Josh Martin for a while. Yet for some reason he could not follow his instincts.

"Give me another month on it," Fuller said.

"A month? Jesus, Jack. You're going to figure it out in a month? What are you going to do that hasn't already been done?"

"What are the alternatives? Let it sit there?"

"Jack, we have to move on. Not every case gets solved. You know that. Not even all of your cases get solved. We have no suspects. No leads. The case will still be open. We just have to put our focus on other things right now."

"So we just sit and wait for someone to come forward with new information or evidence or something?" Fuller asked.

"That's what we have to do," McAvoy said. "Josh Martin is a missing person. As of right now, he hasn't been killed no matter what your gut says. So unless someone comes forward with new information or a body is found, it's time to move on."

Fuller sat quietly for a moment. He looked around McAvoy's office. There was not much to it. There were no pictures on the walls. McAvoy had the pictures on his desk, a chair that Fuller was sitting in, and a few files cabinets. Is this what Fuller was striving for? One last promotion to sit in a crappy office like this?

"Maybe I should take a leave of absence," Fuller said.

"You want a leave of absence?"

"Well, I have vacation days don't I? What about just a vacation?" Fuller asked.

"You would normally need notice for that, but I can arrange it for you, Jack. You are important to us here, a great detective. So yeah, take two weeks and come back refreshed with a clear mind and ready to work on something new."

"I think I can do that," Fuller said.

"Good."

"You want me to bring those files down to storage, Ronald?"

"Thanks, Jack."

McAvoy put the files he had on his desk back in the cardboard box he had taken them out of an hour ago. Fuller picked up the box and headed out of the office.

"See you in two weeks, Jack."

Fuller nodded. He then turned and began walking in the direction of the stairs. The department stored its old files in the basement, and prayed it would not flood. It was a prayer not always answered.

When Fuller reached the stairs, he did not go down them. Instead he swung to the right down a hallway where there were restrooms and vending machines. This hallway reached a T, where Fuller made another right turn toward the main reception area. He walked past the receptionist, with the file box in hand, and out the front door of the station.

The Martin files were in his possession, and he had two weeks of pay coming to him. Fuller was not sure if he would ever set foot in the station again, and that thought suited him just fine.

10

March 23, 7:34 a.m.

A coffee shop seemed like as good a place as any to meet. It was not like Alicia Martin was doing something illegal. It still felt wrong, though. It felt like this meeting should happen in private. Surely these plans were not hatched in coffee shops. Were they?

Alicia was fidgety – continuously checking the time on her cell phone as she sat with a grande latte. Her acquaintance was not late yet, but Alicia's stomach was still in a knot. She thought about bolting out the door and rescheduling the meeting for another time. It did not matter how noble her intentions were, or how pretty her face was, Alicia knew what she was undertaking was not going to be viewed in a positive light by nearly everyone who would hear about it. Alicia checked the time on her cellphone again. If Bridget did not arrive in the next two minutes, Alicia was prepared to walk out of the coffee shop and reschedule the meeting. She would say something had come up with one of her kids. They were sick or had a school project to finish.

As those thoughts of escape were racing through her head, a tall, blonde woman in a sharp black blazer and black dress pants walked through the door. She was wearing a low-cut yellow shirt, and flats. Even though Alicia had only spoken to her on the phone, she knew immediately that Bridget Cass had just walked in the door.

Alicia gave a slight, nervous wave. It caught Bridget's eye, and she smiled as she approached.

-11-

April 7, 12:22 p.m.

Where the hell is Jack Fuller?

That was the question rolling around McAvoy's head for the last three hours. Fuller was supposed to return from his two-week vacation/sabbatical/leave of absence today. McAvoy had a new case waiting for him. Yet Fuller was not at the station.

McAvoy had called Fuller's cell phone three times and not once did it even ring, going straight to voicemail instead. The Captain was really tired of hearing "You have reached Jack Fuller, leave me a message."

McAvoy hoped Fuller was not face down in a ditch somewhere. McAvoy had figured the break would re-ignite Fuller, not wear him down more. The Captain walked out of his office into the bullpen.

"Has anyone here heard from Jack Fuller in the last two weeks?" McAvoy shouted.

"I talked to him," Jim Warner said.

"Warner? When did you talk to him?"

"Last week. I met Fuller for a beer. We talked mostly about the Martin case."

"Shit," McAvoy said. "Has he called you since?"

"Nope. Nothing since."

"Did he say he was coming back to work today?"

"He didn't mention anything," Warner said.

"Shit. Has anyone else heard from Fuller?" McAvoy said.

There was nothing but silence.

"Back to work."

McAvoy went back into his office and sat down. There was a very real chance he was going to have to fire Jack Fuller. That is, if Fuller ever showed up again.

Part II
The Devil is at the Door

12

October 24, 3:24 p.m.

Houston West was driving down the road, aimlessly thinking of Lauren. Her actions never quite lived up to her words. She would always say things like "I want to see you, Houston," or "Some days I really miss you." But whenever he would call her to set something up she was always busy.

He would get a commitment, and then she would back out.

"Oh, something came up tonight, I'll call you next week for dinner." And when next Friday had rolled around, there had been no phone call. Perhaps there was a message he was not getting. Perhaps she was just being nice.

The back and forth is what got to him. He wished she would either be a total bitch or an angel, instead of something in between. Because if it were one or the other his heart could decide on what his mind had been telling him to do for a long time.

As he drove he felt a burning sensation on the top right side of his head. It stung. Stung deep inside. His throat clenched up, and tears almost fell from his eyes. Sometimes, he really hated that girl. But this feeling was not solely from her. It felt more sinister. It felt dark. Houston was surprised that he enjoyed the feeling a little, even though he was in quite a bit of pain.

6:15 p.m.

Josh Martin was doing homework when his mom called him for dinner. That was five minutes ago. He was still seated at his desk buried in his math homework when he heard a knock at his door.

"Yeah," he said.

The door was already open a crack. Alicia Martin pushed it fully open and stood in the entryway.

"We are waiting on you for dinner," she said.

Josh put down his pencil and rubbed his forehead.

"Okay, okay," he said. "I'll be right there."

The family – Alicia, Josh, Macy, Sam and Angel – sat down to a meal of chicken casserole with sides of potatoes and corn. There was also a salad in the middle of the table for everyone to serve themselves from. The children ate quietly and quickly. Chicken casserole was a family favorite.

Alicia broke the silence.

"Halloween is just a few days away, kids," she said.

"Yay!" Macy, Sam and Angel said in unison. Josh was silent.

"Are you all excited?"

"I can't wait to wear my princess costume," Angel said.

"I'm glad to hear it," Alicia said. "What about you, Josh? Are you excited?"

He pushed some corn around his plate with his head down.

"A little, I guess. It is just Halloween."

Alicia nodded, and took a sip from the glass of water in front of her.

"You'll have fun like you always do," she said. "I've got pumpkin pie and ice cream for dessert tonight."

This drew another round of yays from her youngest three children.

"I'll pass," Josh said.

After dinner, Alicia, Macy, Sam and Angel ate their pie and ice cream. Josh retreated to his room to finish his homework. Halfway through one of the thirty math problems he had to complete he sighed and looked up at the ceiling.

He hoped his mother did not embarrass him on Halloween.

13

October 25, 10:15 a.m.

"Your mom got the house all ready for Halloween, Joshie?" Tommy Basil said.

"Shut up, Tommy," Josh replied.

"I'm just kidding, man. No worries." Tommy paused for a second. "So what is she dressing you as? Cinderella or the fairy godmother?"

Everyone they were standing with – Ritchie McGill, Johnny Vincent, and Caroline Ambers – started laughing. Josh's cheeks went flush. He really hated how his mom treated Halloween; acting like it was the grandest celebration of the year. He was looking forward to the first day of November.

The bell rang, releasing the students from Mr. Mitchell's third period biology class. Josh was headed to English; Caroline followed him. She caught up with him quickly and threw her hip into his.

"So your mom likes Halloween, huh?"

"Yeah," Josh said. "She really gets into it. The guys always give me trouble about it."

Josh met Caroline the previous year, but they had said only the word "hey" to each other a couple of time. This year they had a few classes together, and Josh noticed Caroline was talking to him more. He did not mind the extra attention.

"Well, I think it's pretty cool," Caroline said. "I wish my parents were into something. They seem so dull."

"I just wish she was into something else. Halloween is so cheesy."

"It can be fun. You get to dress up, and be silly for a night."

"Fun for kids. I'd just rather not, I guess," Josh said.

"It's not just for kids. I'm dressing up," Caroline said.

"You still dress up?"

"Yup. Every year. I'm going as a bumble bee this year."

Josh pictured Caroline in a giant fluffy bumble bee outfit with black tights covering her legs.

"A bumble bee?"

"Well it's probably not what you are thinking. It's like a tight leotard that is yellow and black striped with little wings. My mom doesn't like it."

A new image popped into Josh's head. He liked this one much more than the fluffy outfit.

"Did you do the reading?" Josh said.

Caroline's hand twirled through her hair.

"I totally forgot. What happened?"

Josh rolled his eyes.

"How could you forget?" he said.

"I don't know," Caroline responded. "I was hanging with Amber, and then I went home to have dinner, and I just spaced."

Josh smiled and shook his head.

"So are you going to help me out or am I going to have to ask someone else?" she said.

Josh laughed. "Alright, but you owe me."

"I know, I know. I owe you again. Just tell me."

"You remember how Jem is running away from the Radley place and his pants get all torn up?"

Caroline shook her head. "Is that from the last chapter? Because I didn't read that either."

"Jeez, Caroline. Well he's running away from the Radley place and sneaks under the fence and his pants get caught. They get ripped and he kicks them off and runs home."

"With no pants on? That's funny."

"Yeah," Josh said. "With no pants on. So in this chapter, Jem tells Scout that he found the pants sewn back together and hung over the fence. Then they find a bunch of things in this knothole in a tree. There's some twine, then two figures that look like Jem and Scout that are carved out of soap. It's like a mystery."

"That's so weird. Who's doing that?"

They had reached the doorway to the English class but stood outside so Mrs. Yocum would not hear them talking about the reading.

"We don't find out who is responsible. But after they find a few more items, they go back to the tree and the knothole is plugged with cement. They find Mr. Radley and ask him what's up, and he says the tree is sick so he plugged the hole up"

"That's strange. I don't like *To Kill a Mockingbird*, I liked *Great Gatsby* a lot more."

"You aren't even reading *Mockingbird*," Josh said with a laugh. "And you barely read *Gatsby*."

"Hey!" Caroline said. "Not cool."

"But *Mockingbird* is awesome. And you should start reading it. For other reasons than me having to bail you out. It's really good."

Caroline laughed. "Okay. I'll do the reading tonight. For you, Josh." She laughed again. "So, are you going to Tommy's party?" Caroline said.

"I think so. Are you?"

"If you're going to be there, I think I might. All dressed up like a bumble bee. A good-looking bumble bee."

Josh smiled, but he tried to keep it from getting too big. The image of Caroline in a skimpy bumble bee costume popped back in Josh's head as the two walked into the class together and took their seats.

-14-

October 26, 7:30 a.m.

The Deerfield River was so still it looked like a sheet of glass. There were no sounds crackling through the air either. Most of the birds had already flown south. The air was cool, and hints of Jack Fuller's breath were visible on this fall morning. The Detective was sitting in a fishing boat with Charlie Bradwell. Charlie was an investment banker who loved to fish, and also the owner of the fishing boat. They had caught a couple of fish so far. None of them were worth keeping. Charlie's voice tore through the silent air.

"You want to move along? Not much biting here."

Fuller nodded. "Go ahead," he said.

Charlie fired up the motor and steered the boat out of the small cove. The small engine sounded like the biggest powerboat in the marina when it roared to life on this silent morning. Fuller smiled as the breeze from the boat kicking into gear hit his cheeks. Late October was his favorite time to fish. The scenery was divine at this time of year. God truly had his paintbrush out.

Fuller and Charlie had met in Florida – the same trip where Fuller last saw his son, Daniel. In between benders, Fuller managed to book a deep-sea fishing trip. It had seemed like a good way to take his mind off his failed parenting while not causing his liver as much damage. The sun was hot, and the water was choppy on the day of the voyage; an awful combination for a man who had enjoyed his fair share of tequila the night before. Fuller's stomach on that day, already queasy from the tequila, had wanted to return its contents to the outside world about thirty minutes into the boat expedition. With much effort Fuller kept himself from vomiting. Charlie was not taking well to the choppy waves that day either. From a mutual case of hangovers and seasickness, a friendship was formed. The fact that both men were from the Boston area was whipped cream on top of the sundae. Shortly after Fuller returned from Florida he received a call from Charlie asking him to go fishing. Since then many fishing trips had been taken – all of which were enjoyable.

Charlie had three great passions – fishing, cooking, and women. If he could have done it all over again, he would have opened a restaurant instead of becoming a banker. He knew he was not a five-star chef, but his food was damn good. There were never any complaints.

After four more hours of fishing, and catching twelve keepers, the pair went back to Charlie's house for their customary post-trip meal. Charlie worked his magic in the kitchen while Fuller enjoyed a drink and provided the best company he could. The conversation had turned to women rather quickly, because Charlie really only talked about those three things he loved so much – fishing, food and women. The first two subjects had been covered at length while the men were in the boat.

"Meet any good-looking women lately?" Fuller asked.

"Oh, I've had my luck. In my business, though, there are a lot more women around than in yours. And lately it's been younger women. I went out with a twenty-five-year old two weeks ago. Best sex I've had in my life. Unfortunately, she hasn't returned my calls. That's the way they are, I guess."

"You're the greatest, Charlie. I haven't had luck like that. That's for sure."

"You get so wrapped up in your work, Jack. That makes it tough. Plus you work strange hours."

Fuller nodded his head.

"I'll just keep living through you, Charlie."

"I can live with that," Charlie said with a chuckle. "I'll keep trying to live enough for the both of us. Grab your plate. This is nearly ready."

The dinner was top notch. Charlie had seared the fish and served it with roasted potatoes and a salad. Fuller was amazed at how simple everything looked. The flavors in his mouth did not match what his eyes saw.

"Charlie, I don't know how you do it," Fuller said. "This is incredible."

"You saw me working, Jack. There isn't much to it."

"You truly are a master."

Charlie smiled and took a sip of his beer.

"Too kind, Jack. You are far too kind."

7:15 p.m.

Lauren should have arrived fifteen minutes ago. Sometimes Houston felt like she descended into her own world, and it drove him crazy. Time must have not existed in the place she went to. Most people watched TV to pass the time while they were waiting to be picked up. Houston could not do that. He had to watch the outside of his apartment. He had to watch for her.

Her tardiness sent his mind into a frenzied state. Pretty soon he realized that he was no longer in control of his breathing. He was almost panting as he waited, like an excited dog waiting for his dinner. He knew he should calm down and play it cool. This rational thought was no match for the compulsion that he had to look out of the only front-facing window in his apartment to see if she had arrived. The more he tried to relax, the more his head began to swell with pain. It began to hurt on top of his head toward the back, and slowly worked its way to the front.

He forced himself to shake off the pain in his head as he saw her silver Mercedes, a college graduation gift from her parents, pull into the parking lot. Lauren Funst was working as a junior associate in an investment-banking firm, pulling down roughly sixty grand a year. She had spent most of her four years of college on the party scene drinking heavily and experimenting with drugs. Though making good money, Lauren's "I want the best of everything" lifestyle was beyond her means. He father continued to give her a monthly allowance so she could maintain her image. Houston knew he was smarter than her by a long shot, but he did not have a college degree. Sometimes he resented her for it.

Houston opened his front door and went down the steps towards Lauren's car. He always felt extremely aware of himself on the short walk to a waiting car. It was like he was on display, and he did not enjoy it. He worried about how he looked and how he walked. Houston never felt in control during these walks, and he always hurried because of it, which only made him look worse. He had worn his nicest dress shirt, a pair of jeans, and black dress shoes. His hair was styled and his face was shaved, revealing his square jaw. He was treating the evening as much like a date as he could. He hoped he looked the part.

"Hi, Houston," Lauren said in her most gleeful tone when he opened the passenger door. The sound of her voice made him tingle.

"Hey, Lauren," Houston said. He was trying to keep his tone as cool and relaxed as possible, but the words did not come out that way. Lauren could tell he was eager and excited.

"You're going to love this place we are going tonight," Lauren said. "It's called Andrietti's. Italian food. It's the best."

Lauren's mother was full-blooded Italian. Her father was of mixed European descent – an American mutt. She had blonde hair and blue eyes from her father's side, and gorgeous olive skin from her mother's side. She had a look that caught his eye in high school, and she never grew out of it or changed it. His eyes still lingered on her for a beat too long, even though he could draw her from memory. She backed the Mercedes away from his apartment complex and headed in the direction of Andrietti's.

"So how've you been, Houston? It's been a little bit since I've seen you. Totally my fault, of course."

Houston admired how Lauren seemed so casual all the time. It was as if nothing bothered her. Houston always had his guard up when he was around other people, and around Lauren he was constantly conscious of his actions. He was obsessed with her, and Houston was pretty sure Lauren knew it. He tried to mask his feelings, and play it cool. Acting was not something that came naturally, though. His veil was, in fact, see through.

"I've been good. Still at the same bullshit job. I'm debating what my next move should be."

This line was standard for Houston. He knew he needed to make changes in his life, but he was not sure which way he should go.

"Well I think you need to go finish school. You're so smart. You always helped me so much in high school."

Francis Seward High School is where Houston and Lauren met – in a math class. Houston had always breezed through his classes without much effort. He loved when Lauren asked him questions about how to do certain problems. He always wanted to talk to her. He did not care if the subject matter was they x's, y's, and z's of differential equations. So long as they were talking, he was happy.

"I'm thinking about it. College just wasn't challenging me. I wanted to be out in the world."

The conversation revolved around Houston's future for the rest of the drive to the restaurant. Houston tried his best to alter his gaze from her to the road during the conversation. He could not help but stare at her from time to time. He hoped she did not notice.

When they arrived at Andrietti's they were seated at a booth near the rear of the restaurant. It was away from the kitchen and the bathrooms, and tucked into a cozy corner. While it was Houston who called Lauren two days ago to try to see her, it was Lauren who picked the restaurant and made the reservation. Houston was thrilled to see it was a nice place, and that she had reserved a quiet table. He could not help thinking that maybe this was more than two friends getting together to catch up. Maybe Lauren saw it as a date too.

When the waitress came over, Lauren ordered a bottle of wine and a bruschetta appetizer. Houston looked at her and smiled.

They had seldom been out together as just the two of them. Usually they were in a group or at a party when they saw each other. He felt a pulse of euphoria course through his body. More chitchat ensued while they waited for the wine and bruschetta to arrive. It was mainly talk about each other's families, and about what they would order for dinner.

They were both pretty quiet during the meal, which surprised Houston. Normally with Lauren he did not have to force the conversation. She usually took care of that. But tonight he seemed to be the one initiating every exchange, and he was running low on things to talk about. The food was excellent, but you could only talk so much about how good your meal was. Lauren poured herself another glass of wine, which finished off the bottle, and broke a minute-long silence between the two.

"What are we doing when we get out of here?"

The question caught Houston by surprise. He did not imagine anything more than dinner.

"Um, I don't care," he responded. "Anything you want to do."

His heart raced. Houston's mind jumped forward in time. He saw flashes of all kinds of ways this night could end. He tried to suppress a smile, tried to act cool, but he could not quite pull it off.

"I want to dance and get some drinks somewhere."

The drinks sounded great. The dancing did not. The smile Houston could not hold back just moments before quickly vanished. This was not a scenario that had flashed in his head.

"Lauren, I don't really dance. Not well anyway," Houston mumbled. Any feeling of confidence had quickly drained. He felt helpless.

"Oh come on," she said, instantly picking his mood back up. "You'll be with me. No reason to be embarrassed. It's just me and you, and I promise I won't judge your moves. Just have fun."

Her insistence was a refreshing change. Normally it was Houston who was insisting on spending more time with Lauren, not the other way around. *What was she trying to get out of this night?*

"I suppose it will be fun."

"I'll buy you a couple of shots to loosen those hips up."

That was an invitation Houston could not refuse.

*   *   *   *   *

Houston's heart was racing by the time he and Lauren arrived at a bar called The Old Pine, which always had a live band playing. The place was crowded, and Lauren grabbed Houston's hand to lead him to the bar. She ordered two shots of tequila, and after licking salt off of their hands they threw them back. The band was loud. Lauren leaned in, and put her lips toward Houston's ear. He could not help but feel a rush of excitement. It had nothing to do with the tequila and everything to do with her lips.

"Are you ready to dance with me? Or do you need another shot?" she said.

Houston leaned back and smiled at her. His thoughts of trying to act cool had faded. He had gotten this far. From here, he thought it would be easy.

He held up his index finger. "One more."

A sly smile spread across Lauren's face.

Houston's dancing was sloppy, but he was making an effort. He did not like to dance, and he did not try it very often because of that fact. Lauren, on the other hand, was a great dancer. Houston was trying to keep pace. Every now and then Lauren would grab his hand, or turn around and rub her butt on his crotch. These were moments he had dreamed of happening. The reality was far better than the dream.

It was starting to get late, but there was still another two hours before the bar closed. The band had taken a break twenty minutes ago, and Lauren had again led Houston to the bar by his hand to take two more shots. Houston was really feeling the tequila now. He made a note to decline any more shots Lauren wanted to take. The alcohol was causing the night to race by. The band was getting set to start again on stage, in what Houston figured would

117

be its final hour of music. He began walking toward the dance floor when Lauren grabbed his hand again and gave him a slight tug.

He turned around and leaned into her to hear her say, "Do you want to get out of here?"

Lauren said she would leave her car at the bar since neither of them was in any shape to drive it. Houston hailed a cab, and Lauren gave the driver directions to his apartment.

"You can take me back to my car in the morning, right?"

"Of course," Houston said. Now that they were alone in the taxi, the feeling to remain cool once again rose up in Houston's chest. He was not sure this was really happening. Again, the reality felt better than the dream.

The walk up the stairs to his apartment was over in a flash. It was even quicker for the two to get into bed. Houston had never felt such a rush of excitement. He wanted everything to slow down. He wanted to live in this moment forever.

They might have been making out for two minutes or two hours, Houston could not tell, but it was Lauren who started taking off his clothes first. From there things went way too fast for Houston. He lost control in a fit of excitement as their bodies heaved against one another. His years of fantasizing about that moment had come to a realization in a matter of minutes. It did not matter that the moment was brief. He was happy. Lauren nuzzled into his arms. Both of them slept naked.

In the morning, Houston hoped for more, but received only a couple of kisses from his overnight guest. He drove Lauren to her car, and asked if she wanted to go out for breakfast. She declined, saying she was meeting up with her sister for some shopping. Before she got out of the car, she leaned over the center console and gave Houston a hug and a kiss on the cheek.

"I had a lot of fun last night," she said.

"Me too," he responded. He could not help but smile.

He leaned in and kissed her on the lips. It was a good, long kiss – the best he could offer. She pulled away first, but did not fully back away. Instead she rested her forehead on his. Her lips were inches away from his mouth. She stayed like that for a few seconds without saying anything. Then she picked her head up, and looked Houston in the eyes.

"I'll see you soon," she said.

Lauren grabbed her purse, and the old grocery bag Houston had given her for her clothes from last night. She opened the door of Houston's car and got out. She was wearing an old hockey t-shirt of his, and a pair of his sweatpants.

"Don't I look great?" she said with a giggle.

Houston laughed. "Of course you do. I'll see you soon."

"Bye sweetie," she said and then closed the door.

"Goodbye," Houston said to himself. He waved at her as she drove off.

October 29, 1:15 p.m.

The American cheese was beginning to drip onto the frying pan when Alicia Martin flipped her grilled cheese sandwich over to toast the other side. A pot of tomato soup was simmering next to it. Then she set a plate for herself and poured a glass of water from the bottled dispenser that was in a corner of her kitchen. When she returned to the stove to check on her soup and sandwich, she found both done and ready to eat.

Alicia flipped the grilled cheese out of the pan and onto her plate with a spatula. She then tossed the spatula and dirty pan into the sink to be washed at a later time. While she chewed on her grilled cheese and spooned tomato soup out of the bowl she had prepared, Alicia scanned her kitchen with delight.

The last of her Halloween decorations – some pumpkins and black cats – were finally in their proper places in her kitchen. The house was officially ready for the big day. It took her longer to set up this year because she was busier with the children. Alicia hoped she had not neglected them in her preparation for Halloween. She made a mental note to devote more attention to them once her favorite holiday was over.

4:11 p.m.

He feared her being away from him. He feared her charm would make someone else feel the same way he did about her, and that her sexy nature would follow. He feared her meeting someone else. And mostly he feared that she would care about that new someone a lot more than she cared about him. These feelings had only intensified since their night together. His obsession had only grown.

What really frightened Houston was that he could not get a hold of Lauren, so he opened his cell phone, and pressed the send button once again.

*   *   *   *   *

He was about to orgasm. She could tell as she looked up into his dark brown eyes. She hoped her afternoon rendezvous was not going to be spoiled. She had ditched out of work early for this, and she had yet to get hers.

She stopped, got up from her knees, and lightly pressed her hands onto his shoulders. He fell backward into the bed, and she kissed him. Sex was next. That would be the easiest way, no lying on the bed waiting for him to make his move. Sometimes, the girl has to be the aggressor.

She heard her phone buzz in her purse.

That was Houston, she thought. It was probably the fifth time he had called in the last twenty minutes. Making it four times since she had been naked.

Lauren was exhilarated when Houston touched her naked body a few nights ago. She did care for him, which compounded the rush that sex had given her. It had been a while since she had emotional sex, and her orgasm that night was more satisfying because of it. She knew Houston loved her. The feeling was not mutual. Lauren knew it was not fair to Houston to have sex with him – knowing he would interpret it wrong. But she needed to know what it was like to be with someone who cared deeply for her. It was something her body had craved for a little while – an itch that needed to be scratched.

She pushed Houston from her thoughts and began to have sex with Ed Baines, a fellow investment banker she had met at an out-of-office function earlier in the month. He was good, ultimately justifying skipping the end of the workday. Despite her pleasure, Lauren did not think she would see him again. He was not *that* good, and she really did not like investment bankers all that much anyway.

6:40 p.m.

It was dark in Jack Fuller's apartment. He thought about how short the days seemed now that the sun was setting earlier. There was little food in his fridge, so Fuller had stopped at Randy's Burgers on the way home. Randy's was a greasy little joint that made six-ounce burgers, great shakes, and had a drive-thru window. It was a favorite of Fuller's, especially when his cupboards were bare and he was jonesing for something fast, something hot, and something loaded with cholesterol.

He sat down, and spread the contents of his drive thru bag over the kitchen table. The container of fries was already half empty because Fuller had been snacking on them on the drive home. He could never resist this temptation. The fries from Randy's Burgers simply tasted better when you ate them right away. It was some kind of physical law, and Fuller had long since given up disputing it. He took a sip of the chocolate shake and dug into the first of three burgers, sighing loudly after the first bite.

His mind drifted to his son, Daniel, and life before the divorce. His life had been busier then. Now he felt it had been better despite the bustle. He wished he had given his family more attention. Fuller thought of the fishing trips he had taken with friends of his and the extra hours he had put in at his job. As he sat eating burgers alone in his kitchen he realized neither of those activities had gotten him what he truly wanted in life. He thought the fishing helped him relax, and it did, but perhaps more time with his family would have bettered him in the long run. At the time, Fuller thought he was making progress by putting in long hours on cases at the station, but now he realized he was stealing time from Heidi and Daniel. Perhaps his life of solitude now was punishment for his previous actions. There had been few women in his life since Heidi left for Florida. None of his relationships had ever technically started or ended. There was usually a dinner or two. A night or two in bed. And eventually a fading into nothing. Neither side ever said they did not want to see the other. The communication on either end simply stopped.

Fuller dug back into the burgers. This time with more focus. He devoured them without another thought of his estranged son and ex-wife. He vowed to not let memories of them, and the thoughts of his failures, plague him. Fuller had another fishing trip planned for the upcoming weekend. He was very much looking forward to it.

-16-

October 30, 3:32 a.m.

Late nights no longer bothered Houston. During his first few weeks as a janitor at the Vanguard police station he could barely make it through his shifts. He thought of quitting several times during that span, and probably should have.

Currently, Houston was full of energy. He had stumbled upon something intriguing during his rounds mopping the floors.

* * * * *

Jim Warner was a very forgetful man.

He always had a backup plan in case his forgetfulness cropped up. An extra watch in the top, left-hand drawer of his office desk, a second set of keys for his house and car sitting next to the watch. He even had a second cell phone. People knew if they did not reach him on one phone to try the other because he probably left it somewhere foolish.

It was no surprise to anyone at the police station – except maybe Houston, who did not know Jim Warner from Jim Morrison – that the padlock hanging off Warner's locker was left open. From there, Houston's task was simple.

-17-

October 31, 5:15 p.m.

"Dude, Caroline likes you, I'm telling you," Tommy Basil said to Josh Martin.

Josh shook his head again.

"She does, man, she really does," Johnny Vincent chimed in.

"How do you guys know?" Josh said. "Did she tell you?"

"She didn't tell me, but I sit by her and Amy Mitchell in foods class and Caroline has been asking about you lately," Tommy said. "No joke, dude. Not kidding at all."

The three were sitting on the couch in Tommy's basement with Ritchie McGill, Frank Saunders and Nick Abbottello. Josh tried to contain a smile. It danced across his lips despite his best effort.

"See, you like her too," Johnny said.

The smile burst across Josh's face, and he laughed a nervous laugh.

"So what if I do?" he said.

"Then you should go for it," Tommy said. "You know. Ask her out. Tonight. She'll be here tonight,"

"You think? Tonight? I mean, Halloween?" Josh said.

"Yeah, man. Totally. Halloween is perfect," Tommy said.

Josh nodded his head, but was thinking of all the ways that Halloween was not the perfect night to ask out the girl you had been crushing on since the first week of school. It was cheesy, for one, and usually people associated Halloween with scary things. Scary movies, scary costumes, and all sorts of things that went bump in the night. The first day of November had a much better ring to it. But Josh was being pressured by his friends, and he did not want them embarrassing him when Caroline did show up at

Tommy's house. Plus, he knew if he put it off until November 1st that it would turn into November 2nd and then November 3rd and so on. Procrastination had a way of compounding itself.

"I'll do it," Josh said. "What time is she coming over?"

"I'm not sure," Tommy said. "But probably after seven. Plenty of time for you to run home to get your cell phone."

"Cool," Josh said. "I'll roll out of here in a little bit, and then be back before seven."

"You might want to ditch the Yankees hat and freshen up your hair a bit," Johnny said. "You want to look good for her."

Josh cringed a little bit. He did not like being the center of everyone's attention. He preferred to blend in to the scenery. That was not going to be an option on this night. He really did like Caroline, and there was not going to be a way to keep it a secret when everyone was hanging out in Tommy's basement. He knew he would have to ask her out tonight, and he would need to do it early on in the party. Josh hoped his friends would allow him to ask Caroline out on his own terms.

"Right," Josh said. "Good thinking. I'll do that."

6:12 p.m.

He had been driving for thirty-five minutes, but he was not sure of where he was or where he had been. It had all been a daze to him.

A right here. A left there. Right, left, left, left, right, left.

Lauren had not returned his calls or texts, and each new day seemed like a week. Houston had not felt like himself lately. He felt dark, almost as if he was dying from the inside out. He wanted Lauren for another night. His mind had become so focused on her that he occasionally lost track of what else was going on. Their night in bed had done nothing to cure his obsession.

He glanced out the passenger window of his car and saw a kid walking down the street wearing a Yankees hat. The kid was walking by himself, with his head down. Houston pulled over and got out of the car.

"Hey buddy, I'm a bit lost. Could you direct me back to Wilson Street?" he said.

"Um, sure," the kid said, obviously gathering where he was and the best route to get to Wilson. "You're going to want to turn around and go the opposite direction on Randall here…"

As the boy said this he turned his back to Houston to point out the direction, Houston pulled out the nightstick that had been nestled in the back of his pants and clubbed the boy across the back of the head. Immediately the boy's knees buckled, and he fell into some bushes. The boy was unconscious, and bleeding from where he had been hit. Quickly, Houston reached out and pulled the kid from the bushes. He hurried over to his car, and threw him in the trunk.

A quick glance around and Houston determined that nobody had seen him. It was just after six, a lull in the trick-or-treating for the night. The younger children had gone home for dinner, and the older ones were not all out yet.

Unfortunately, Josh Martin was out. But instead of knocking on a door for candy, he was unconscious in Houston West's trunk.

7:45 p.m.

Dude, where are you? Caroline showed up an hour ago and she's been asking about you non-stop. Get over here.

Tommy Basil hit send on the text message to Josh. It was the third one he sent since Caroline had arrived. Caroline had asked about Josh repeatedly since her arrival.

"Tommy, where's Josh?" Caroline asked again from her seat on the couch. Tommy wished Josh would just show back up already so that she would stop asking about him.

"I just sent him another text. He hasn't responded to any of them. You want his number? You want to text him?"

Caroline smiled shyly.

"No," she said. "I don't want to text him. I just, you know, was wondering where he was. He told me he was going to be here."

"He was here," Tommy said. "But he had to run home to get his cell phone. He should be back any second. Maybe he's walking and it's on silent or something."

"Ok," Caroline said with a smile.

Tommy thought Josh was taking Johnny's comment about fixing his hair too literally. He knew Josh was manic about certain things. He was probably at home doing and re-doing his hair over and over again. Or maybe his mom had made him stay. She did make a big deal out of Halloween.

"I'm sure he'll be here soon," Tommy said.

8:10 p.m.

Houston found himself standing in field. Tall grass encircled a clearing. He was not sure how he had arrived at this place. His last memory was of him asking a teenaged boy for directions back to Wilson Street. There were several other gaps in time Houston could not account for from his day. The headlights from his car illuminated the clearing in front of him. Houston turned to see he was twenty yards away from his car, and that the driver side door was ajar.

While he was looking at his car, Houston heard a rustle from the tall grass. The grunt of an animal followed. Houston stepped towards the sound, and his hand gripped a knife that hung from his belt. He was not sure where he had bought the knife or when he had strapped it to his belt. Houston was mighty happy he had it now, as the animal that was causing the grass to move grew closer. The beast was about to reach the clearing when Houston heard another rustle to his left. He heard a third rustle of grass come from his right a second later. Houston slowly backed toward his car.

What emerged from the tall grass was not what Houston expected. They looked like large crocodiles. Houston thought his mind was playing a trick on him. Surely there were no crocs in New

England. The crocs charged in unison. Houston noticed a glint of silver dangling from their necks. It looked like a necklace with a heart pendant at the end of it. Again, Houston thought his mind was playing a trick.

Regardless of whether or not these animals were real or imagined, Houston instinctively drew the knife that he had no recollection of buying from his belt. When the first croc, the one charging hard from the center, neared him, Houston drew the knife over his head with both hands on the handle, and drove it down into the crocodile's back with all the force he had.

It was then that the nightmare ceased. Houston saw no crocodiles. He was standing behind his car, and saw that the knife was driven deep into the chest of a teenaged boy.

What had he done?

A flash of Houston clubbing the kid over his head and throwing him in his trunk pulsated through his brain.

What had he done?

What followed was a rush of memories. It was as though 100,000 volts had been shot through him. He closed his trunk and ran around to the front of the car.

Where was he?

It was so dark he could not tell what was going on. It seemed like he was in a secluded area, but he was not sure. He needed to get out of there. He needed to get moving.

Dirt and rocks kicked up as Houston's car sped off a gravel parking lot and hit pavement. He realized he was at a forest preserve on the edge of town. He had come here with Lauren and some of her friends one gorgeous day two summers ago. He had no recollection of driving to the forest preserve on this night, though. His mind was blank. He only heard a voice in his head now. It was repeating one word over and over again.

Drive.

Drive.

Drive.

8:48 p.m.

As he drove his anticipation grew. Adrenaline was racing through his veins. He felt something dark and sinister running through his body. It made him feel alive, yet empty. The outside world did not matter. Consequences were unimportant. Traffic was a little heavier than usual. He kept reminding himself that the body was in his trunk and that no one could see it from inside their cars. And for some reason he felt protected even if he were to be stopped. Houston felt this dark and sinister force inside of him was more important than anything in the outside world.

He pulled into the parking lot of his apartment complex and raced up the stairs to his unit on the second floor. He burst in through the front door and frantically searched through the house. He needed something large.

He spotted his hockey bag. He could fit a few hockey sticks as well as all his other gear into it. He grabbed for it, only to realize it was still full of gear. He could not lift it from where he was standing. Quickly, he unzipped the bag and dumped the contents onto the floor. Like the guts of a bug being squished, Houston's hockey gear spread across his floor. He was out the front door in a flash.

He rushed to his car, and went past the driver side door. It was the trunk that he was after. He slowed to a brisk walk so as not to draw anyone's attention. Quickly, he opened the trunk and stared at the crumpled body of the teenaged boy. Blood was beginning to soak into the mats that lined the floor.

Houston tossed the hockey bag in the trunk next to the body. He then reached in and patted the dead boy's pockets, looking for some form of identification. He found only one item, a wallet, and quickly snagged it.

Houston attempted to put the body into the hockey bag, but he heard a car pull into the parking lot in the distance. Instinctively, Houston slammed the door to his trunk shut and headed up the stairs to his apartment. The wallet was still in his hand.

The door to Houston's apartment had not closed all the way. He pushed it opened, tossed the wallet onto his coffee table, and sat down on his couch. He took a breath, then searched through the contents of the wallet. There was a twenty-dollar bill, and a few scraps of paper with phone numbers written on them. A school ID card was in a slot with a clear plastic coating on it, so it could be shown without taking it out of the wallet. Houston stared at Josh Martin's name and picture, and saw his address listed below them. A small sweat was breaking on Houston's forehead. He took the ID and the twenty out of Josh's wallet, and went to throw the wallet in the trash can. Houston's hand, with the wallet still in it, hovered above the cylinder. He realized he should not throw it away in his house. He slipped the wallet into his pocket, and grabbed a bottle of water from the fridge. Houston walked into his bedroom and headed for his closet. He needed a fresh shirt.

As he opened the closet door he saw the police uniform he had stolen from the station last night after work. Houston thought it would make a great Halloween costume for the party he was supposed to be attending tonight. Now it did not look like he would make it there. It's a shame because he would have looked like a real cop.

Maybe he could find another use for the uniform. He looked at Josh Martin's ID, still in his hand. Maybe he could even use it tonight, and perhaps make it to the party. He would arrive late. Very late.

11:19 p.m.

"Ms. Martin?"

"Yes," Alicia answered.

"My name is Officer Warner, may I come in?"

"Sure," she said with a nervous twinge in her voice.

She stepped back enough to allow the slender officer into her home. She was just about to head to her bedroom to turn in for the night when she heard a knock on the door. She knew it was too late for trick-or-treaters. The young officer looked fine, but something did not feel right. It felt like he did not come alone. Alicia felt another presence in the room – a dark presence.

"The kitchen is over here, what is this about?" she asked, her voice quickening with every word.

"Well, Ms. Martin, do you know where your son is tonight?"

"Josh? He's at a friend's house. They are having a Halloween party. The boys, his group of friends, are going to sleep over at the house and then go to school in the morning. Why? Has Josh got himself into trouble? He's just a kid you know, it couldn't be that bad."

She hoped her last sentence was true. Some of those "kids-being-kids" moments had turned into felony crimes. She had seen as much on TV. The feeling of an outside presence faded a bit, but it still lingered.

"Perhaps you should sit down, Ms. Martin," the officer said with a calm voice that made the hair on Alicia's neck stand up. Suddenly she felt very cold.

"What did Josh do?"

"Your son didn't do anything. He was merely in the wrong place and the wrong moment in time with the wrong person very near by."

The more the officer spoke, the more unsettled Alicia became by his tone of voice. It was as though he prepared this speech, like he was auditioning for a TV series. He must have thought about what he would say on the way to the house. But still, it seemed so unnatural. His eyes looked hollow and dull – black almost.

"What did Josh do? Is he in your car? Or is he down at the station?"

The officer paused a moment to collect his thoughts. He had not expected that jump in questioning.

"Ms. Martin, your son is dead."

An odd wave of stunned calmness, anger and a thousand little needles filled with pain shot over her. She slouched in her chair, and her head dropped to the table as tears poured out of her eyes. The officer placed a hand on her back.

"Ms. Martin, this is difficult, and it is very late. I would suggest handling the details with the body in the morning. I'll be in early tomorrow morning to start working on this. You can stop by the station at any time tomorrow and deal with it all then."

That idea sounded like the right one for Alicia. Although taking out the large butcher knife in the top right-hand drawer by the stove and roaming the streets for Josh's killer sounded like a good idea too. Alicia would have done anything that anybody suggested right now, her body was in the chair in her kitchen, but her mind was in another dimension.

"Think it over, Ms. Martin, we could always go down there right now, but it is not necessary. Josh's body will be there. It's really best if you wait until morning. They are processing it for evidence now. You'd have to wait a long, long time."

Yes, she thought. And she did not want to wake her other three children at midnight to tell them their older brother had died. She could not fathom telling them about murder. *Was it even murder?*

"Officer, was it a murder?"

"From what we can tell, it was. There was a gunshot wound, and it does not appear to be suicide since the body was partially covered out in the woods."

More tears fell.

"I'll be there first thing in the morning. I don't know how I am going to tell my other kids."

The officer's ears perked at the mention of other children. Sorrow hit him for a moment, just a moment.

"I could stay if you would like."

"No, officer, I think I would like to be alone right now."

The officer wanted to reach out and touch her hand, console her a bit. Almost apologize for being this messenger. But he could not force himself to do it. He froze. All he could think to say was, "I'll let myself out."

More tears fell as the officer walked out the door.

When he got back to the car parked outside Alicia Martin's house, the officer was already holding the shiny gold nametag emblazoned with "Warner" in his hand. He removed his hat and opened the trunk of the car, a car that was not painted black and white like the other police cars. At that point, Houston West smiled to himself. It was all in the details. The littlest thing would have thrown off what he just did. It had been perfect, even on short notice.

With that he turned the key on the trunk and tossed his hat, nametag and badge on the body of Josh Martin. He bent over to touch the teenaged boy; his skin was ice cold.

Part III
Magical Nightmares

18

March 23, 7:14 a.m.

Fuller had not slept the night before. He had cruised through the tough hours on adrenaline, but his eyes grew heavy now as he sat on his couch with documents from the Josh Martin file covering his coffee table. Some had even formed into piles on the floor.

His review of the Josh Martin case was not going anywhere. It was the same details, and his hope of finding something new had faded away. Yesterday, when he sat down on his couch and began sifting though the case files, he had a feeling in his gut that something he had missed before would make sense now. None of it did.

They did not even have a body, let alone a crime scene to investigate. His frustration mounted.

7:45 a.m.

Bridget Cass sat across from Alicia with a medium cup of black coffee in front of her. The butterflies that had been in Alicia's stomach were beginning to settle down, perhaps that was because of the slice of banana bread Bridget insisted Alicia eat.

"Always eat before a meeting," Bridget chirped.

The first few minutes of the conversation were a blur for Alicia. Bridget was doing all of the talking, and it was at a breakneck pace. Alicia could barely keep up as Bridget described her services and experience.

"By the way," Bridget said, "I am so sorry, once again, that my office is under renovation right now. This is definitely not the way I usually meet a new client. Well, should I say potential new client for now."

"Oh it's no problem at all," Alicia said with a smile. "I was a little nervous about meeting in public, but my house is not in great shape right now."

"Don't worry," Bridget said. "None of these people are listening. Most of them are half asleep. And who could blame you for a little untidiness at home? You've been through so much."

"Thank you."

Bridget Cass was an attorney, and a founding partner of Cass and Young, a small in size, but big in success, firm. Bridget had a wealth of experience in bringing suits against big companies and government agencies that had wronged employees, customers, common citizens, and those with special needs. Alicia had Googled "lawsuits against police departments," and Cass and Young's website came up as the top hit.

Bridget's bio on the site impressed Alicia, notably the fact that she was heavily involved with a group called Our Missing that provided support and assistance for those with missing children.

"I know we spoke on the phone at length yesterday, Alicia," Bridget said while pulling a legal pad and a pen from her briefcase, "but tell me again about Josh."

The conversation lasted for nearly an hour before Alicia cut it off. She recapped everything she could remember about Josh's disappearance. Alicia described the man who came to her house dressed as a Vanguard police officer and who identified himself as Jim Warner. She told Bridget about meeting the real Jim Warner, and how Detective Jack Fuller had headed the investigation. Alicia finished up by talking about how the investigation had gone nowhere, or at least nowhere that she had been informed of by the department. Alicia felt cut out of the loop and forgotten. She deeply missed her son, and she felt the police were not doing anything to find him or find the man who came to her house on Halloween night.

"I think that is all I can say at this time," Alicia said with tears in her eyes. At that moment she wished she was not in a coffee shop so she could properly break down and cry.

"That's more than enough, Alicia," Bridget said. "I'm on your side. I'm your lawyer now. Something will be done about this, I promise you."

"Thank you so much."

"Of course. I know you have my number, but here's my card just in case. I'm also putting my cellphone number right here on the bottom. You call me any time you need me. We'll be in touch in the next couple of days, and I'll get the ball rolling from there."

Alicia took the card, which was a rich cream color with deep black ink on it. It was, like the rest of Bridget Cass to this point, impressive.

"Oh," Bridget said. "I nearly forgot. Forgive me. Here is the number for Beth Monk, the head of Our Missing. You should give her a call."

Bridget copied the phone number for Beth from her cell phone onto a sheet of the legal pad, tore it off, and gave it to Alicia.

"They do so much good. It is a great organization. Tell her I gave you her number."

"I will do that," Alicia said.

"Good."

With that, Bridget gathered her things, wrapped Alicia in a warm, yet professional hug, and headed for the door. Alicia felt things starting to turn her way ever so slightly. Retaining Bridget's services was a good thing. As she watched Bridget slip behind the wheel of her sparkling white SUV, Alicia smiled ever so slightly.

12:30 p.m.

The sun was shining brightly through the windows of Fuller's living room, but he was sound asleep on the couch. He had been lying there for the past three hours. He woke with a jump, as if someone had clapped their hands next to his ear. He suddenly felt very cold, and reached for the blanket that was dangling off one of the arms of the couch.

The dream he woke from was startling. He had seen Josh Martin in Orchard Park. Josh was standing on the path between the two baseball backstops, in the very spot Fuller had seen that thing – the dark entity. Josh was staring at Fuller. His mouth had been moving, but Fuller was out of earshot. It seemed to take Fuller an eternity to reach Josh Martin in his dream. Fuller had called out to the boy many times. "Louder, Josh! Louder!"

Fuller was standing face to face with Josh, and Josh's mouth was about to open when Fuller woke up. It was after his eyes opened from his dream that he heard what Josh was saying.

Come find me, Jack. Come find me again.

The words were not from Josh Martin. They sounded the same as what Fuller had heard several months ago. It was a deep, baritone voice. So deep it could not have been from this world. It spoke calmly, like a person always in control.

When you need me, you'll find me, but first you must wake from this dream.

Come find me, Jack. Come find me again.

19

March 24, 12:37 p.m.

Alicia Martin's children were at school, and her house was correspondingly quiet. This morning she had managed to tidy up the place, and was happy it now was presentable for guests. Outside it was sunny, but cool. The calendar was inching toward spring even though the temperature was not keeping pace. It was the kind of weather where any kind of jacket would do, but without one, you surely would feel the spring chill.

Alicia was in the kitchen preparing soup and sandwiches. A small platter of cheese and crackers sat on the table. Three bottles of wine sat on the counter of the elegant, but not extravagant, kitchen. Alicia hoped the wine bottles would catch her guest's eye, and she would suggest a glass. Alicia did not want to be presumptuous in this meeting. She had never met Beth Monk before, just as a day before she had not met Bridget Cass. Like Bridget, Alicia's phone conversation with Beth was pleasant. Still, she did not know what to expect from the meeting. At least this time it was in the comfort of her home. Butterflies were not present.

Beth Monk arrived without presumption or flair. Unlike Bridget Cass's sleek SUV, Beth drove a modest mini-van. Instead of the dark blazer and pants with the eye-popping yellow shirt, Beth wore a simple white blouse and jeans. Beth did not have a business card, let alone one with as much modest style as Bridget. The day before Alicia kept pulling the business card out of her purse to look at it. She felt honored to have it. Never before had a small piece of paper mesmerized her so much. Beth, however, appeared far more average than Bridget, and Alicia could not help but feel a bit of a letdown after being dazzled the day before.

"Are you hungry?" Alicia asked after their brief introductions.

"Yes, why thank you," Beth said.

"I hope soup and sandwiches are ok."

"That sounds perfect. Can I help?"

"Oh no," Alicia said. "Please, sit."

Beth took a seat at Alicia's kitchen table, and grabbed two squares of cheese and a cracker from the plate that sat before her. Alicia noticed that Beth had not looked at the wine.

"So how do you know Bridget?" Alicia asked, as she walked toward the cabinet directly above the wine bottles, and pulled out a cup, hoping to draw Beth's gaze.

"She didn't tell you, did she?" Beth said. "Well, that's typical for her. She sometimes forgets the minor details."

"What do you mean?" Alicia said, as she paced back toward the sink and filled the cup with water. "I'm sorry do you want anything to drink?"

"Thank you, water is fine with me."

It was not the answer Alicia was hoping for. She walked back to the cabinet, glanced at the wine bottles, and pulled another cup from above.

"Bridget is my younger sister," Beth said.

"Oh really?" Alicia said with surprise. "I had no idea. Different last names and all."

"Yes. We are both married. And it's stuff like that that slips her mind from time to time. She's brilliant, don't get me wrong. I know she is your lawyer now. And she's exceptional. But with me and her, it's just how it is sometimes."

Alicia felt foolish even though there was no family resemblance to be seen between Bridget and Beth. How could she have known the two were sisters? Even if they were in the same room together, gossiping away like teenagers, Alicia would have never guessed they were related.

"Well, now that we have that little awkward piece of information out of the way, how about we talk about Josh," Beth said.

Alicia brought over two half sandwiches of turkey, Swiss cheese, lettuce and tomato that were lightly topped with a sweet onion vinaigrette. The soup she ladled into the bowls she had set was creamy baked potato with bits of bacon, and a generous shaving of cheddar cheese layered on top.

Alicia took a deep breath, and brought a spoonful of soup to her mouth.

"Josh was," she paused, "*is* my oldest child. He's a sweet boy who blends in with the crowd. He's not a peacock out front; sometimes you have to look to find him. And on October thirty-first of last year, Halloween, my favorite holiday, I lost him. I haven't seen or heard from him since. That night a man came to my house dressed as a police officer. He told me Josh was dead – that someone murdered him. He told me they had the body at the police station, and that since it was so late – did I mention it was really late? Like almost midnight."

Beth shook her head.

"Well it was. And since it was so late, he said I should come down to the station in the morning and identify Josh's body and begin sorting through things then. I am a single mom with three other children. They are all pretty young. As badly as I wanted to go to the station that night, I figured it would be best if I waited until morning. The officer, whoever he was, kind of talked me into staying home. I was just so numb."

"Alicia, that is understandable," Beth said. "Do not beat yourself up over that."

"When I went to the station the next morning, the man who came to my house, who said his name was Officer Warner, and had a badge and nameplate and everything, was not the Officer Warner who works for the Vanguard Police. They said no officer had been sent to my house and there was no body of a teenager named Josh Martin at the station. They checked to see if it could have possibly been another station, but it was not. They had never heard of anything I was talking about. And yet my son was missing; gone without a trace."

Beth sat quietly, eating the comforting lunch. Bridget had sent her a brief e-mail with a primer of Alicia Martin's story. The first paragraph said the purpose of the e-mail was so that Beth could brace herself for the tale. Beth had heard worse stories of parents losing their children one way or another, but she could not recall a story more bizarre.

"I was so torn. I went to bed on Halloween night, or more accurately fell asleep at the kitchen table here, believing my son was dead. When I walked out of that police station the next day, I didn't know what to believe. I guess I still don't. The police were heavily involved for a while, but I haven't heard anything from them in months."

There was silence for a moment as both women took a bite of their sandwiches and sipped on their soup. Beth was keeping quiet, hoping Alicia would say more. She had the feeling Alicia had not talked much about Josh since last Halloween. Opening up is the first step in grieving and understanding. The room remained quiet, though. Alicia did not wish to talk anymore. Beth knew Josh's disappearance would eat Alicia from the inside if she did not talk about it.

"I want to start off by trying to manage your expectations a little bit," Beth said. "I cannot make any grand promises, because there is no telling if I can keep them. My sister is definitely more the promise maker. I choose not to be. I am more of a realist."

Alicia's eyes cleared when hearing Beth's direct statement. The watery onset of tears dried up in an instant.

"Hope is a dangerous thing," Beth continued. "I don't want to provide false hope that I can personally find your son. That isn't what I do. I am not an investigator. I am someone who once lost a child – she was kidnapped seven years ago. I have not seen her since. I hope one day to see her again. And I miss her every moment."

Alicia knew this fact about Beth from reading Our Missing's website, but it did not make hearing it in person any easier. Tears were beginning to form again.

"What I did was form an organization that can help bring awareness to cases of missing children. Sort of like a watchdog for the police force. Understandably, they get busy and certain cases get pushed down the list on their agenda. We at Our Missing want to make sure that cases of missing children are not the ones that get knocked down the rung of priorities.

"What I can do for you is simple, provide exposure for your case, and make it difficult for the police to put it on the back-burner. While the amount of time that has passed is not excessive, it appears the involvement of the police force is starting to wane, and I do not want that to happen. It sounds like they mismanaged this from the start, what with someone coming to your house dressed as an officer, and telling you that your son is dead. We have a rally coming up in two weeks to promote our cause and bring some cases to the forefront. If you are comfortable with it, I would like you to tell your story – the story you just told me – at the rally."

Alicia had been sipping her soup while Beth was talking. The thought of speaking in public about Josh irked her in some way she could not fully describe. She wanted all the things Beth had spoke of, but she did not want to be the one behind the microphone telling the story.

"A rally?" Alicia said. "What kind of rally?"

Beth held up a hand.

"It's not what you think," she said. "This is not a bunch of mothers standing up on a stage outside of the police department shouting chants to bring their children home. While that might get a blurb on the news stations – especially the more sensational channels on a slow day – it doesn't tend to work. It is easy for the police to ignore it as a bunch of cranks who want attention more for themselves than for their kids."

Alicia cautiously nodded.

"We will be setting up in that small park right in downtown Vanguard," Beth said. "You know, the one that doesn't have a name."

"I know the place," Alicia said while nodding her head again.

"It won't last any longer than a few hours. Our permit allows us to be there for three hours. You will not be the only speaker. It is not your responsibility to fill all of the time. The way our rallies usually work is we have speakers for about an hour, and then we use the remaining time to interact with those who came out. It is very therapeutic."

Beth paused a moment to allow Alicia the opportunity to say something. Alicia did not jump at the chance, sitting quietly instead.

"I think it would be good for you," Beth said. "I know it would be good for our group, and we can help you begin to kick start police involvement once again. Besides that, I think attending the rally and telling your story can help you personally. I think you will see that we are a great support group."

Alicia slowly nodded her head. The proposal seemed innocent enough. All she wanted was to know the truth about Josh. If he was out there alive, she wanted him back. If he was indeed dead, she wanted to know for sure so she could put her doubts to rest and begin moving forward. Her feelings of helplessness started to fade in the last few weeks. She no longer felt paralyzed with grief.

"I think I can do this," Alicia said. "But I don't know what to say during my time on stage."

"You just need to tell your story, Alicia," Beth said. "Just like you told me. I can help you polish it up a bit. I can help you practice. The important thing to know is that you are no longer alone in facing this. You have a support system now. I am here for you. Bridget is here for you. You will meet other members of Our Missing and you will see how wonderful they are and how much help they can be."

"Yes," Alicia said. "I will speak. I just want to know what happened to Josh."

The words sprung from Alicia's lips without much thought. It was as though they were pushed out of her. In her heart she still felt conflicted about speaking at the rally, yet a part of Alicia felt the need to quickly accept Beth Monk's offer.

"I do too, Alicia. I do too."

Lunch was finished, and Alicia cleaned up as they chitchatted more about Our Missing. By the time Beth left, Alicia could see the family resemblance between her and Bridget. It was nothing physical. Bridget had a face and body for television and magazine covers. She truly was stunning. Beth was not blessed with the same looks. She was never going to wow a room simply by entering it. While the packaging of Bridget impressed Alicia, it was the substance of Beth that left a stronger impression.

The family resemblance came from the comforting feeling Alicia felt after meeting with both Beth and Bridget. Alicia no longer felt the dark depression creeping through her mind. She was thinking clearly, and focused on inner peace.

Alicia hoped the feeling would last.

20

March 25, 8:40 p.m.

When going into a conversation with something to hide, a good poker face comes in handy, but it is not the most important thing. The most important thing is having a plan. One could have the best stone-face in the world, but if that person says the wrong thing – or trips up – the truth will be found out. Jack Fuller was set to meet Jim Warner at a bar called Willy's at a little after nine. Fuller was currently going over the final details of his plan.

Warner was absent-minded – everyone at the station knew that – but he was not an idiot. He was still a cop, and would be able to tell Fuller was lying if Fuller could not keep his story straight. One problem facing Fuller is that he did not know what word was being spread around the station about his absence. Rumors were good. Something official from McAvoy's mouth would be tricky. Part one of Fuller's plan was to get Warner talking about what he had heard regarding Fuller's absence from work. Jack hoped the first words out of Warner's mouth were not, "So where have you been?"

Part two of Fuller's plan was to circle around to Josh Martin. It was one of only a few cases Warner and Fuller had been involved in together. Of course, it was the most recent and prominent. He figured part two of this plan would be something Warner had figured out before showing up. He had to know the reason for the meeting would involve Josh Martin. The final step was to find out anything more about Alicia. Fuller was curious if anyone had been keeping tabs on her lately.

Willy's was not Fuller's favorite bar, but he was not opposed to the occasional visit. The lighting was dim, and the drinks were moderately priced. On most of Fuller's visits to Willy's the scent of urine mixed with the odor of stale beer lingered in the air. This trip was no exception. When Fuller arrived, he scanned the small bar area, and saw no sign of Warner. There were about a dozen small tables near the bar, but Warner was nowhere to be found there either. Fuller's watch read exactly nine o'clock.

A standard jukebox hung from a wall near the bar. It was one of the modern ones with enough digital songs to keep music playing for three months straight without hearing a repeat if the user was so inclined. Currently the Rolling Stones' "Jumping Jack Flash" was vibrating through the sound system.

He saddled up to the bar, ordered a beer, and turned his attention to the tip-off of a basketball game between the Lakers and Clippers. Fuller was not a fan of either team, but enjoyed watching the NBA. Five minutes into the quarter, Warner arrived. He gained Fuller's attention with a friendly pat on the shoulder.

"Jack, how's it going?" Warner said.

"Jim," Fuller said while turning his head. "Good. Good. How are you?"

"Can't complain," Warner said. He had not yet taken his seat.

"Always a good thing," Fuller said. "Grab a seat. Grab a beer."

"Thanks," Warner said. "What do we have here? Lakers and Clippers? Nice."

"I didn't know you were a basketball fan."

"Big fan," Warner said. "Don't watch many of the West Coast games, but I don't mind watching them when I get a chance."

"I agree with you there," Fuller said.

The bartender brought Warner's beer, and Fuller ordered a second one for himself.

"So, this is about Josh Martin, right?"

Fuller nodded. He did not need part one of the plan. Warner walked right into part two.

"Jack, that thing is a dead end," Warner said. "I mean, no body, minor evidence. All we have to go on is that guy who showed up at the mother's house saying her son was dead."

"Isn't that pretty convincing, though?" Fuller said. "That's the part I can't get out of my head. The fact that someone dressed as a cop, well, not just a cop, dressed as you, shows up and tells Alicia that her son is dead and to come to the station in the morning."

"Jack," Warner tried to interject, but Fuller waved him off.

"Then, her son really is gone. I mean, nobody has seen him. Nobody has found him."

"Jack, I know. I know it makes no sense. I agree with what you have thought all along. That the kid is dead. But how do we find this guy? How do we even know the messenger is the killer?"

Fuller took a swing of his beer.

"It's him. I know it's him."

Warner rolled his eyes.

"Jack, I want to catch this guy as much as anyone, but where else do we turn? We questioned other officers, the people who work at the station, guys who were in lockup before the crime. Everyone had a good story. Everyone had an alibi. I don't know how the guy got my uniform. I mean, maybe it wasn't even mine. I know I had a uniform go missing, but that's happened before. I've got a pretty common last name too. Maybe it was someone who just knew I was a cop. Someone who knew a man named Jim Warner worked at the station."

This seemed unlikely to Fuller. Usually the path of least resistance was the answer to these mysteries. There was always some sort of tangible connection. Something to bring everything together.

"Don't you think that is unlikely, Jim? Don't you think there is some sort of simple connection from our station to the killer to Josh Martin?"

Warner smiled. It struck Fuller as odd that the man would smile at a time like this. Maybe it was a nervous, subconscious reaction. Warner probably did not even realize he was doing it. It made Warner look like a dismissive idiot to Fuller.

"I know that's usually the case. And I want to believe that, but apparently it isn't that simple this time around."

He was an idiot, Fuller thought. A lazy idiot who did not want to dig any deeper into the case. Warner had taken McAvoy's company line. Put it on the shelf and wait for something to fall into your lap. No more digging. Josh Martin's killer was going to have to knock on the police station door and announce that he was guilty to be caught by these fools. Fuller would have none of it. He would not stop until he found Josh Martin's killer.

"Have you heard about the mother?" Warner said. "Alicia."

Fuller shook his head. "No," he said, very happy to be moving to part three of his plan without much effort.

"I couldn't remember if you were out on your vacation before the word spread around the station. She's starting her own campaign soon. Kind of like a crusade. Word is she is going to be attacking us for the work we did, or as she claims, did not do. She's going to try to band together with other people who think they have been wronged by the department. She's going to be at the forefront, though."

To Fuller, those did not sound like actions Alicia would resort to. He felt he knew her well enough to make that judgment. Apparently he was wrong. Warner had also offered up the other bit of information Fuller was looking for out of this meeting – that Fuller was on "vacation."

"That is surprising," Fuller said. "It doesn't seem like her."

"Well, it's coming, Jack. Be ready. You might be in the crosshairs."

"Thanks for the heads-up."

The two men had finished their beers. The bartender came over to check on them.

"Another round?" the bartender said.

Warner started to nod his head.

"No," Fuller said. He had executed the steps in his plan, and gotten the answers he was seeking. "We're done."

Warner quickly changed his course. "Just the check," he mumbled.

21

March 26, 7:30 p.m.

The aroma of freshly cooked biscuits swirled through the rooms near the kitchen in the Martin house. The biscuits were sitting in the middle of the kitchen table in a wicker basket; slight vapors of steam could be seen coming off of them if one were to look closely. Macy, Sam and Angel all had their eyes on them. Three big sets of eyes. None of them blinked. Alicia set two frying pans onto hot pads. One pan held vegetables that smelled sticky sweet. The other was filled with diced Italian sausage, browned to perfection. The eyes did not move from the biscuits despite these additions to the dinner table.

"Dig in," Alicia said as she sat.

Three hands darted for the biscuits. Amongst the rush, Alicia spooned vegetables onto her plate. The meal was pleasantly quiet for Alicia. It felt more normal around the house during the last few weeks, perhaps because Alicia was beginning to feel like herself again.

"I have some news for all of you," Alicia said.

The children's eyes turned toward their mother. Macy, Sam and Angel had started to slowly trust her again. The bizarre actions had ceased, and she was acting like the mother they had known before Halloween of the previous year. Life was almost normal for the children again.

"I'm going to be bringing some attention to our family," Alicia said. "I'm becoming involved with an organization called Our Missing, and I will be speaking at a rally."

"What is this organization about?" Macy asked.

"It's for those who have lost a child. I'm going to be speaking about Josh."

Macy pushed her vegetables into a pile on one of the edges of her plate. Sam forked sausage into his mouth. Angel took a bite of her biscuit. They stared at their plates. None of them said anything.

"Is that okay with all of you?" Alicia asked.

Josh's name had not been mentioned by the children in quite some time. Speaking about him had brought out the worst in their mother – a side none of them had ever seen before. There had been times when Alicia believed Josh to still be alive and sitting at the table with them while they ate dinner. There were also times when she told the children Josh was dead and never coming back. This confusion had made life at home difficult for Macy, Sam and Angel. They had learned to avoid talking about Josh for fear of their mother's reaction. One night, while the three were seated on the floor in Macy and Angel's room, a pact had been made to not speak of Josh around their mother.

"It's okay with us, mom," Macy said after a long silence.

Sam shot a glance her way. His eyes wide and stern. His mouth tight. His eyebrows furrowed.

Alicia breathed a sigh.

"Thank you for that, Macy," she said. "I want all of you to know that this will not take my focus away from you. This is going to be something that helps us. I will not allow it to hurt us."

Macy nodded. Sam and Angel sat quietly while they finished their dinner.

8:18 p.m.

The cheese from the Hot Pocket was sizzling as it oozed onto the plate Jack Fuller removed from his microwave. He carried it into his living room and set it on his coffee table next to the beer he had been drinking. The heat of the plate had just started to burn his fingers when he set it down. Fuller now rubbed his hand to alleviate the brief pain. He cursed while doing so. Fuller sat on the couch and, despite all of the signs that he should allow his dinner to cool, took a bite of the Hot Pocket. It burned the roof of his mouth. Fuller slurped in the cheese and meat between gasps for breath. He reached for his beer, and guzzled the remainder of it in an attempt to quell the heat. After walking to the kitchen to grab another beer from the fridge, Fuller took a second bite of his dinner. This one went much better, though he felt slight irritation on the roof of his mouth.

Another basketball game, this time Indiana at Chicago, was on his television. He enjoyed the last of the second quarter while finishing his meal. When the game went to halftime, Fuller channel surfed, and found nothing to his liking. He returned to the broadcast, and was inundated with commercials, boring analysis, and highlights of other NBA action. During this time his mind went idle, and eventually drifted to Alicia Martin. The news Jim Warner had given him the night before was off-putting at the time, but now Fuller thought it was rational. McAvoy and the rest of the Vanguard PD had dropped the ball on the Martin case. Sure, Fuller was frustrated with himself for not producing enough evidence to compel McAvoy to continue moving forward, but he felt McAvoy was flat-out wrong for pushing this case to the back burner.

Perhaps a meeting with Alicia Martin would help. If Alicia really was moving forward with a crusade, as Warner had put it, Fuller thought he could be a powerful ally. Fuller knew everything that had gone on with the Josh Martin case, who better to help? The question that remained for Fuller was whether or not he was willing to concede his career as a detective over this decision. He did not have any intention of working for McAvoy again, but if he joined up with Alicia Martin, it would create enough of a stir that no department would touch him in the future. He could explain the abrupt exit as the result of a difference of opinion. And he was sure that, in time, McAvoy would be a positive referral and corroborate Fuller's reasoning behind quitting so suddenly. What Fuller would not be able to explain is his being a traitor, and shedding light on what went on inside the walls of a police department during an investigation.

It was something he would have to sleep on. Regardless of which side Fuller would choose, he wanted to see Alicia Martin again.

10:49 p.m.

The day had been a surprisingly warm 75 degrees, and the temperature in Alicia's bedroom reflected it. Despite having the windows open for the past few hours, she had not been able to cool off completely. Now the outside temperature had dipped into the low 50s. Alicia walked the line between sleep and awake. She heard her bathroom door creak slightly as a breeze came through her open window. A moment later a shiver tiptoed down her spine. Inch by inch waking up her nerves along the way. Alicia felt as if there was something – or someone – in the room with her. A cold and dark sensation crept over her body.

When Alicia woke the next morning, she would not be sure if what she felt was real or if she had been dreaming.

22

March 27, 10:00 a.m.

Whether or not what Alicia felt the previous night was a dream or reality did not matter to her this morning. She was determined not to let her mind be affected by thoughts of a dark nature anymore. Her battle with her mental demons throughout the winter had toughened her, and she was better prepared now. Today was a day to herself. The kids were at school, the house was clean, and she had nothing on the agenda. Alicia felt it was going to be a good day. It came as a surprise to her when the doorbell rang.

Jack Fuller was standing on her small front stoop when Alicia opened the door. It took a moment for Alicia to place him. Once she recognized Fuller, Alicia saw that his face looked worn since the last time she had seen him. His sharp features and cool demeanor had morphed into something softer and sloppier. Through the prism of Alicia's eyes, Fuller looked weak. His eyes looked heavy, and his clothes were not crisp. It looked like he had taken a nap in them, even though it was not yet noon.

"Ms. Martin," Fuller said with a smile. "It's good to see you again."

Alicia nodded.

"Same to you, Detective Fuller," she said with an abrasive tone that Fuller took as confirmation of Warner's story.

There was a brief silence.

"What brings you to my door once again, Detective?"

Fuller looked down at his shoes. He looked like a teenager who so badly wanted to ask his crush to be his girlfriend, but did not know the right words. The sun peeked from behind a cloud, and Alicia spotted gray hairs on the detective's head that she had not seen before.

Fuller did not know how to proceed. He thought Alicia would be a little more welcoming than this, and that things would flow more naturally. That was not the case. He decided to lay his cards on the table. No secrets. No bluffing.

"I hear you are going to go public with your side of the story about Josh," Fuller said.

This surprised Alicia. She did not think anyone knew about her agenda. Surely Bridget could not have said anything. Alicia was her client. There must be some kind of privilege. And it did not seem like Beth was one to blab, especially to the police. Beth did run an organization, though. Surely she had told some of the members. Perhaps someone at Our Missing had a big mouth, and that person had told someone else who had a big mouth.

"Well that news didn't take too long to spread," Alicia said. "That's what you came here for? To try to scare me into not talking about Josh? To try to tell me the police have done everything they can to find my son?"

"No. That's not why I came, Ms. Martin. I came to apologize. We failed you. We could have done more to find Josh, and find out what happened to him. You deserved better."

Alicia looked away from Fuller to collect herself. Those words were good to hear, but she needed to keep the fire burning inside if she was going to be able to make her disapproval of the police's investigation a public matter.

"As nice as that is to hear, it does not change anything," Alicia said.

"I know," Fuller said. "And it shouldn't."

"If that is all you came here for, Detective, then I think you should leave."

Alicia turned her back to Fuller and walked into her house. Fuller knew he should leave, walk back to the car, and not say anything else. Then he recalled McAvoy telling him that he was off the case; telling him they were no longer going to pursue any leads.

"Ms. Martin?"

She turned around with a look of annoyance across her face.

"There's something else you should know."

10:07 a.m.

"Alright children, put down your pencils. Time is up."

The words floated through the room with a gentle coax. They were emitted from the voice box of Ms. Madigan, who was Macy Martin's seventh grade teacher. The class was taking a practice exam for the upcoming Constitution test. It was a state-mandated exam for seventh graders in Massachusetts. Macy's exam was a little over half done. She had not been able to focus on the questions during the test.

"Now remember, this was just a practice test," Ms. Madigan said. "The real exam will be in two weeks. We'll have one more practice early next week, and then it will be for real. We're going to go over the answers now. Don't feel embarrassed if you get any wrong. This is the time for correcting errors."

Ms. Madigan reviewed the exam by calling on members of the class to give their answers. Macy was called on for the second question and the twentieth question of the 100-question exam. Both of her answers for those questions were correct, as Ms. Madigan assumed they would be. Macy was one of her best students, if not her best student. She knew she could call on Macy when the tougher questions came up.

Macy looked at her answer sheet and saw that question number forty-two was the final question she had an answer for. She hoped Ms. Madigan would not call on her after that. When question number thirty-seven rolled around, Macy was called on again. This time her answer was wrong. It was the first question she had answered incorrectly. Most of the class missed it as well. Shortly after that, question number forty-two came and went. Macy's eyes began to dart around the room. Luckily, Ms. Madigan was reading each question off before she asked for an answer. All Macy needed to do was focus, and she could get through this without much more embarrassment. She did not like getting questions wrong in front of her peers. She had developed a reputation for being a smart child, and she very much enjoyed living up to it.

"Macy? What did you get for number forty-seven?" Ms. Madigan asked.

Macy had spaced. She had not been paying attention. She had spent her brainpower telling herself to pay attention, but had lost Ms. Madigan along the way. She glanced down at her exam, and saw a paragraph of text for the question. It was one of the longer, more detailed questions of the entire exam.

"I didn't get an answer for that one," Macy said in a dejected voice.

Ms. Madigan was surprised, but she did not want to put Macy on the spot any further.

"Not to worry, Macy. It is just a practice exam. Remember, it's not going to hurt you to guess an answer on this test. So even if you don't know for sure, just take your best guess."

Macy nodded a disappointed nod, and fixed her eyes on the exam. Ms. Madigan called on her three more times before the review was over. Macy was alert for each question, and responded with the correct answer. None of that covered up her embarrassment of not having an answer for question number forty-seven.

10:28 a.m.

Not much had been said in the last ten minutes. Alicia was preparing coffee while Fuller sat at her kitchen table. She thought about how much of a role the table had played in these events. It was where she found out about Josh. It was where she told her children about Josh. It was a place where she had fallen to some of her deepest depths, and yet, a place where the light of hope and positivity had returned to her when Beth Monk sat down for lunch with Alicia. Now, Detective Jack Fuller sat at her kitchen table. She did not want him in her house long. The coffee was ready, and Alicia poured a cup for Fuller. She did not want any.

"Thank you," Fuller said when Alicia placed the cup in front of him.

Alicia nodded, but did not say anything.

"Ms. Martin, what you need to know..." Fuller's voice drifted off. He was not sure how to proceed, or if he should proceed at all. "Well, the reason I came here this morning..."

"Yes, Detective?"

All of the conflicting thoughts from the previous night rushed back to Fuller. He knew he should not be sitting in Alicia Martin's kitchen. Sabbatical, or vacation, or whatever Ronald McAvoy wanted to call these two weeks where Fuller did not have to report to the station notwithstanding, Fuller was still a paid employee. The rule may not have been explicitly laid out in some police handbook, but it was generally understood that you do not give damning information to someone who is going to use it against you. That went for any workplace, but rang especially true in this setting. Fuller knew he should tell Alicia his coming to her house was a mistake. He knew he should walk – no, run – to the door and never come back.

Fuller took a sip of his coffee to gather himself. He inhaled a short breath of air and turned his eyes to meet Alicia's.

"The police force is pushing your son's case to the back burner."

10:33 a.m.

Sam was staring out of his classroom window when his teacher, Miss Rosen called on him. Sam did not respond.

"Sam?" Miss Rosen said.

"Um, yes? I'm sorry what was the question?" Sam said.

"I was asking what the capital of Washington was."

"Seattle?"

"No, Sam. It is not Seattle. Does anyone know the capital of Washington?"

Several students raised their hands. Sam wondered why Miss Rosen did not take this approach in the first place.

"Yes, Jenny," Miss Rosen said.

"It's Olympia," Jenny Brouch said with a smile on her face.

"That's right," Miss Rosen said.

Miss Rosen continued to go around the class asking students the capitals of states. Sam turned his attention back to the window. The sky was darkening outside. Sam did not see any rain clouds rolling in. It just looked darker outside, as if the pale blue sky was sucked up into the ether by some powerful vacuum.

10:38 a.m.

"Excuse me," Alicia said. "What did you say?"

Fuller was surprised the words leapt from his tongue so smoothly. He had not wanted to say them. He felt so close to leaving, but something inside of him forced the words out before he could catch them. Now there was no way to undo what was already set in motion. He might as well answer Alicia's question.

"They are putting it on the back burner," Fuller said. "No longer actively pursuing leads."

"What does that mean?" Alicia asked.

"It means the case is still open, but they will not be dedicating much time or staff to it."

The part of Fuller that wanted to bolt for the door was keeping his answers short, and hoping Alicia did not ask questions. But that part of him had already lost the battle. Fuller took a deep breath, and told himself to be more open.

"What it means, Ms. Martin, is that there will not be an army of police officers looking for Josh. If something breaks on its own, the police will track it down. But they are not going to be out there pounding the pavement in an attempt to make a break on their own."

Alicia was surprised.

"So no one will be looking for my son?"

"Not in an official capacity. No."

"What does that mean?"

Fuller had talked himself to another point he was not sure he wanted to reveal.

"I'm not going to stop looking, Ms. Martin. I'm going to find out what happened to Josh. I promise you that."

"Detective Fuller, you have just told me that the police force you work for is putting this case on the back burner. How are you going to find him? Aren't you part of the back burner plan? Haven't you been sent here to break the news to me because you are the one who has dealt with me the most?"

"No," Fuller said. "I am not any of those things. I came here to tell you because I thought you should know about it. I am not sure how I am going to find out what happened to Josh, but one way or another I am going to find out. I was not sent here by anyone. Officially, I am on leave from the force. What they don't know is that I will never work for them again."

Alicia was again surprised by the straightforward approach Fuller was taking.

"You're quitting?"

"Yes."

"I'm very surprised, Detective. I don't understand why you are choosing to tell me this, though."

"I heard you were going public with the story of Josh," Fuller said. "This is something that is going to bring some heat on the police force. It could be a little. It could be a lot. I can't really say for certain. But there will be attention where they don't want it."

Fuller paused a moment to take a sip from his coffee. Alicia Martin's eyes were fixed on the Detective.

"Perhaps I can be a silent partner in your quest," he said.

10:47 a.m.

Angel glared at her classmates. They were standing in a group getting a lecture from their teacher, Mrs. Phillips. It was recess, well, first recess as it was called. The children in kindergarten through second grade got two recesses. It was more of a break for the teachers than the students – another chance to get away from the classroom. Another chance to tire the little devils out.

Angel was sitting by herself on a bench about ten yards away from the lecture group, watching Mrs. Phillips talk. Angel knew she should not have done what she did. It had not made her feel any better.

Tommy Timbers would heal. He deserved it anyway.

Mrs. Phillips turned away from the group, and they slowly broke apart and resumed playing on the blacktop. She strode toward Angel. Angel's eyes filled with tears. It was her turn now. Mrs. Phillips took a seat next to her on the bench.

"Angel, you can't do what you did. Do you understand that?"

Angel wiped the wetness away from her eyes and nodded.

"I need you to answer me, Angel," Mrs. Phillips said.

"Yes," Angel said.

"Tommy could have really been hurt. That rock you threw could have hit him in the eye. Luckily it didn't."

"But he," Angel started, but was cut off.

"I know. I know. He said something about your brother. I know. That's why I talked to the whole class. I told them things like that are not good to say, and that they can hurt people with their

166

words. But Angel, you can't throw rocks at people. You have to come to me and tell me if anyone says something like that."

"Ok," Angel said. "I'm sorry, Mrs. Phillips."

"I need you to apologize to Tommy. And he will apologize to you. Ok?"

Angel nodded. She did not want to say she was sorry to Tommy Timbers, but she understood it was the only way out of this situation.

11:05 a.m.

Alicia tidied up her kitchen after walking Fuller to the door. Fuller had laid out in broad strokes what the police had done in trying to find out what happened to Josh. To Alicia it sounded like the police had done their job to the best of their ability, which was disconcerting. Her end result in joining the Our Missing rally and hiring Bridget was to finally get an answer about Josh. She thought getting the police to focus more attention on his case was the path to getting that answer. Now she was not so sure.

The part about the police basically dropping the investigation was infuriating, but that had only come about recently according to Fuller. Still, that was a good bit of information that she did not already have. She would still need to focus her attention on Josh and making everyone see him as she did. She knew criticism and some backlash would probably come her way if she attacked the police too forcefully. She hoped she was strong enough to take it.

23

March 29, 2:30 p.m.

Bridget Cass walked from one room to the next without saying much. She was observing, and her contractor, who was explaining the renovations to Cass and Young's office space, followed close behind. Everything looked good to Bridget. She was no expert on carpentry and electrical work, but the aesthetics of the renovation were pleasing. Jan Young, her co-founding partner, was the third member of the group. As was Jan's style, she was completely silent. Jan would undoubtedly give detailed comments to Bridget after they left the worksite, but she would not say anything in front of the contractor.

The brief tour concluded with handshakes, smiles, and standard nods of approval. The contractor went back inside the office suite to resume working while Bridget and Jan walked outside and to a nearby Starbucks.

"I like it a lot," Jan said. "The design looks great. I know I liked what I saw in the drawings they did, but to see it in person really looks good. Great work, Bridget."

"Thanks," Bridget said. "I agree with you. Everything is great. This is money well spent. We needed more space, and we needed an upgrade."

"Having that large conference room along with the two small ones we already had is going to be wonderful. The possibility of hosting a large-party deposition is something that I'm looking forward to."

Not long ago, Cass and Young had signed a long-term lease with their office building. Included in the terms of that lease was that the vacant office space next to Cass and Young's current space would be absorbed by the law firm. Renovations would be made to bring the spaces together in a pleasing manner. Cass and Young would foot the cost of the renovations, and in exchange for that the monthly rent would only increase by five hundred dollars for the term of the lease. Both Bridget and Jan viewed it as a great deal.

"It sure will be nice for the Wayland case, huh?" Bridget said.

"Oh yeah. Those drives into the city are a pain. I'm glad I'll be able to host a few," Jan said.

The pair arrived at the same Starbucks Bridget had met Alicia Martin at nearly a week ago. It jogged Bridget's memory.

"You know, I didn't tell you. It totally slipped my mind," Bridget said. "We have a new client."

"Oh really?" Jan said.

"Yeah. I met her here a few days ago. Totally blanked on telling you. This whole working remotely thing has broken down communication a bit," Bridget said with a laugh.

"Who is it?" Jan said.

"Alicia Martin is her name. It might ring a bell for you. She was mentioned in the papers briefly last fall. Her kid disappeared. Police don't know if he's dead or alive, and it doesn't sound like they are looking too hard. She wants to sue."

Jan nodded.

"I don't recall the name. Is there a case?"

"Maybe," Bridget said. "Maybe the police will pay to shut her up. If not, at least we'll shed a little light on her son. Maybe give them a kick in the pants."

Jan nodded again.

"We doing a retainer?" Jan asked.

"Haven't worked all that out with her yet. I was hoping to maybe get five grand out of her up front, then a smaller percentage of anything we get from the police. We'll see how the case progresses."

"At least try to get the five," Jan said. "This re-model isn't cheap."

Jan was always worried about the firm's finances, even though Bridget had a better grasp on them.

"Don't worry," Bridget said. "We're in a good spot. We can absolutely afford the re-model without five thousand dollars from Alicia Martin."

"It wouldn't hurt, though," Jan said.

Bridget smiled.

"I'm going to be following up with her when we are done here. So I'll let you know."

"Good," Jan said.

The chitchat turned to personal affairs, and general small talk as they finished their coffees. Jan stood up to leave.

"Let me know about Alicia Martin," she said. "Otherwise, I'll talk to you tomorrow."

Bridget nodded, smiled, and picked up her cell phone. Jan headed for the door. Bridget pulled up the number for Alicia and clicked on it to make the call. Alicia answered on the second ring.

"Hi, Alicia. Bridget Cass here."

"Hi, Bridget. How are you?" Alicia said.

"I'm doing well. How are you today?"

"I'm feeling pretty good," Alicia said.

"That's great to hear," Bridget said. "Are your spirits still up?"

"Yes," Alicia said. "Everything has felt so positive lately."

"That's the most important part. Listen, Alicia, I'm calling not only to check in on your well being, but to discuss a formal agreement between you and us at Cass and Young."

"Oh," Alicia said, slightly caught off guard. "Of course. Go ahead."

"I think we have grounds for a suit," Bridget said. "But before we do that, I need to meet with you again so we can sign a retainer agreement, which appoints me as your attorney."

"Of course, of course," Alicia said. "That's so wonderful to hear. And it makes perfect sense that I need to sign something."

"Good," Bridget said. "I'm glad you understand. Now, Alicia, I'm going to charge you an up-front fee of five thousand dollars to retain the services of my associates and me. That, and whatever expenses are associated with this case, are all you will have to pay out of your own pocket. If we receive any kind of settlement from the police department, Cass and Young will take thirty percent of that sum. Now, that number is slightly lower than what I can take by law, but that is because you are paying an up-front fee."

Alicia was quiet on the other end. The five thousand dollar amount had come as a bit of a surprise. She knew she was going to have to pay Bridget somehow, she just did not think she would have to shell out five grand so soon.

"Does all this make sense, Alicia? You're awfully quiet," Bridget said.

"It makes sense," Alicia said.

To Bridget she sounded very uneasy.

"Alicia, you can express any concerns you have now. I don't want this to be something that bogs down our relationship. I don't want you thinking about this agreement and it keeping you up at night. And I don't want you walking into a meeting we have two months from now and we start arguing about the retainer agreement. That will not be productive in any way. So, if you have any concerns, please, speak now or forever hold your peace."

Alicia was still quiet on her end of the line for a moment.

"I guess it is just a little more than I expected," Alicia said. "But I've never hired a lawyer before. I have the money. My business has been successful."

Alicia was not lying by saying that she had the money or that her home furnishings business had been successful, but since Josh had gone missing Alicia had not been working. She finished up a few existing jobs for clients after Josh's disappearance. In the months since then she had not taken on anything new. Alicia even declined two project offers via e-mail. In the past, only occasionally had she passed on a project, and she had never done so via e-mail. She had always spoken directly to a client, either in person or by phone. If Bridget Cass was going to be looking for more fees and expenses, it was time for Alicia to get back to work.

"I'll be honest with you, Alicia," Bridget said. "The number is a little high. Often when we do a plaintiff's case, we don't ask for anything up front and the case is done on a contingency. But this case is a little different, and I need to have some assurances for my business. You say your business has been successful, so I think you understand the nature of this."

"I do," Alicia said. "And I agree to those terms."

"Wonderful. When can we meet to have you sign the paperwork and cut the check?"

"Tomorrow?"

"That is perfect. How about eleven in the morning? I can come to your home if that is alright with you."

"That is fine. I'll see you at eleven."

"Thank you, Alicia. See you then."

After ending the phone call, Alicia walked straight to her computer and logged into her bank account. She saw a little over forty thousand dollars in her checking account. Plenty more was in her savings. She scrolled back on the registry to the last transaction before Halloween. It was a check she had written for seven hundred and fifty-five dollars on October 29. Alicia could not recall what exactly the check was for. The balance of her account after that check read sixty-six thousand dollars and change.

Alicia logged out of her banking account, and logged into her e-mail. There were five new messages. None of them had anything to do with work. A slight shiver crept across her shoulders.

7:12 p.m.

Fuller was in the small second bedroom of his apartment, the one he had turned into an office. The stolen boxes of files pertaining to the Josh Martin case sat open on the floor. There was a stack of folders face up on the left side of his desk and a stack of folders face down on the right side of his desk. Fuller sat between the two stacks, sifting through an open file folder. A pen rested on the legal pad placed next to the file. He held a pen in his right hand as he sifted through the contents of the folder. On the floor behind him were two more neat stacks of file folders, tall enough to look impressive, but not tall enough to topple over. Not without a push at least, though he was often tempted.

The stack of files to his left was what he wanted to get through tonight. The stack to his right was what was already done. The two stacks behind him represented the last two days of work. His legal pad was a little more than half full with notes. Fuller's hope was that the notes were clear enough to understand when he needed to review them later. While his spirits were up, Fuller felt no closer to finding new information about what had happened to Josh Martin. Most of the notes in the legal pad were small congratulations, stating that the police force had done things properly during their investigation.

He sighed and looked at the clock that hung on his office wall. He knew he should eat, but he did not have much of an appetite. There was nothing appealing in his cabinets or refrigerator anyway. Maybe he would run to Randy's Burgers later, when he could no longer ignore the hunger.

Fuller turned his attention back to the open file in front of him. In a deep recess of his mind a thought began to grow. A thought Fuller did not like. A thought that there might not be anything that could be done about finding out what happened to Josh Martin. The thought that started to grow was that this case could never be solved. It was so tiny at this time that Fuller did not even realize it was there as he continued to read through documents and take notes.

But it was there, and once it was, it would not be easily forgotten.

24

March 30, 11:00 a.m.

After their telephone conversation the previous day, Bridget Cass was surprised when she pulled into Alicia Martin's driveway. The home was lovely, and large. It was not an expansive mansion by any means, but it was not run down and in disrepair either. The yard was large – Bridget estimated it was a little under an acre. She could imagine Alicia and her children having a very nice life here. With Alicia's apprehension about the retainer fee the day before, Bridget assumed money was a little tight. That did not appear to be the case with the look and upkeep of Alicia Martin's home.

It only took a few seconds for Alicia to reach the door after Bridget had rung the bell. Bridget noticed there was no sound of a dog barking, which she welcomed. It was not that Bridget was against dogs. Sometimes she found them annoying. And in the hands of an irresponsible owner, the pooch would be a nuisance. She preferred no pets at all.

"Hello, you're right on time," Alicia said with a warm smile.

"Punctuality is important," Bridget replied as she stepped through the threshold. "Your home is beautiful."

"Thank you. I appreciate that."

Alicia's kitchen once again served as her conference room, the kitchen table once again the focal point. Alicia supposed she could have held the meeting in her office up on the second floor, but it was small and cluttered. She had no desire to clean it up.

Bridget pulled a slender folder from her briefcase, an elegant looking handbag made of dark leather. She set the file on the counter as Alicia asked her if she wanted anything to drink.

"Coffee please, if you have it," Bridget said.

"It'll take a second to make a fresh pot," Alicia said. "Is that alright?"

"You know what, don't worry about it. This isn't going to take very long. A glass of water is fine."

"Are you sure? It isn't much trouble."

"I'm sure. Thank you, Alicia."

Alicia filled two glasses with water from the water cooler, and placed one in front of Bridget. She then took her seat across the table. It was the one Alicia always sat in. A seat with some good memories and some bad. A seat with one horrible memory that still haunted Alicia.

"So," Bridget began after taking a sip of water. "This is our retainer agreement. The language in this document is standard across the board. Please read through it, and let me know if you have any questions."

Alicia took the document from Bridget and began at the top of the page, which was marked with today's date below Cass and Young's letterhead. The document was addressed to her and read:

Thank you for retaining our services to represent your interests. This letter sets forth the terms of our representation.

OUR RESPONSIBILITIES:

We will provide counsel and representation for all matters surrounding the Vanguard Police Department's involvement in the case of Josh Martin, your son. We will keep you promptly advised of all developments in this matter, and make no substantive decisions without your knowledge and approval.

CLIENT RESPONSIBILITIES:

You agree to cooperate with us in all respects. Your cooperation may include discussing the matter with us, making decisions regarding negotiations, providing us with information necessary to represent your interests, attending conferences either in person or by phone, as well as reviewing and executing documents necessary to complete the negotiations. You also agree to pay our fees as set forth below, on a timely basis.

OUR FEES:

A one-time $5,000 payment will retain the services of Cass and Young. Your case will primarily be handled by Bridget Cass, but input may be sought from the other attorneys at the firm. Rest assured, you have the entire legal force of Cass and Young behind you.

After the one-time payment, Cass and Young will receive 30 percent of any settlement fees received from the Vanguard Police Department or any other currently unknown entity that arises in this matter.

Regarding costs, our statements will include disbursements expended on your behalf, copy charges, fax expenses, messenger service, etc. Copies are billed at .25 per page; faxes are billed at $3.00 per fax regardless of length. All other costs are billed to you at our cost with no add-ons or surcharges.

If any terms of this agreement are broken, be it financial or otherwise, Cass and Young reserves the right to withdraw their representation of you.

The purpose of this letter is to memorialize the terms of our representation. If the terms, as set forth in this letter, are consistent with your understanding of our agreement, please sign where indicated below. I look forward to working with you towards a successful resolution of this matter

Very truly yours,

Bridget Cass

BC/jas

ABOVE TERMS AGREED TO AND ACCEPTED:

_____

Date

It was an intimidating document to read, and Alicia was worried a little bit about the future costs of copies and faxes. Once again, television was clouding her mind. She imagined all the papers she saw shuffling back and forth between her favorite TV attorneys. What she did not know was that Cass and Young handled nearly ninety percent of its documents electronically.

"This is all standard?" Alicia asked.

"Of course it is," Bridget said. "Alicia, this isn't some deal with the devil. We are your attorneys now."

Alicia moved her head slightly from side to side like a metronome.

"Alright," she said, and signed her name to the bottom of the document. She then stood up and opened a file folder of her own that was sitting on the counter behind her. She took one last look at the check before handing it over to Bridget Cass.

Bridget took the check, and Alicia saw a quick smile brush across her face. It was only there for an instant, but it had existed. Bridget could not cover it up or talk it away.

"Thank you," Bridget said. And stuck out her hand. Instinctively, Alicia shook it.

"Is there anything you would like to discuss about your case while you have me here?"

"Actually there is," Alicia said. She hoped Bridget would not be angry. Alicia's gut felt her attorney might not react favorably. "Detective Jack Fuller came to my house two days ago. I took a sort of impromptu meeting with him right here at this very table."

Bridget felt a rage begin boil in her belly. She was able to control it, though. Years of being a lawyer had taught her how to control herself. A lawyer could not have an outburst at a judge in court without some kind of adverse consequence. Being cordial with opposing counsel was also a good strategy, no matter how much one wanted to wring their neck. Clients too. Calmness was a necessity of the job. Real life lawyering was not like lawyering on the big screen, or more commonly, the small screen. The day-to-day dramatics were not there. They happened from time to time, but lawyers really had to pick their battles. This was not a spot for Bridget to unleash her fury.

Alicia thought she saw a flash of red in Bridget's eyes when she told her about Detective Fuller. It was not a metaphor, either. Alicia could swear a small red flame burst brightly through the whites of Bridget's eyes and then quickly dissipated. There was no other evidence of how she felt about the meeting between Alicia and Detective Fuller taking place. Not yet, at least. Bridget kept the same pleasant expression on her face.

"Is that so?" Bridget said.

"Yes."

"Did he call to set it up?"

"No. He just showed up at my door. He's been here before. He was the lead detective on Josh's case."

"What did you two talk about?"

Alicia was pleased with how smooth this was going. She thought Bridget would have been a little upset. Instead, the lawyer seemed quite pleasant despite the initial flash of red in her eyes.

"He told me that the police were dropping Josh's case. Well, not really dropping it, but not actively pursuing leads. He said that he was no longer working for the police force, although they don't know that yet. I guess he is on some sort of sabbatical, but he has no intention of returning. He also said he would like to help me. That he heard I was going to be suing the department and that I might be stirring up some shit. And that he wouldn't mind lending an invisible hand to help stir."

Bridget digested the information. She did her best to maintain a poker face despite the fury she felt. Bridget figured that this Detective Fuller character was lying to Alicia, and that Alicia had bought into the lie. Bridget assumed the Vanguard PD would get wind of what was coming, and that Detective Fuller must have been chosen as the point man of deception because he had a familiar relationship with Alicia, and she would believe his story. Bridget did not like this sudden interest by a member of the Vanguard PD. Not one bit.

"Alicia," Bridget said in the calmest tone she could muster. "This is all interesting information. But do you really believe it?"

Alicia considered the question for a moment.

"I do. I believe what Detective Fuller told me."

The fury in Bridget's belly boiled a little more intensely now. She was not sure whom she was angrier with: Alicia for her gullibility or the police department for preying on this poor woman who was trying to put her life back together.

"I don't," Bridget said. "I think this Fuller was sent here because he knows you, and because you trust him. I think the powers that be in the Vanguard PD sent him here looking for an inside track on what you are going to do so they can get out front in defending themselves."

"I … I … there's no way. That's …"

"Unbelievable?" Bridget said.

"Yes," Alicia said. Then again quietly to herself, "Yes."

"Well that's what I believe. Did you tell him anything?"

Alicia thought for a moment.

"No. He did most of the talking. I was doubtful of his story at first too, Bridget, but I assure you he is telling the truth."

"I don't buy it. I just don't. You don't need to convince me of it either. If you didn't tell him anything that gives us an answer right there. They already know we are going to file suit and bring this case out into the light on a grand scale. The Vanguard PD knowing that they will be sued doesn't change anything that we are going to do."

"What about him helping us?"

"Absolutely not," Bridget said. "I do not want you having any contact with Fuller or anyone else from the Vanguard PD. If they come to your door, tell them you cannot talk to them without me present. Then, call me immediately."

This was a little more in line with how Alicia originally thought Bridget would react.

"I will do that. I'm sorry, Bridget."

"You have nothing to be sorry about. He came to your door. You didn't need to let him in, but it is Fuller who is at fault."

"Are you going to call over to the station and find out what happened?"

Bridget had considered this before Alicia had mentioned it, but quickly dismissed it. You do not send ground troops into a country that you are going to drop a nuclear bomb on. While Bridget did not consider Alicia Martin's suit against the Vanguard Police Department nuclear by any definition of the word before this morning, she was surely going to make it as nuclear as possible in light of this new information.

One thing that Bridget always did well was take care of her clients. The other side, when it came down to brass tacks, could go fuck themselves in her opinion. Most of them looked down on her because she was a woman anyway. So fuck them. She hated people messing with her clients. She was like a mother duck protecting her eggs. Her wings were about to be spread, and her beak was about to start squawking.

"No," Bridget said. "I am not going to call the station. It would serve no purpose. They know the lawsuit is coming. And maybe they know that they might be front-page news in the local papers someday soon because of you speaking at the Our Missing event with Beth. But, no, I'm not going to go digging into why Fuller came to your house. I already have my opinion on the matter, and that is enough for me."

Alicia nodded.

"Is there anything else you would like to add? Any more instances of police intimidation?"

Alicia thought those words were a little strong, and she liked Bridget Cass a little less for saying them. Alicia told Bridget she had nothing else to report. Bridget gathered her things, and pleasantly headed for the door. The fire in her belly was under control.

"We'll be in touch," she said before walking out to her car.

Alicia did not respond. She wanted to believe what Fuller had told her, but orders from her lawyer were orders. Alicia had just paid Bridget five thousand dollars after all. Advice was what she was paying for. She would stay away from Fuller, and if he came back to her house she would have to tell him to leave immediately. It made her stomach twinge a little bit to think this way. Alicia felt Fuller was on her side, and that he had told her the truth. Bridget had left her with no other option. Alicia knew she needed to listen to her attorney's advice.

25

April 1, 6:22 a.m.

Sam Martin lay awake in his bed awaiting the scream. He had been up for half an hour with excitement. Slowly the happenings in the Martin household had been returning to normal. Sam thought maybe this would help. If it did not, at least it would make his sisters jump a little bit.

The first shriek escaped from Macy and Angel's room and reached Alicia's ears. Alicia was confused at first. A second shriek followed shortly after the first. Alicia hurried out of her bathroom and down the hall toward her daughters' room. A wry smile crossed Sam's face as he heard the shrieks and pitter-patter of feet. *They've found out,* he thought. *Finally.*

Sam heard his mother reach the doorway to his sisters' room. His door was across the hall, and cracked open slightly. He had to strain his ears to hear the conversation.

"What's going on?" his mother said.

"My teddy is gone!"

That must have been Angel. Sam could not tell for sure by her voice. She was too far away. The word *teddy* came through loud and clear, so he knew it must be her.

"And Charlie is missing too!"

That was Macy. Sam could tell from her voice. It was louder and more pronounced. Plus, he knew Charlie was her stuffed dog. While Macy was slowly drifting away from her stuffed animals, Charlie was always at her side while she slept. Always.

"They're gone?" Alicia said. She processed the scene for a moment, then turned to see Sam's door open slightly. He usually slept with it all the way closed.

"I think I know where they are," Alicia said.

The tears that had started to well in Angel's eyes disappeared as quickly as they came. The same went for the redness forming in Macy's cheeks.

"Where?" Macy said. She was irritated. Nobody messed with her Charlie.

Alicia brought her voice down to a whisper. "I think they are in there," she said while pointing at Sam's door.

Macy stormed out of the room and flung Sam's door wide open. Angel was a step behind her.

"April fools!" he shouted with a delightful cackle of laughter.

"Not funny, Sam!" Macy retorted.

"My bear!" Angel shouted.

Sam was lying in his bed with Angel's bear snuggled into his left arm and Macy's Charlie snuggled into his right. Macy scooted around the edge of the bed, snatched Charlie and stormed back into her room. Angel bounded on top of the bed to grab her bear. She was a little more forgiving, wrestling with her brother a bit to get her precious bear back, and then sitting on Sam's bed for a moment to look the bear up and down before leaving.

Even though her daughters started the morning with a little bit of emotional distress, Alicia could not help but smile at the scene she saw unfold. It did seem like things were beginning to settle a little bit around the house.

"Pretty funny, Sam," she said. "But next time try to do it in a way that doesn't pick on your sisters."

"Sure, Mom," he said with a grin.

"Or me," Alicia added.

"Noted."

Alicia headed back to her bathroom to continue getting ready for the day. Sam found his way to the shower and began his own morning routine. Macy was already half dressed, with Charlie back in her rightful spot on the bed. Angel sat on the floor of their room and hugged her bear tightly.

26

April 3, 10:30 a.m.

Jack Fuller's home office desk was completely clean of files from the Josh Martin case. The stacks that had accumulated on the floor of his second bedroom were cleaned up and put back in their respective boxes, which now had their lids back on top.

Fuller was still asleep. He'd found that his energy peaked at night during these last few days, and he had gradually been sleeping to a later hour. If he were asked how this made him feel, he would say he enjoyed his new routine. Unfortunately, it had not yielded any results. He was no closer to Josh Martin or Josh Martin's killer than he was when he took the boxes on the way out of the police station days ago. Nor was he any closer than he was months ago when he was working the investigation nearly round the clock.

He had not discovered any new missteps by the department to feed Alicia Martin either, but that was not the end of the world. He could still be helpful in her desire to hang the Vanguard PD out to dry. The large calendar that lay on his desk had a note on it for today. It read: *Check in on Alicia.*

12:47 p.m.

Alicia looked up at her only audience member. She was not expecting applause. It would have been a positive feeling after an otherwise nerve-racking experience. The echo of clapping did not reverberate through Alicia's living room. Beth Monk stood from her seat on Alicia's couch and walked toward the future Our Missing speaker. Beth swung around so she was shoulder-to-shoulder with Alicia. Alicia was slightly taller than Beth.

"That was very good, Alicia," Beth said without turning to look at her. She was staring at Alicia's couch. It was as though she was picturing the crowd she would see in the town square in a few days. Beth assured Alicia it would not be a large crowd, but it would likely be the largest she had ever spoken in front of. Alicia hoped she could keep her nerves in control.

"Don't worry about your nerves," Beth said, as though she was reading Alicia's mind. "Don't allow them to control you. Everyone gets nervous. Especially when speaking in front of a crowd. You can do this, and you will do this. I have faith in you."

Alicia turned to see Beth's face. Beth did not do the same.

"Thank you, Beth," Alicia said.

"Don't mention it," Beth said.

"You need to go through it again, though. From the beginning. Nice and slow. Don't rush these folks. This is a slow burn speech. Keep them hanging."

Alicia was not sure she understood all the terminology Beth had just laid on her, but nodded her head anyway. She liked the phrase "slow burn." It echoed in her head a few times before she began speaking again.

1:35 p.m.

It had not been ten minutes since Beth Monk left Alicia's house when the doorbell rang again. Alicia was in her cluttered home office checking a few e-mails when she heard it. *So much for getting back to work.* Mildly annoyed, she got up from her chair and went to the front door. Seeing that Jack Fuller was on the other side brought about conflicting feelings. Alicia knew she had to follow the line Bridget had drawn in the sand. Jack Fuller was not on their side even though Alicia wanted to trust him. Alicia had no other choice.

"I cannot speak with you," Alicia said.

Her words cut through Fuller's brief opening line before he got too far. Alicia had not heard what he said. A puzzled look crossed Fuller's face. One that simply said *Oh*. He briefly looked down at his shoes, and then back at Alicia.

"Is this a bad time? I would have called, but I didn't have your number."

This was a lie. Fuller had her number tucked away in the file boxes of her son's case, and he had considered using it. He figured his first unannounced visit had gone so well that he might as well try it again. It was tougher to read a person over the phone. It was also tougher to say no to a person's face.

"It isn't that this is a bad time," Alicia said. "My lawyer has instructed me not to speak to you. And that if anyone from the police department wishes to speak to me, that she must be present."

The *Oh* look deepened on Fuller's face. He understood what was happening now. His help was not needed nor wanted.

"Ah. I understand. I'll let you be. I'm sorry," he said.

Alicia wanted to say something nice to let him know that she thought he could really help, but she decided to maintain her tough approach to Jack Fuller's second visit of the week. She simply closed the door, turned around, and walked back to her office.

Fuller was a little surprised by Alicia's actions. He walked down Alicia's front steps toward his car in the driveway wondering how anyone could try to sell something door-to-door. It certainly did not feel good having a door somewhat rudely closed on him just now. He could not imagine it happening several times a day every Monday through Friday of a week.

Back in her office, Alicia dialed Bridget Cass. Again, it was something she really did not want to do, but she was following orders.

"Alicia, hi. How are you?" Bridget said when she answered the phone.

Alicia felt a sense of importance. Her number was programmed into Bridget's mighty cell phone.

"I'm fine today," Alicia said in an upbeat tone. She was trying to give off the vibe of calmness. "Detective Jack Fuller just came to my door again. I told him I could not speak with him."

That fucker is what went through Bridget's head. She refrained from saying those words it into the phone.

"Good, Alicia. Good. Hopefully that settles the matter and sends the proper message to the Vanguard police."

"I hope so," Alicia said.

"Any other news?"

"I met with your sister to go over my speech today. It's coming along well."

"That's wonderful to hear. Speaking for Our Missing is going to be a big part of this. I'm so happy you will be doing that."

"I'm looking forward to it."

Bridget smiled on her end of the line. She was proud of what Alicia had been doing these last few days.

"This is all good news," Bridget said. "Let's keep the good news coming. We'll be in touch when we are getting closer to filing the complaint against the police."

"Sounds good."

"Have a great day, Alicia."

"Thanks. You too."

Alicia set her cell phone on top of a stack of papers on the desk and opened up her e-mails. There was one from the friend of a client Alicia had done a lot of work for over the years. The friend, Tania Mills, was looking for a new living room set and had really liked Alicia's past work. Alicia created a new file on her computer with Tania Mills' name, and also created a subfolder in her e-mail titled Mills Correspondence. She dropped the e-mail into the correspondence file, and replied saying she was on the job.

*   *   *   *   *

Pressing send on the e-mail to accept the new job was the high point of Alicia Martin's emotional ride since Houston West came to her door dressed as Officer Jim Warner and told her that Josh was dead. Alicia thought she would continue to climb higher on this sheer vertical cliff that led out of the depths of depression. She could not imagine that her fingers would slip from their grip – with the help of a force nobody understood – and that she would plummet back toward the jagged rocks at the base of the cliff unable to stop herself along the way.

Neither could Alicia envision the safety harness held in place by her will would snap this time, failing her when she needed it most.

27

April 7, 12:22 p.m.

Jack Fuller knew today was the day he was supposed to return to work at the Vanguard police station. This date had a large black box drawn around it on his desk calendar. The box had grown in size each time he traced and retraced the perfectly square outlines that made up the box that the seventh day of April lived in. Fuller had powered off his phone before going to bed last night in preparation of several incoming calls from McAvoy today. He did not want to be bothered by the constant ringing. He would turn his phone on after work hours were done. Fuller had no desire to speak with McAvoy today – or ever again for that matter.

Fuller was sure McAvoy was pissed. He was also sure McAvoy did not have the whole picture yet. The guess around the station was probably that Fuller was just late on his first day back on the job. Surely no one thought he had quit. It was highly unlikely anyone working there had figured out Fuller would never set foot in the Vanguard police station again. There were some smart people working there, but none of them had psychic abilities. Fuller wondered how long it would take everyone to realize he truly was gone. *Maybe by tomorrow?* Surely not *everyone* would be convinced by then.

Fuller had been nervous in anticipation of this day. Last night he had not slept well as a result. He tossed and turned in his bed for what felt like hours, always holding a pillow like it was a football – a habit he had picked up at some undefined point in his life. Fuller was not sure when it had started, but now it was the only way he could fall asleep.

3:45 p.m.

McAvoy's day was in its final quarter mile. He liked to be at the station by 6:30 in the morning on most days. Which, during the month of April in Vanguard, was still before the rooster's crow. Any hope of reaching Fuller was lost. McAvoy had given up trying shortly after he finished his chicken salad sandwich for lunch. The idea that Fuller could have forgotten that today was scheduled to be his first day back had crossed McAvoy's mind. After mulling the thought over, McAvoy decided it was an unlikely answer. Jack Fuller was much too smart and organized for an error like that. McAvoy knew something was up, and he did not like it.

Part of him hoped Fuller was not injured or sick. Regardless of their differences at times, McAvoy had tremendous respect for Fuller. He always thought of Fuller as a true professional who worked hard, often to a fault. Like the boxer who must be stopped by his own corner because he does not realize the damage he is causing to his own body by continuing to fight. That was Jack Fuller. A police force needed some alphas, and Jack Fuller had always been one in McAvoy's eyes. After a few hours had passed in the early morning, and it became apparent that Fuller was either extremely tardy or not showing up at all, McAvoy was hoping to get word of an injury or an illness. He liked those options better than the alternative.

Even though he did not want to believe it, McAvoy had already settled on the notion that Jack Fuller had finished working at the Vanguard Police Department. He was surprised Fuller had essentially chosen one case over the job as a whole. Alpha or not, Fuller was a cop through and through. Plus, McAvoy knew when he told Fuller to take two weeks off it would cause him to stew. Alphas needed to show their dominance over a group. They did not function well when cast out on their own. McAvoy figured Fuller would come back motivated to prove wrong the powers that be and show them the Martin case could be handled efficiently even with everything else going on. Much like Kobe Bryant, when age started to pile on his back, McAvoy expected Fuller to win with determination and will. He expected Fuller to disobey orders, go rogue, refuse other assignments, and maybe even try to lure other officers and detectives to his side in his personal battle against McAvoy. This is what McAvoy thought the department needed. A good kick in the pants, as his father used to say.

Apparently the Captain's mind game, and his feeling that he knew Jack Fuller down to his stubborn core, had backfired. McAvoy never foresaw a future at the Vanguard Police Department without Jack Fuller there as his best detective. If that was now the situation, then McAvoy did not know what to do about it.

McAvoy decided he had enough for the day, and left the station. It was an early departure for him. The sun was still firmly above the horizon line. He was not tired. He simply had enough of a frustrating day. It had not felt normal from the start, and McAvoy hoped a good night's sleep would put normal back into his life. The walk to his car was uneventful. He did not tell anyone he was leaving for the day, but people noticed. Word spread rather quickly, and the question of whether or not Jack Fuller was finished at the Vanguard Police Department was bursting out of everyone's lips.

5:30 p.m.

D-day will be tomorrow. Or, perhaps Bridget should call it C-Day for Complaint Day. She had put the final touches on the complaint that was going to be filed at the Suffolk County Courthouse sometime before noon tomorrow on behalf of Alicia Martin. A draft had been e-mailed to Alicia this afternoon, and Alicia had responded quickly, verifying all of the allegations as true. Bridget then gave it a final read through, touched up a few areas, and sent it to her home office printer. She wished the firm's renovated office space was complete. It looked like it was going to be another two weeks before everything was ready for them to move back in.

These moments were always exhilarating for Bridget. The beginning of a new lawsuit brought a needed change to the daily routines of being a lawyer. The possibilities of the case were limitless, and Bridget was always excited for what obstacles she would need to conquer in order to receive the best result for her client. The feeling it most resembled for her was the day before a new school year began. Discovering who was in her classes and what her teachers were like was always a thrill for Bridget. These moments were life-altering events shaped by computer programs that made the master schedules. A new friend could emerge simply because a computer had selected that person to be in the same class as Bridget. The thrill she felt now was the same. A path had been set by forces outside of Bridget and Alicia Martin's control. The journey down this path would be taken together, and Bridget felt the end destination would be satisfying and successful.

She created a brief e-mail to Alicia and pressed send.

5:42 p.m.

Alicia was sitting in her office looking over material for her new client, Tania Mills. She was putting together a sample package of materials to send to Tania. In the living room, Macy, Sam and Angel were watching TV. Alicia knew she was going to have to start preparing dinner soon. Her e-mail pinged. It was a message from Bridget. Alicia opened it.

Complaint is final. Tomorrow our journey begins. Looking forward to it.

Bridget's standard e-mail signature listing her contact information and the address of Cass and Young's office was underneath her message. Alicia's stomach filled with butterflies after reading the message. She was not sure if she was ready for this chapter of her life to begin. Not only was the complaint being filed, but in five short days she was going to be speaking at the Our Missing event. Public life awaited. The excitement she thought would come with it was not present. Instead, she felt darkness beginning to set in again. Alicia unsuccessfully tried to push the feeling away. She closed the message and headed to the kitchen to begin making dinner for her children.

28

April 9, 9:40 a.m.

The Sheriff knew the first address on his list very well, although he was a bit surprised to be serving a summons there. Regardless, the job was the job, and he dutifully got into his car and began driving in the direction of his destination.

Roger Mullins had been a sheriff for the last eight years. Serving a summons was not the most fun part of the job, but he did not complain. His wife, Rita, enjoyed hearing that this was one of his responsibilities because she felt it was safe. Any day where he had to serve multiple summonses was a good day for her. She only wanted him out of harms way during the day, and home for dinner at night.

The Vanguard Police Department was where Roger Mullins got his start before working his way up the ladder and becoming a Suffolk County Sheriff. He knew Ronald McAvoy from their days together as low-level cops at Vanguard. They had not been partners, but they had been friendly enough for the occasional beer after work and the even less occasional barbecue at one of their homes. Since Roger went on his path to become a sheriff, he had lost touch with McAvoy. Today, Roger was excited to see his former co-worker even though the circumstances were not ideal.

The drive was only twenty minutes door-to-door, and Roger had the radio in his car tuned to the local sports talk station. He had it turned down just enough to where he could hear his own police radio without any issue. The two hosts were gabbing about the previous day's Red Sox game, the season opener. The Sox had defeated Baltimore 5-2, and, as usual with an Opening Day win in Boston, optimism for the season was high. The station was going to a commercial break as Roger pulled up to the Vanguard Police

Department's parking lot. There were four prime spots marked with visitor parking signs near the main entrance of the building. None of the spots were taken. Roger pulled his car, labeled with Suffolk County Sheriff on the side, into one of the spots and headed for the front door.

Once inside, a receptionist directed him toward McAvoy's office. Roger navigated the halls with ease, his memory of the building coming back to him with remarkable precision. He found McAvoy's office door open, and the Captain looking down, studying papers on his desk. Roger rapped his knuckles on the doorframe and put a smile on his face.

McAvoy looked up, and recognized the man standing in his doorway immediately.

"Roger, holy hell," McAvoy said while standing up and extending his right arm for a handshake. "What are you doing here?"

Roger strode into the room with his right arm extended. Their hands met and locked for a quick three pumps before they released.

"It's good to see you again, Ronald," Roger said. "It's been way too long."

"Way too long," McAvoy echoed. "Sit. Sit. What are you doing here?" he asked again.

"Well," Roger said as he parked his ample posterior into an open chair on the opposite side of McAvoy's desk. "I'm afraid I don't come under the best circumstances."

Roger handed over the envelope that contained the summons and a copy of the complaint filed on behalf of Alicia Martin. McAvoy took the envelope and opened it. He did not read through the entire document. None of it caught him by surprise.

"Well," McAvoy said after a brief silence. "We were expecting this. We heard some rumors that she might sue us."

Roger brightened a little at this. He was glad his old friend was not caught off guard.

"It's good that you had a head's up. Sometimes these things really catch people by surprise."

McAvoy nodded. And set the envelope on his desk.

"Enough about this," he said. "How are you doing, Rog? How's the Sheriff's Office?"

"I'm doing good. Packed on a few pounds since we last saw each other, but I'm healthy as a horse. Or so my doctor's say. The Sheriff's Office is great. Love what I do. Couldn't think of a better place to work."

McAvoy was happy to hear all of this. He had noticed that Roger had probably gained a solid fifty pounds since the last time the two saw each other, which had to have been eight or nine years ago by McAvoy's recollection.

"That's great to hear," McAvoy said. "Things here have been great. As you can see, I'm the Captain now. No more patrol cop work for me. It's nice being able to oversee everything."

"That's awesome. Just awesome. What do you think of the Sox this year?"

McAvoy grinned.

"They looked great yesterday. I think they've got a great team. Hopefully they stay healthy. They could really be something this year."

"Totally agree," Roger said. "I love their pitching staff. If those horses stay healthy, they'll go far."

"Definitely," McAvoy said.

Both sides sensed the conversation was beginning to run its course. Roger jumped first at an exit strategy.

"Well, I gotta get going," he said. "More people to serve this morning. Sorry I had to be the bearer of bad news for you."

"I'd rather have it be you than someone else," McAvoy said. "It was great getting to see you again. We have to get together for a beer soon. It's been way too long."

"Definitely," Roger said. "Maybe catch a Sox game on TV."

"That would be perfect."

The two shook hands, and Roger headed back to the front of the building to find his car and continue on his morning task. He had three more summonses to serve. He hoped they all went as smoothly as his visit with Ronald McAvoy had. Some people were really adverse to these types of situations, and Roger understood that. He did his best to explain to them that he was not there to arrest them, but to merely serve them with papers saying they are being sued. Not everyone listened. Some ran. Roger thought those people were idiots.

McAvoy looked at the papers his old friend Roger Mullins had given him. He wanted to throw them in the trash and forget all about them. Unfortunately, he knew this was not an option. The number for Christopher Bronstein, Vanguard PD's attorney, was stored in the contacts folder on his computer. McAvoy pulled up the number for Bronstein's direct line and dialed.

"Christopher Bronstein."

"Chris, it's Ronald McAvoy of the Vanguard Police Department. How are you today?"

"Hello, Ronald. I'm doing ok. What's up?"

"Well, you know how we discussed that a suit might be headed our way?"

"Yes."

"We got served today."

"Can you e-mail a copy of that over to me? And the summons too?"

"Of course."

"I'll be filing an appearance on the Department's behalf later today. Thanks for sending that stuff over, Ronald. We'll take care of this."

"Thanks, Chris. I'll get this to you as soon as we are off the phone."

"Wonderful. Have a great day."

"You too."

McAvoy hung up his phone, scanned the documents using his desktop scanner, and e-mailed them off to Bronstein. He hoped he would not have to do anything else with this matter for quite a while.

29

April 12, 7:30 a.m.

Winter was not ready to relinquish its grasp on the weather to spring. Try as spring might, today was a battle it was going to lose. Beth Monk clicked the weather app on her cell phone and saw that the temperature reading was thirty-nine degrees. The high was going to be a chilly forty-two despite clear skies and minimal wind. Beth wore her winter jacket and a headband that covered her ears. Her face felt numb as she sipped a fresh cup of coffee. She had been at the site of this morning's Our Missing gathering since five o'clock to oversee assembly of the small stage and help with the P.A. system. Alicia Martin and her other speaker for the morning, Jane Rotolowski, should be arriving at any moment. The show was set to begin at nine – the earliest their noise permit allowed even though the park where they were set up did not have many residences nearby. It was a small park near the "historic" downtown of Vanguard. The only reason the town's council members deemed Vanguard's downtown "historic" was because it was old. Not a lot of history had actually happened in Vanguard. At least not a lot of major history. Sure, every town had local history: a high school team that won a state championship, a moderately famous politician, a few major notable crimes. Vanguard even once had a lottery winner. Nothing major, just a four million dollar jackpot in the state lottery. It had kept the people of the town buzzing for a couple of months.

Beth saw Alicia approaching from a parking lot not far from the park. Alicia's children were in tow. Beth did not care if Jane Rotolowski showed up. Beth could fill that time. Alicia was the new star. She was the important part of today. Beth found Jane a little annoying, even if she was saddened that Jane's daughter had fallen into drugs at the age of thirteen and run off a year later.

"Good morning, Alicia. I hope you are feeling warm on this chilly morning."

Alicia had a stylish winter hat on her head, and a sleek brown leather jacket that was zipped all the way to the top. A red scarf was wrapped neatly around her neck. Her exterior appearance masked her inner feelings well. Beth could not see the despair that had been creeping into Alicia's mind.

"I am so far. Hopefully it warms up a little. Or we may not have much of a crowd."

"I'm not discouraged by the temperature," Beth said. "I think the people will still show. It's a pretty committed group for the most part. And who do we have here?"

Beth looked into Sam, Macy and Angel's eyes as she said this.

"These are my children," Alicia said, and introduced each of them. "I'm sorry you haven't had a chance to meet them until now."

The children each took turns shaking Beth's hand, and smiled as best they could. They did not like being roused from bed at an early hour on a day off of school.

"When I am speaking you three are going to hang with Mrs. Monk. Is that understood?" Alicia said.

Sam, Macy and Angel nodded in unison.

"And as far as you three are concerned Mrs. Monk is me, okay? I want you on your best behavior."

The trio nodded again.

"We have a small trailer with a heater, some coffee and some snacks set up behind the stage. Kind of like a green room," Beth said. "Would you follow me there?"

"That sounds wonderful," Alicia said.

The trailer was indeed small, but everyone was able to fit comfortably. Alicia was sipping on a coffee when the door burst open without warning. Alicia jumped slightly, splashing coffee on her upper lip. It burned. She hoped it did not leave a mark.

The woman who entered was short, and Alicia hated that the first thought in her head was that the new resident of the green room trailer was overweight. She felt guilty for her thoughts.

Jane Rotolowski was short, and she was fat. She would admit it to anyone. She liked to eat and did not like to exercise. Especially since her daughter, Brittney, had disappeared nearly three years ago.

"It's freezing out there!" Jane shouted and slammed the door closed.

"Good morning, Jane. How are you?" Beth said.

"Freezing."

Jane made a beeline for the pastry assortment. She ignored the bowl of fruit.

"And hungry."

Jane scooped up two scones and a blueberry muffin – a third of the pastries that were set out. Alicia doubted there were any more hidden away in the trailer.

"So," Jane said with her mouth full of scone, "I'm leading off this morning?"

"That's right," Beth said. "You're going first and Alicia, oh my, I'm so sorry. Alicia, this is Jane Rotolowski, our other speaker this morning. Jane this is Alicia Martin. She's new to our group."

Jane gave a polite wave, and smile, but did not move from her place near the pastries. Alicia declined to get up from the folding chair she was sitting on. She also waved and smiled.

"Anyway," Beth continued while turning her attention back to Jane, "you're going first, and Alicia is going second. I'll wrap it up as I usually do."

"Works for me," Jane said. She had polished off the first scone, and her mouth was full of her first bite of the second.

"Do you need me to look over anything in your speech?" Beth said.

"Nope. I'm well practiced at this by now," Jane said.

"Wonderful. Alicia? What about you?"

"I'm good," Alicia said with a nod of her head. "Just a little nervous."

"Don't be," Jane said. "There aren't that many people at these things. And they are all here for the same reason. We're all trying to find strength to deal with the loss of our loved ones."

Alicia found these words comforting even though they had come from a mouth that was filled with scone. She hoped her children were not picking up any habits from Jane.

The adults made small talk in the green room trailer while the children sat quietly. They were bored. Macy, Sam and Angel had already had enough of this morning adventure and were ready to go back home. There was TV to be watched and video games to be played. Alicia had insisted that each of them bring something to pass the time, and those items were housed in a tote bag that sat on the floor between Alicia's feet. Angel made a move for the bag. Alicia saw this. She picked it up before Angel got to it and handed it to her youngest daughter.

From the bag Angel pulled a coloring book and a box of crayons. Sam and Macy each snagged their iPods, popped their earbuds in and selected their favorite song. The adult chitchat continued. At least now Macy and Sam were spared from listening. Angel did not seem to mind the conversation.

Alicia was mostly playing the role of listener between Jane and Beth. Jane had explained that her daughter had become involved with a bad group of kids and had gotten into the drug scene. When Jane found out, she came down hard on Brittney. Grounding her and forbidding her from seeing her friends. This only made Brittney want to see them more. She would constantly sneak out of her room. One night she snuck out and Jane never saw her again. Jane hoped she was still alive out there, but with each day it became tougher.

A knock came at the green room trailer door, and in entered a small man dressed in a work uniform.

"We are all set up, Beth," the man said. "Some people are starting to arrive."

"Thank you, Danny," Beth said. "We'll be starting in a few minutes."

The butterflies returned to Alicia's stomach.

*   *   *   *   *

Alicia stood off stage while Jane gave her speech. It was essentially the same material Alicia had heard in the trailer twenty minutes ago. The second time through did not make it any easier to listen to. Jane's speech went fast. Too fast. Alicia had tried to peek out at the crowd to see how many people were in attendance. She could not get a good look from where she was standing.

Beth Monk sidled up to her.

"How do you feel?" Beth said.

"Nervous. Not ready."

"You're ready, Alicia. Just do as we practiced and you'll do great. There are not many people here. Don't worry about them. They don't exist as far as you are concerned. It is just me and you in your living room. You are standing and giving your speech. I am sitting on your couch eating up every word."

Alicia nodded. She would do her best to visualize this scene Beth had described.

"I'm going to check on your kids," Beth said. "Then, I'm going to be standing right here during your speech. It is going to go great."

Beth gave Alicia a gentle rub on her back, and headed toward the green room trailer. Jane was wrapping up.

"Now, our next speaker is new to Our Missing. Please welcome Alicia Martin."

Alicia heard her name, but it did not register in her brain. It was as if she was dangling above the stage, watching the show from her own special spot. The comfort Beth had bestowed upon her slipped away – a distant memory already. Alicia felt her feet begin to move despite her brain seemingly not ordering them to do so. The full crowd came into view, and Alicia's nerves released a little.

There could not have been more than seventy people standing in front of the stage. Most of them were women around the same age as Alicia. She felt comforted by this fact.

Alicia reached the microphone stand, which was in the middle of a stage that Alicia now realized was far too big for the purpose it was serving this morning. A rock band with eight members could have fit comfortably on this stage with all of their sound equipment and speakers. This thought made Alicia feel small again.

"Thank you," Alicia said into the microphone. She scanned the crowd briefly and then glanced to her left in the direction from which she came. She could see Jane Rotolowski headed toward the green room trailer, probably to finish off another couple of pastries. Jane passed Beth on the way. Alicia saw Beth smile and give Jane a quick hug. For that moment, and that moment alone, Alicia wished she was Jane Rotolowski instead of Alicia Martin.

Alicia turned her focus back to the crowd. All eyes were on her. She took a deep breath, and began.

"I'm here to tell you about my son, Josh. He's a high school freshman right here in Vanguard. Right on the cusp of those independent years. I thought of him still as a little boy. I always did. I guess I always will. The last time I saw Josh was last Halloween. He went to his friends' house for a party. He was supposed to spend the night."

She took a deep breath here. She had written a note for herself to do so on one of her notecards. She tried to slow down. She felt she was talking too fast.

"From what his friends tell me, he made it to their house for the party, but he had forgotten his cell phone at home. Josh was smart, but he was forgetful sometimes. I suppose all teenagers are. So he left the party to walk back home to get it. He never made it home. His friends figured I wouldn't let him go back to the party. Halloween has always been my favorite holiday. They told me they figured I had something planned for the whole family and had made Josh stay with us.

"I never knew my son ever left that party. Never knew he walked back home to find his cell phone. That night a man came to my door. It was late, just before midnight. This man – who was very young – was dressed in a Vanguard Police uniform. I found out later that he was not from the police station. I invited this man into my house, and asked him to sit down with me at my kitchen table. He told me Josh was dead. That they had found the body. That my son had been murdered. It was the worst moment of my life. At the time I was not thinking straight. I did not know what to do.

"This man – who said his name was Officer Warner and had the name badge to prove it – said that it was very late, and I was clearly upset. He said I could come to the station in the morning and work out all the details then. It sounded like a great idea to me at the time. Like I said, it was late. I am a single mom, and I have three other young children. They were all asleep, and I didn't want to wake them up. The officer convinced me that in the light of day things would be better. Even just a little better is all I needed."

Alicia paused again, and looked over at where Beth was standing. Beth gave her a thumbs up. Alicia felt tears welling. She refused to let them fall.

"The next morning, when I went to the police station the man they said was Officer Warner was not the same man who had come to my house the night before. Nobody at the station knew anything about Josh Martin. I didn't know whether to think my son was dead or if someone was playing an awful joke on me. From there an investigation began, but it was a joke from the beginning. To this day they haven't found a body. There is no trace of my son other than a baseball cap they found in the bushes. But as much that I hope he is out there, I feel that my Josh is gone. And that the man who came to my door took him from me."

That was where what Alicia had written ended. The rest of her speech was penned by Beth.

"Our Missing exists to help people like me and all the others out there who have lost a child for one reason or another. I am proud to join this cause, and to try to shed light on what happened to Josh. I hope all of you continue to stay strong in memory and pursuit of your loved ones. While I believe Josh is gone, many of your missing are still out there somewhere. Hope can help bring them home. Never lose that hope."

Alicia had not liked the closing of her speech very much. It was not something she believed in. Beth had told her she needed to end with something positive, though. Regardless of the fact that Alicia felt Josh was gone; she had to portray a message of hope to the audience. Reluctantly, Alicia had agreed to this request.

Alicia walked off the stage to where Beth was standing. A small ripple of applause drifted through the crowd. Beth gave Alicia a hug just as she had given to Jane.

"Great job," she whispered in Alicia's ear.

"Thank you."

"Go be with your children."

Alicia nodded and headed for the green room trailer. Beth walked to the microphone.

"Thank you everyone for coming out this morning and braving these chilly temperatures. As always, we have coffee and doughnuts at the tables in the back. If you have not helped yourselves already, please do so. We also have our donation and information tent set up back there as well. Please stop by, and if you can, please make a donation to Our Missing. Every dollar helps us continue to support those who have lost a child. Thank you all so much for being here. If you've been here before, you know that now is when we begin to converse on a more personal level. I'm willing to speak with any of you about the children or nieces or nephews you have lost. It's also important to talk to the person standing next to you. Maybe they have had a similar experience to yours, or maybe they can help in one way or another. I know not everyone here has lost a child, and I am thankful for those who come out to support our cause when they have not been impacted directly. Once again, thank you all for being here today."

There was another small ripple of applause. Beth smiled and waved. She then headed down the front steps of the stage to mingle with the crowd. It had been a successful morning. She was proud of Alicia, and, as always, Jane had done very well with her speech. She hoped the donations were good this morning.

30

June 8, 10:15 p.m.

Since her speech at the Our Missing event in the unnamed park near "historic" downtown Vanguard, Alicia Martin had not heard from Beth Monk. Not a phone call. Not an e-mail. Nothing. Alicia had been on the Our Missing website since then and saw a picture of her taken while she was giving her speech. There was a small article headlined "Vanguard, Mass. Mother Alicia Martin Joins the Our Missing Cause." Alicia had not given any permission for her image to be used on the website.

She felt used, and it bothered her. It was like the whole event was a one-night stand. The coaching and the meetings had been equivalent to being buttered up with drinks. The calm reassurances before the speech were the same assurances that yes, he really was a good guy. And yes, he really did care about you. The speech was the act itself. Scary and exhilarating at the same time. Beth hugging her on the side stage was the brief goodbye the next morning. Once again being assured of good-guy status.

And now, silence. Nothing. Alicia had called Beth twice and left messages only to have them not returned. She sent an e-mail as well and got nothing back. Alicia tried calling Bridget, only to get her voicemail. Bridget responded to Alicia's message not with a phone call, but with an e-mail that gave a brief update on her lawsuit. There was no mention of Beth or Our Missing in Bridget's e-mail, despite the fact that Alicia had asked about them in her message.

This troubled Alicia because she had not wanted to get involved with Our Missing in the first place. Bridget had suggested it, and Alicia had gone along. Alicia's heart was never committed to the cause. Perhaps Beth had sensed Alicia's uncertainty, and that was the reason for Beth's lack of contact. Alicia also thought Beth could be busy preparing for another event; prepping another new member. If Jane Rotolowski was invited back time after time, surely Alicia would have been.

The last few months had left Alicia feeling alone and forgotten. The rush she had received in late March and early April was gone. She felt weak.

During this time period a recurring dream had been haunting Alicia. The dream started shortly after her speech and had occurred more and more frequently as each week passed. In the dream Alicia was in her house, alone, moving boxes from one room to the next. There seemed to be no end or beginning. The boxes were piled everywhere, and Alicia was dutifully sorting through them – constantly stacking and restacking, box after box.

Currently, Alicia was dreaming again. She was in Josh's room, but none of the furniture or clothes that occupied the room in real life was there. It was only boxes, stacked from floor to ceiling with a narrow gap in the middle for Alicia to walk through. One at a time, she was moving the boxes from Josh's room into the hallway. The entire house was dark. A spotlight followed Alicia as she moved. She looked like a prison escapee from a black and white movie – trapped against a black background by a brilliant white light.

This dream differed slightly from the rest. As Alicia moved the boxes, she heard a voice from inside Josh's room. In all her recurrences, she had never heard a sound aside from her own breathing and the slight muffed noise of one cardboard box being set on top of another. But this dream had a sound. The first time the sound was made, Alicia was not even sure it was there. She continued to move boxes as if nothing had happened. It took two or three trips for the sound to get loud enough for her to hear it. It sounded like one of her children calling her name.

Alicia put down the box she was holding and stood still. Then she heard it again.

"Mom!"

It was muffled and far away, as if the person was yelling at her from underwater. This time she heard it. She knew which child was calling out to her. Her reaction was immediate.

"Josh?!?"

"Yes! Help!"

In a panic, Alicia began to tear down the stacks of boxes. Two stacks tumbled to the ground in disarray. The contents – which Alicia had never seen in any of her dreams until now – spilled to the floor. Each box was filled to the brim with paper of all different colors. Each piece was filled with writing from top to bottom. The text consisted of only one word written over and over: HELP!

"Not like that," Josh said. He sounded farther away now. "You're burying me. Don't let them spill. You have to move them one at a time."

As fast as she could, Alicia piled the papers back into the boxes. She moved the boxes one at a time. Sprinting from one point to the next. Sweat began to pour down her face. The corner of Josh's room where the voice was coming from was becoming visible. The boxes were starting to fill up the hallway. Alicia feared she would not have enough room to stack them all. She hurried back into Josh's room and took the first box out of the next stack. When she did so she saw a hand on the other side.

"Josh!"

"Mom!"

His voice was strong now. Alicia hurried through that stack, revealing more of her son as she did. She pulled a box from the next stack, and could see his head. He was lying on his side, completely covered by boxes. It flashed through Alicia's mind that she had been moving boxes for months. How long exactly has she been looking for Josh? How long had it taken her to find him?

She put her hands on his face.

"I'm here, Josh. Mom's here."

"Mom," he said. "It's too late. You did your best, but it is too late."

With that he vanished. She screamed. It was loud, almost deafening.

She heard Josh's voice boom from overhead.

"Come be with me, Mom. I need you. It was hard. I was so scared."

Alicia had tears running down her face as she sat in his room, surrounded by boxes.

"Tomorrow night," her son's voice boomed again. "Tomorrow night come join me. They will be ok. They are strong. I am weak and scared. I need you, Mom."

Alicia clasped her hands over her ears. She could not leave her children to be with her son. As much as she wanted to, she just could not do it. Then, suddenly and beyond her will, like when her feet had moved her to the microphone at the Our Missing rally, Alicia began muttering to herself. Her voice was barely above a whisper.

"Tomorrow night. Tomorrow night. Tomorrow night."

As she lay asleep in her bed, with sweat covering her face, her lips formed the words.

Tomorrow night.

31

June 9, 9:30 p.m.

Alicia rose from where she was seated on the end of her bed. She walked out of her room and headed towards her children's bedrooms. Alicia had started a movie for Macy and Angel in their room nearly two hours ago. The door was now closed. Alicia quietly opened it and peeked her head inside. The TV was still on, but it was on the load screen for the DVD. The movie was over and her children had fallen asleep some time before the end.

Alicia stepped into the room, and turned off the TV. She walked towards Macy's bed, bent down, and kissed her forehead. She did the same for Angel. She turned out the light and closed the door, then she headed for Sam's room.

The door to Sam's room was closed as well. She opened it and stared into the darkness. It appeared Sam was also asleep. Alicia could not bring herself to cross the threshold, so instead she whispered, "Goodnight, Sam." Then quietly closed the door.

Sam was not quite asleep. Later Sam would be questioned whether he had correctly heard what his mother said.

Alicia headed back to her bedroom. She did not want to go back there. She felt forced to. Something was pulling at her. There were two bottles of pills on her bedside table. Sitting next to the pills was a glass of water. She took a sip of the water and filled her hand with pills.

"I miss you, Josh," she said.

She put as many pills in her mouth as she could, took a drink of water, and swallowed. Then she filled her hand with pills from the other bottle and repeated the process. The labels clearly said they should not be taken together.

Alicia rested her head on her pillow. The pain was greater than she anticipated. Then, a peaceful feeling rolled over her. The dark provided by her closed eyes flashed to a brilliant white light before subsiding forever.

32

June 12, 2:17 a.m.

Fuller sat motionless with his head on his desk. A half-empty bottle of scotch was next to him. The office that was the second bedroom of his apartment had become the only room he occupied for any length of time over the past few weeks. He ate there, and slept there. His work had engulfed him. He was going through the boxes of files again. And again. And again. He could not stop. He had become focused on his quest and his quest alone. Nothing else mattered to Fuller. He had to fix the debacle of the Martin case. He was not sure how things had gone this far without a resolution or some kind of break, at the very least. It seemed like the police force did everything right at the time, but now it seemed like a giant clusterfuck.

His eyes blinked and automatically attempted to focus on the papers directly in front of them. Fuller did not want things to clear up. The blur was his only desire at the moment. Well, one of two desires, with the bottle to his left claiming the top slot.

He lifted his head, picked up the newspaper from yesterday morning, and read the article again. It was at least the twentieth time he had read it. He placed the paper back on his desk, set his head in the same place it had been for the last eight hours, and began to cry.

33

June 13, 9:30 a.m.

Ronald McAvoy's cell phone buzzed to life. He fished it out of his pants pocket, but did not recognize the number displayed on the screen. He chose not to answer, and went back to reviewing the paperwork in front of him. Moments later, it buzzed again. The same number came up on the screen. This time McAvoy answered.

"Ronald McAvoy."

There was silence on the other end.

"Hello? Is anyone there?" McAvoy said.

After another moment, a voice came through. McAvoy recognized it immediately.

"Don't get any crazy ideas like trying to trace this call."

"Jack," McAvoy said. "What are you doing?"

"Oh, a little of this and a little of that. Kind of freelancing my way around."

Fuller's voice sounded empty, and drunk. The words came slowly.

"I mean what are you doing calling me? I don't have time for this."

Fuller sighed.

"I just wanted to let you know that Alicia Martin is dead."

"I saw the newspaper article," McAvoy said. "Thank you for calling."

McAvoy wanted to end the call right there, but could not disconnect fast enough before Fuller's response.

"And it's your fault, Ronnie," Fuller said.

McAvoy filled with rage instantly. The accusation was ludicrous, and he hated being called Ronnie.

"I had nothing to do with this woman," McAvoy grumbled. "This is no one's fault but her own."

"You were the one who stopped the investigation of her son's death," Fuller said, still speaking slowly. "You were the one who took away this woman's hope."

McAvoy shook his head. He could not understand how Fuller, an experienced detective, could become so wrapped up in one case.

"Jack, we haven't spoken in a while. You stopped coming in to work without a word. I have to ask, are you still chasing this?"

Fuller was sitting in his makeshift home office; the burner phone he purchased was in his hand. Around him was an array of papers. All of them pertained to the Martin case.

"Yes," Fuller said. "I'm still chasing this."

"Have you gotten anywhere?"

Fuller said nothing.

McAvoy paused, and took a long breath.

"Why don't you come in, Jack. We can work you back into your old position. We still haven't filled it."

Fuller considered McAvoy's words. He did want more structure. He did want a better environment. His nightmares had been getting worse. The dark cloud that recently started chasing him through life was growing stronger. Perhaps getting back into a normal routine would help him feel more grounded. He wanted to say yes, but he felt something pull inside of him and force him to say no.

"I can't. This is too important," Fuller said. He could not believe he had said the words. It was not what he wanted to say. The words did not feel like his own. Fuller felt like there was someone else in the room with a gun pointed to his head.

McAvoy began to say something else, but Fuller hung up the phone before he heard it. Fuller stood up from his desk and walked to his office door. He did not recall closing it. He tried to turn the handle, but the door would not budge.

You need to work, Jack.

It sounded as if those words were whispered in his ear. The hair on the back of his neck stood up. He was frozen.

"Leave me alone!" Fuller yelled.

He tried the handle again. It still would not move. Fuller went back to working his way through the Josh Martin files again. Two hours into it, he dozed off. He woke after thirty minutes of sleep. The door to his office stood wide open.

34

October 31, 6:00 p.m.

A car pulled to a stop in the small parking lot for Orchard Park. The sun was completely below the horizon, a shimmer of light was still showing. It was not dark enough for a child to be afraid yet. Jack Fuller stepped out of his car and looked around. There was a group of trick-or-treaters standing at the door of a nearby house. Fuller smiled as the tallest child rang the bell.

He turned his attention to the path that cut through Orchard Park. His smile vanished. These grounds brought foul memories to mind, along with thoughts of the demon he could not shake. He began to walk the path, peering into the lit windows of the houses that backed up to the park. When the path reached the two baseball backstops that backed up to one another, Fuller stopped, just as he had nearly a year ago. It was one year ago exactly that Josh Martin walked between the backstops and headed toward Roberts Road on his way home.

This same spot was where Fuller first encountered the dark entity that haunted his dreams. It had never manifested itself again, yet he felt its presence inside of him. He could feel it constantly. Fuller's thoughts had not felt his own for quite some time. Evil had been present in all he thought of – murder, torture, and so on. He only thought of it in relation to Josh Martin's killer. Fuller could not imagine going through with any of it. He was appalled he was even thinking such things. He felt his mind continuously betrayed him.

Fuller looked skyward, and saw the ever so slight appearance of the moon. He exhaled. Fuller had not come back to Orchard Park for any specific reason. He knew there would not be any clue present now that a year had gone by. Yet, he felt he needed to come back. It was the only explanation he could think of. He closed his eyes and exhaled once more.

When he opened them and leveled his head, the dark entity was in front of him once more. Fuller fell to his knees. His breath became short.

What took you so long to return?

This voice was no whisper like Fuller heard when he was locked in his office. It was a deep baritone, like the voice a movie would use for the voice of God. Fuller was not sure if only he heard the voice or if it was echoing through the park. Surely if others had heard it they would have opened their back doors after the thunderous sound.

Fuller was unsure how to answer. Should he speak his response aloud? Or merely think it in his head? He opted to speak.

"I never considered it. I figured this place was a dead end."

The dead end exists in your office. In those notes. This is where the path began for you. And this is where it will continue to the ultimate end point.

Fuller had not risen from his knees yet. He looked up at the darkness, with its red heart necklace beating ever so slowly. The unformed body was as terrifying as ever.

"Where does it end? Tell me where it ends?"

The entity moved slightly to Fuller's right, as though it were revealing something behind it. Fuller saw the image of a small apartment building appear between the backstops. His mouth opened.

It ends here.

"What is that? An apartment building? Where is that?"

It is in the West. You will need to find it. You will need to find Houston.

Another image appeared. This time it was of a young man. He was clean-shaven and had a buzz cut. Fuller did not recognize him.

"I don't know who that is. Where do I find him?"

You can find him in the West. He has served his purpose. And you will have served yours when it is done.

"When what is done?"

When he is dead.

Fuller shook his head. "I'm not killing anyone. Not because some spirit told me to. They'll lock me up."

Fuller felt a sharp pain rush through his spine. Suddenly he could not feel his legs.

You will do it. Or you will die.

"Why don't you kill him?"

The pain was moving toward his neck. Fuller slouched over and fell to the ground. He could not feel his arms.

Because it will bring you peace. It needs to be you.

"Is this him?" Fuller's voice was barely a whisper. He could feel the air being pushed out of his lungs. His heartbeat was beginning to slow.

Yes. This is Houston. You will find him in the West.

"I'll do it."

Immediately Fuller felt a release of the pain in his spine. He sucked in a big breath of air. Fuller looked around and realized he was already on his feet. He did not recall pushing his way off the ground. Just as it was a year ago, there was no sign of the dark entity. Fuller walked to his car feeling no ill effects.

When he opened the door to his car and sat down in the driver seat, he examined his palms in the light. There were no scrapes or marks of any kind. He checked his face in the rear view mirror and found it to look the same as it had before he strolled into the park. He rolled up his pant legs, where he was sure he would see a mark from when he fell to his knees. There was nothing to be seen. There was not a scratch on him.

He closed the door and sat still as the overhead light dimmed.

This is Houston. You will find him in the West.

Fuller had no idea how he was going to find Houston, but that face was etched in his brain. It was similar to the face Alicia Martin had described to the sketch artist – the face of the man posing as Officer Jim Warner. All Fuller knew was that he was going West. The rest would be in fate's hands. Or perhaps, in the hands of the dark entity.

When you need me, you'll find me, but first you must wake from this dream.

Come find me, Jack. Come find me again.

This is Houston. You will find him in the West.

11:30 p.m.

Fuller had been asleep on his couch for almost two hours. The TV was still on. His mind had been blank until this moment. Now he began to dream.

It started quickly, as all dreams do. He was at an airport. The familiar sounds of people talking and announcements being made were not there. It was perfectly silent, even though people were all around him. Fuller was standing near a large window that reached well above his head. He was looking out at the tarmac, and could see several planes coming and going.

There was a ding from overhead, and a voice came onto the loud speaker. "We will now begin boarding Flight 241 with non-stop service to Cheyenne. All first class passengers can begin boarding."

Fuller looked at his ticket and saw it was first class. Without realizing it, he was already on the plane. It had taken off, and Fuller was looking out the window with a cup of ice water in his hand. As he looked out the window, a face appeared. The same face he had seen in Orchard Park.

This is Houston. You will find him in the West.

The TV in Fuller's living room switched from the local news to a sitcom re-run. The theme music came blasting through the speakers, and startled Fuller awake. He turned off the TV and stumbled toward his bedroom, not really certain of his movements.

In the morning he would remember his dream.

November 1, 9:10 a.m.

Everything inside the Farnelli Bakery and Pastry Shop looked the same as it always did, and the aroma of fresh pastries smelled the same. But Fuller felt very different as he sat with his coffee waiting patiently for the waitress to take his order.

When he woke this morning he felt rested for the first time in a long time. For weeks, or perhaps months, Fuller constantly felt half asleep. He would catch himself dozing off during the day, yet he was unable to sleep through the night. The nightmares did not help. Each one felt remarkably real and had a lasting impact on him when he startled awake in the middle of the night. Most nights it felt as though his heart would leap from his chest. Usually it took two to three hours to relax and drift back to sleep.

The waitress entered his field of vision, and Fuller instinctively glanced down at the menu. He knew what he was going to order, but looked at the description on the menu one more time.

"Have you decided on what you'd like?" Joan, the waitress, asked in a sweet tone. Fuller would not call her young, but she was younger than he was. He instantly found her attractive.

"I'm going to have the southwest omelet," Fuller said. It was a delicious combination of chorizo sausage, jalapeno peppers, onions, cheese and eggs. Fuller usually topped it off with a generous helping of Tabasco sauce.

"That comes with breakfast potatoes and your choice of a pastry," Joan said.

"I'll have a banana muffin." Fuller knew that was not really a pastry, but they counted it as one here.

"Anything else for you?" Joan said with a smile as she grabbed the menu from the table.

"A side of bacon, please. And could you bring the muffin first?"

Joan jotted down the order on her notepad, and without looking up said, "Of course."

She was back in less than a minute with his muffin, and Fuller popped the top off as soon as she put it down. He unwrapped the muffin stump and ate it first, then started in on the muffin top. He had been eating muffins this way since he was a kid, and he was never going to stop. It tasted too good.

Fuller's dream from the night before was still playing in his head. The details were becoming less and less clear, but he knew it was about going to Cheyenne. He was also positive about seeing the face from Orchard Park again, and hearing the same voice he had heard in Orchard Park say the same two sentences. *This is Houston. You will find him in the West.* The feeling in his gut was strong, but his mind thought it was a crazy idea.

Are you really going to fly to Cheyenne because you had a dream about it?

Joan returned with his omelet.

"That muffin was awful, I see," she said.

Fuller looked down and saw the empty wrapper sitting on the table. He chuckled. "It was the worst thing I've ever had. I demand the rest of the breakfast be free."

Joan reached over and grabbed the wrapper. Her hand grazed Fuller's forearm along the way. Fuller felt a jolt of electricity when she touched him.

"You shocked me," he said.

"Whoops. Well, I am electric," Joan said.

"That one's coming out of your tip."

She laughed. It was a good laugh; one Fuller wished he could hear more often.

"I'll refill your coffee."

"Thank you."

Fuller dug into his omelet. By the time he was finished he had arrived at two conclusions. First, he was going to Cheyenne. It felt right. He would find a flight in the next few days. He was not sure what he was going to do when he got out there. It was going to be his starting point on his journey. Cheyenne was in the West, and apparently so too was Houston.

The second conclusion was that he was going to sleep with Joan before his trip to Cheyenne. He sat still until she came over with the bill.

"Here's your check," she said. "Was everything alright?"

"Everything was delicious."

Fuller looked at the bill and reached for his wallet as she cleared the table.

"Say Joan," Fuller said as he laid a twenty-dollar bill down for his thirteen-dollar check. "Are you free tonight?"

She picked up the check and looked at him. "Free?"

"Yeah, free. Like, get dinner together free."

She hesitated for a moment. The playful look in her eyes had vanished.

"Look, I'm sorry," Fuller said with a wave of his hand. "That was forward. My mistake. I never said it."

She looked down at the bill, and the money Fuller had given her. She seemed embarrassed.

"I'll be right back with your change," she said.

Fuller exhaled. He felt like an idiot. Worst of all was this was one of his favorite places in town to come to. Now he felt like he would be walking on eggshells every time he walked through the door. He saw her coming back. His instinct was to bolt for the door and never look back. Instead he stayed in his seat, frozen there like something from a science fiction film.

She laid the change down on the table, then slid into the seat across from him. Fuller's emotion immediately changed.

"I am free tonight," Joan said. "I'm sorry how I acted a minute ago. I was flustered, I guess."

A sheepish smile crossed Fuller's face. He felt like a teenager.

"So do you want to have dinner?"

"First I need to know your name," she said with a grin. "I don't go out with guys whose names I do not know."

Fuller laughed heartily. "Good point," he said while still chuckling. "My name is Jack Fuller."

"Well it's nice to meet you, Jack Fuller. You can see from this tag on my chest that I'm Joan. Joan Twillson. And I would love to have dinner with you tonight."

"Wonderful," Fuller said with a smile. His confidence was fully restored.

Joan jotted her address and phone number on a piece of paper for Fuller.

"I'll pick you up around seven?" he said.

"Make it seven thirty," she said. "I like to eat dinner a little later than most people do."

"Seven thirty it is, then."

Fuller headed out of the pastry shop toward his car, and Joan went back to work. Both were already smiling in anticipation of dinner.

7:22 p.m.

The address Joan had given to Fuller turned out to be a small house. He was banking on some kind of apartment complex judging by the fact that she was a waitress working at the Farnelli Bakery and Pastry Shop. They made great food, and Jack loved it, but he could not imagine the pay was very good. The tips had to be paltry as well, given that most menu items were quite cheap – under ten dollars. His detective skills were wrong on his prediction of Joan's housing, though. The house was small, but it was very cute and well maintained on the exterior. Fuller could picture a perfect little family living there. He smiled at the thought.

Fuller was not sure if he should call her phone or get out of the car and ring the doorbell. He sat for a minute pondering the possible outcomes before turning off the engine and walking to Joan's door. His mind was unable to focus. If someone were to ask him to describe what he saw on his walk to the door, he would have produced miserably wrong answers.

Fuller pushed the bell and waited.

Two minutes is a long time to stand in front of what amounts to a stranger's house. Each second seemed longer than the previous. Fuller felt like he was sweating. A wipe of his brow proved he was not. He wondered if he should push the bell again. The wait was agonizing.

After another minute, which felt like an hour to Fuller, he rang the bell again. This time he heard shuffling inside. He sighed in relief when the door opened.

"So you are home. I was beginning to worry," Fuller said.

"What do you mean?" Joan said with a smile. "I only heard the bell just ring."

"Oh. I rang a few minutes ago and there was no response. That ring you heard was my second effort."

"I'm sorry," Joan said. "I had the music cranked up pretty loud while I was getting ready."

"Ah. Well are you ready now?"

"I am. Just let me grab my coat real quick."

She was back at the door faster than she brought Fuller's banana muffin earlier in the day. Joan looked good. Her outfit suited her far better than the long sleeve t-shirt she wore at Farnelli's that morning. She wore a tight V-neck sweater that accentuated her breasts, and a pair of dark jeans. The leather jacket she had on was stylish, and gave off that vibe that she had a bit of an edge. Fuller felt he had no business having dinner with Joan. She seemed like a cute waitress earlier in the day, but now was a dark and sexy woman.

The drive to the restaurant was quiet. Fuller felt intimidated and Joan did not have much to say. Fuller hoped a couple of margaritas would loosen both their tongues. They pulled into Miguel's, Fuller's favorite Mexican restaurant, and were seated right away.

"What's your drink of choice," Joan said.

"Gotta go with a margarita when you're at Miguel's," Fuller said. "What about you?"

"You want to do a tequila shot before the margarita?"

"I haven't done many tequila shots since college."

"I'm a fan of shots," Joan said. "What do you say?"

"I'm down."

The waitress came over and Fuller ordered two Patron shots, and a classic margarita for himself. Joan ordered a frozen margarita.

"I can't believe I'm starting out this night by doing shots," Fuller said.

"Not what you expected?"

"Not at all."

The waitress returned with their drinks. The shot of tequila burned Fuller's throat on the way down. He missed many things from his past, but the stinging sensation after a shot of alcohol was not one of them. A wry smile came across Joan's face as she looked at Fuller.

"How did that feel?"

"It felt like my twenties," he said, and took a sip of the margarita in front of him. "Now that tastes much better."

They each ordered tacos for dinner. They talked about many topics that come up in first dates: where they grew up, where they went to school, what they did now. Fuller told Joan he was a detective. He left out the part about quitting because he did not want to stop looking for Josh Martin.

"A detective, huh? That is not what I expected." Joan said.

"What did you expect?"

"Well, I don't know. Probably some kind of high-level person at a business. Or maybe that you had your own business. Definitely not a detective."

"I'm glad I could surprise you."

Joan took another bite of her taco, and another sip of her margarita.

"Have you been involved with any cases I've heard of?"

"Probably. But I don't know which ones you've heard of. Be specific."

She thought for a moment. "What about that boy that went missing on Halloween? Martin, I think was the name. Were you involved in that one?"

Fuller picked up his second of three tacos and took a large bite; nearly a third of the taco was in his mouth. It was a sound strategy. He was not going to talk with his mouth full. It was a rude thing to do. He nodded his head in response to Joan's question. She did not press him for details.

"That's so cool," Joan said. "I never expected that."

Fuller learned that Joan had been a kindergarten teacher when she graduated from college, but two years ago her job had been cut. She had been bouncing around odd part-time jobs since then as she tried to get back into teaching. Joan started working at the Farnelli Bakery and Pastry Shop six months ago. Fuller could not believe he had not noticed her earlier.

Their meal ended without any more drinks or dessert. The ride back to Joan's house was over far too fast for Fuller's liking.

"I had fun tonight," Joan said. "Call me soon."

"Most definitely," Fuller said with a smile.

The night ended with a kiss, but nothing more than that. Fuller noticed a heart pendant dangling from her neck as she exited the car. It looked shockingly similar to one he had seen before.

9:15 p.m.

The cold mountain air stung his lungs, but he fought through it. Running was a new obsession for Houston West. He needed to pass his nights somehow. He had not met many people since his spontaneous move from Vanguard, and he grew bored quickly. One night a few weeks back he had tried a run. It exhilarated him. When he reached his apartment afterwards he felt motivated and alert.

Every night since then he ran. He felt his legs and lungs grow stronger with each trip. A cold front had rolled in early this morning, and the temperature went no higher than forty degrees. The light sweatshirt he was wearing was not doing much to keep him warm on his run.

Houston's thoughts wandered to the time he spent on the *Catiana*. He was still surprised he had survived. The rest of the crew had a wealth of experience, yet they all went down with the ship. Somehow he was spared. When he first woke up on shore he was terrified, unaware of how he got there. After making it back to town an eerie calm had settled over him. It was as though he knew he would survive no matter what happened to him. It made Houston feel invincible. For some reason his dark tormentor had spared him from death that night. He had no explanation for it – hell, he had no explanation for what the thing was in the first place – but when the *Catiana* was destroyed the dark force seemed to be looking out for him.

He hoped that would not change in the future.

9:30 p.m.

"Where did you get that necklace," Fuller asked Joan. His tone was calm, or at least he thought it was. She was about to close the car door but stopped, and poked her head back in.

"This?" Joan said looking down. "Honestly I don't remember. I saw it in my jewelry box this evening and felt like wearing it. I couldn't tell you for sure where or when I bought it. Jewelry is a passion of mine so I have a lot of pieces."

Fuller chuckled.

"Why do you ask?" she said.

"Oh, no reason in particular. I've just seen one like that before. It's beautiful. Very beautiful."

"Thank you," she said, and leaned into the car to kiss him one more time.

The kiss was sweet, and deeper than the first. Fuller desperately wanted more, but did not press.

"Goodnight," he said.

"Goodnight," she said. "Call me soon."

Fuller nodded as she closed the passenger side door. While she walked in front of his car he swore he saw the red stone in her heart necklace dim to black. If he were grilled on the subject, he would have kept it to himself. Or sworn that the heart on the necklace remained red. But as he sat in the car, he was pretty sure it had changed colors. Perhaps the margaritas were causing his mind to trick him.

11:15 p.m.

Joan lay on her back in her bed. All of the lights in her house were off. She could not hear any sounds coming from her backyard or the street. Twenty minutes ago she had been reading, and her book now rested on her bedside table. She thought of the date she had with Jack Fuller. He was an interesting man, and showed quite a bit of confidence asking her out while she was waiting on him. He had surprised her, and she needed a moment to gather herself before giving him an answer. She also consulted with Courtney, the other waitress working the breakfast shift. Courtney and Joan had become fast friends, and Joan trusted Courtney's judgment.

"I've waited on him before," Courtney had said. "He seems like a nice guy. He tips well, that's for sure."

"What should I tell him? I didn't give him an answer and he backpedaled."

Courtney peeked over at Fuller sitting at his table.

"Go for it. He's a handsome man. I'm sure he's great."

Joan rolled her head from one shoulder to the other.

"Alright. I'll do it. He is good-looking."

As Joan stared up at the ceiling, she smiled at the thought of Fuller. She was happy she said yes. She was a bit perplexed by his question about her necklace, though. Regardless of how much she wracked her brain, she could not remember how she had acquired it.

36

November 2, 3:50 p.m.

Jack Fuller told himself over and over again that he should not call Joan today. He felt it would reek of desperation, and that would scare her off. He had the urge to go to the Farnelli Bakery and Pastry Shop for breakfast, but was able to resist the temptation. Around noon he had a strong urge to call her, and while he had held off until now, as each minute passed it became more difficult to do so.

Once he arrived home after the date he assured himself his mind was tricking him about her necklace. It could not possibly be the same one he had seen that spirit in Orchard Park wear, even if it did look quite similar. Fuller had doodled the heart pendant several times in the margins of a notepad as he continued to contemplate calling Joan.

He could not resist the temptation to call any longer. He dialed Joan's number and put the phone to his ear. Each ring took an eternity. He only had to wait two.

"Hello," Joan said.

"Hi," Fuller said as he exhaled. It was only then that he realized he was holding his breath.

"I was hoping you'd call," she said.

"Really? Why didn't you call me?"

"Cause I'm one of those girls that still thinks the man should call the woman."

Fuller laughed. "I like that. So, I know we just went out last night, but I want to see you again. I know there's supposed to be lag time in between dates, but I can't shake this feeling."

There was silence for a moment.

"And now I've said too much," Fuller joked.

Joan laughed. "No way. You haven't said too much at all. I've felt the same way. I can't really describe it. But I want to see you too. I can't do it tonight, though. What about tomorrow?"

"Tomorrow is perfect," Fuller said. "Shall I pick you up at seven thirty again?"

"Yes you shall," Joan said.

37

November 3, 10:15 p.m.

The second date went even better than the first. Both Joan and Fuller drank more, talked more, and enjoyed themselves more. Fuller felt a good buzz from the alcohol, but was not drunk. He was not so sure about Joan. Her words were coming out a little sloppy.

"That was fun," she said as he pulled into her driveway.

"It most definitely was."

Joan was looking out the passenger side window. Her left hand mindlessly scratched her neck.

"Do you want to come in?" she asked without looking back at Fuller.

"Yes," Fuller said without hesitation.

She turned to face him and smiled. "Good," she said.

After entering her house, she took his coat. Fuller sat on the sofa in her living room. Joan went to the kitchen and returned with two glasses of red wine. She handed one to Fuller, took of sip of hers, and set it on the coffee table.

"I don't know what it is about you, Jack, but I like you. And that's not easy for a girl to say after knowing someone for only two days."

Fuller set his glass down, and smiled. "Three days," he slurred while holding up three fingers on his right hand. "Today makes three days."

She giggled. Then, he leaned in and kissed her deeply.

"I like you too," he said as their lips broke. She pulled back and took another swig of wine. Then leaned in to kiss him again. They kissed like this for a half hour on the couch. Fuller felt like he was back in high school.

Joan broke away and whispered in Fuller's ear, "Do you want to go to the bedroom?"

Fuller looked in her eyes and nodded. He pushed up from being on top of her. She took his hand and led him to the bedroom. The wine glasses remained on the coffee table.

The sex was exhilarating. Joan took control, and Fuller was surprised how aggressive she was. The act was far greater than the anticipation.

When it was over, Joan rested her head on Fuller's chest.

"You're incredible," he said.

"You're pretty damn good yourself," she said.

They were silent for nearly ten minutes. Fuller was dozing when he felt Joan squeeze his belly.

"What's in Cheyenne?" she asked.

Fuller was dazed. He could not tell if he was coming out of a dream or if she had really asked him that question.

"What?" he said. "What did you say?"

She pulled her head off of his chest, but did not look at him.

"What's in Cheyenne?"

"Cheyenne? I don't know. Where did you get Cheyenne?"

"I had this dream last night. You said you were going to Cheyenne. You said you needed to go. I didn't want you to go, but you said you needed to. The dream felt so real. Does Cheyenne mean anything to you?"

Fuller was unsure if he should answer. He liked this girl, but he was afraid she might think he was crazy. He had to speak carefully. He did not want to lose her trust.

"Cheyenne means something," he said. "I might have to go there for work. But I'm not sure yet."

"Work? But you're a detective here. Not a detective in Cheyenne."

"I know, but I still might need to go."

Joan turned to face Fuller. It was the first time she had done so during the conversation.

"Have you seen it?" she whispered.

Fuller's demeanor remained calm. Inside his chest his heart was racing.

"Seen what?" he said hesitantly.

"You have. I know you have. You should go. You should go to Cheyenne. To Wyoming. It wants you to go."

"Joan what are you..."

She cut him off, "You must, Jack. You must go."

Fuller was quiet. He was stunned by this turn of events.

"How do you know about this?"

Her body had not moved since she had turned to look at Fuller.

"It's inside of me. Inside of my head. I see it. I hear it. It wants you to go. You must. If you want to see me again, you must go."

Fuller nodded his head.

"I'll go," he said softly.

She moved her head toward his, and kissed him. Her hand grabbed between his legs. His hand slipped between her thighs.

On her dresser, the red heart of Joan's necklace dimmed to black for a moment before brightening to red again. It repeated this until Joan and Fuller fell asleep. Neither of them noticed.

38

November 4, 9:57 a.m.

A streak of light came through Joan's bedroom window and landed on Fuller's face. Though the drapes were closed, there was a small gap that let the bright morning sun shine through. Fuller stirred. The sun had made him warm. Instinctively, he rolled over to his right into an area of the bed where the light could not touch him. Though he lay there for another ten minutes, he could not fall back to sleep. He opened his eyes again and noticed Joan was not in bed.

Fuller found his pants and undershirt on the floor. He put them on before walking into Joan's living room. She was sitting on the couch with a cup of coffee and a laptop computer.

"Good morning," Fuller said.

Joan set the laptop next to her on the couch and turned to look at Fuller. "Morning," she said with a smile. "Would you like some coffee?"

"Please," he said.

She went to the kitchen and Fuller sat on the couch. He rubbed his eyes, then looked around the room in a daze. He glanced at the laptop and noticed an open webpage for an airline-ticketing site. Thoughts of Cheyenne filled his head.

Joan returned and handed him his coffee. They sat quietly on the couch, not looking at one another. After a minute or two, Joan touched Fuller's arm. He looked into her eyes.

"Will you go?" she asked.

Fuller did not feel as committed to the idea as he had the previous night. His emotions had been reset by the night's sleep. He had almost forgotten his decision to go to Cheyenne – the decision he made while sitting in the Farnelli Bakery and Pastry Shop before asking Joan on a date.

"I'm not sure," Fuller said.

Joan did not blink.

"You must," she said. "What I've dreamed...you must go."

She was no longer the exhilarating sexual partner from the previous night. Her voice did not waver when saying Fuller must go to Wyoming.

"What did you dream of, Joan?"

"It was of you. You told me you had to go to Cheyenne. Then I heard a voice, like a narrator. It said I needed to let you go. I needed to help you. I woke up in a sweat. I was clutching a pillow so tight my hands hurt."

There was a loud creak from somewhere in the house. Joan paused to hear it, then continued on.

"I had this awful feeling, Jack. Just terrible. It was this sense that something horrible would happen if I didn't help you. This feeling did not feel like something my body had created. Or my mind created. It felt like something had infected me. I couldn't shake it. I still can't shake it."

Fuller nodded his head. It was a nod to himself – a body tic of him processing what Joan had said.

"Well Cheyenne has been something on my mind," he said. "It's a place that just kind of got stuck there. Or placed there. I can't shake it either. I feel the need to go, but it seems crazy. I'm a man of evidence. There is no evidence pointing me toward Cheyenne."

She picked up the computer and handed it to him.

"Please. Please go."

He took it and with two clicks booked a ticket that she had already pulled up on the screen. Joan nodded in approval, placed her hand around the back of Fuller's neck, and pulled him close.

"You will be happy," she whispered in his ear. Then turned his head to kiss him on the lips.

Part IV
Cheyenne, Wyoming

39

November 9, 10:45 a.m.

The Wyoming air was different from the air in the east. It seemed cleaner, and the sky looked bluer. Fuller thought the scenery was beautiful. The mountains were an incredible sight, and could be seen in every direction.

Fuller thought of Joan for the duration of the flight. He had not seen her since the morning he had booked the ticket five days ago. He did not know if he would see her again – even though it was because of her that he was here. Without her push, there was no telling if Fuller would have committed to the darkness on his own.

The rental car Fuller booked was a small Ford. He drove it to his hotel while keeping his eyes peeled for places to eat along the way. Fuller brought two bags with him, a suitcase with five different shirts and two pairs of pants plus socks and underwear, and a small duffel bag with as many files from the Martin case as he could cram into it. Both bags were sitting in the backseat.

Fuller found his hotel, The Cheyenne Lodge, and parked the car near the front entrance. The hotel was mediocre. It looked to have been built to be a shade below luxury. Now, with a few decades of age on its foundation and exterior, it had drifted toward an economy-level hotel. Fuller did not need luxury. A clean bed and a hot shower would do.

"Good morning," a front desk employee said. The tag on the left side of her chest indicated her name was Maggie. "Welcome to The Cheyenne Lodge. How may I help you?"

"Good morning," Fuller said. "I have a reservation. I know it's a bit early, but when I called to book the room they said I could possibly have early check-in."

"Let me see. Your name is?"

"Jack Fuller."

Maggie typed on a keyboard Fuller could not see. He glanced around the lobby and smiled at its rustic look. There were a few fish on the walls, and a few animal heads as well. Fuller liked the place.

"It looks like we can accommodate you, Mr. Fuller."

"Fantastic."

Maggie continued pecking away at the keyboard.

"I have you down as staying here for a week. Is that correct?"

"Yes," Fuller said with a nod. "It might be longer, though. Would I be able to extend that if need be?"

"Of course," Maggie said.

Fuller nodded in approval. After a few more standard questions and Fuller handing over his credit card to put on file, Maggie gave Fuller two keys for his room.

"You are in Room 421," she said. "The elevators are located just behind you."

"Thanks," Fuller said. "One more thing. I'm expecting a package. Did it arrive yet?"

Maggie clicked her mouse twice, and looked at her computer screen.

"I'm not seeing anything yet, but I'll check for you and send it up to your room if it is here."

"Perfect," Fuller said. "Thank you."

"You are welcome."

Fuller grabbed his bags and headed for the elevator. There were only five floors in The Cheyenne Lodge. Fuller pressed the button for the fourth floor, and hoped no one else got on the elevator before the doors closed.

His room was standard. Everything looked clean and in order. There was a trout mounted on the wall. Fuller wished he had brought his fishing gear. He thought perhaps he could rent some gear while he was here and take a quick fishing trip. He began unpacking his suitcase and putting his clothes in the dresser. It was the first time he had ever done this at a hotel, always opting to live out of his suitcase on previous hotel stays. When he finished, he sat on the bed and unzipped the bag with his files in it. There was not any information in the files as to why he was in Cheyenne or where he should go now that he had made the trip. Regardless, he had brought them in case they were needed. Looking at the files had become Fuller's addiction. He was afraid of how he might feel if he could not look over them as he pleased.

When Fuller was checking in, he noticed a menu for a restaurant called The Mountains that operated in the Lodge's lobby. He had perused the menu and noticed the restaurant was open all day and offered a standard array of options. Bar food. It was what he wanted. Fuller settled on eating lunch there.

There was a knock at the door. Fuller opened it to see Maggie standing there.

"Mr. Fuller your package did arrive. It was not logged correctly in our computer system. Here it is. I apologize for the error." She presented a banker's box with a FedEx label affixed to the top.

"Thank you, Maggie," Fuller said as he took the box from her. "And don't worry about the small mistake."

"You are welcome. Is your room satisfactory?"

"It's perfect. Thank you."

"Have a nice day, Mr. Fuller."

Fuller nodded and closed the door. He walked to the bed and placed the box on top of it. Fuller took his keys from his pocket and sliced through the packing tape he had sealed the box with two days prior. He removed the lid and tossed it aside.

From the box he pulled his glock. He left the extra bullets he shipped with it inside the banker's box.

40

November 10, 2:10 a.m.

The nightmares were still happening for Fuller. He was now accustomed to lying awake in bed at an early hour of the morning because of a dream. They were not recurring in the sense of the players involved. They were recurring in theme. Fuller was always being chased at the end. He was running until his legs and lungs burned. He would wake with sweat on his forehead most every time. And sometimes he thought his legs were still hurting after he opened his eyes.

Tonight's dream was different. For the first time he was not running. Instead, he was standing still in the middle of a town he did not recognize. There were mountains in every direction he looked. He figured it must be somewhere in Cheyenne. Fuller could not move in this dream, as though his feet were glued to the ground. He was in the center of a town square, and it felt like he was an object on display. People were walking all around the square. No one came within fifty feet of where Fuller was standing.

It felt as if he was standing there for hours. Eventually, a young man emerged from the crowd in front of Fuller. He walked directly toward where Fuller stood. The man was looking at Jack the entire time. When he drew closer, Fuller could see a heart necklace hanging from the young man's neck. Fuller was filled with terror. His body shook in his bed at The Cheyenne Lodge as he tried to wake from the nightmare.

The young man continued to stride toward Fuller, eventually coming to a stop in front of Jack. He was slightly shorter than Fuller. His hair was buzzed. His jaw was square. Fuller recognized the face.

"Hello, Jack," the young man said.

Fuller only nodded in response.

"Do you know who I am?"

Fuller nodded his head again.

The young man placed his left hand on Fuller's shoulder and leaned in. He looked Fuller in the eyes and said, "I'm Houston."

With that a large knife appeared in Houston's hand. He drove it into Fuller's belly with alarming force and speed. Fuller screamed as he tumbled backward. The fall seemed to last an hour. Houston was smiling down on him during his descent. Fuller's hands were wrapped around the handle of the knife, but he could not pull it out. The pain was everywhere on his body.

When he finally hit the concrete, he woke in his bed at The Cheyenne Lodge. That had been twenty minutes ago. He was still shaken by the intensity of the dream. Fuller was unsure if he would sleep again tonight. He tried for another forty minutes, but eventually got out of bed and headed for the shower.

*　　　*　　　*　　　*　　　*

In another part of town, Houston West was awake as well. He too had a nightmare – the same nightmare Fuller had. Houston knew what he was doing was wrong as he strode toward a man he did not recognize standing in the middle of the town square. Houston was trying to run the other way in his mind, but his body would not obey. He looked down and saw a heart necklace hanging from his neck. The giant heart pendant was changing color from black to red at a rapid rate.

When Houston looked up again he was stopped in front of this man. A man who would not speak. Houston called him Jack, but he did not know if that was really his name. Houston's mouth had moved without any thought at all. Somehow a knife appeared in Houston's hand, and he drove it into the man's stomach. Houston stood and watched as the man fell. Blood began to ooze from the wound.

When the man – Jack – hit the ground, Houston turned to walk away. It was as though none of the other people in the square had seen what happened. Houston felt warm, and moved with a confidence he had only felt once before – the night he killed Josh Martin. As he crossed a street that lead to his apartment Houston heard a noise at his feet. He looked down and saw the heart necklace had come unclasped, and clanged to the ground. He reached down to pick it up, but it was surprisingly heavy. So heavy that he could not pull it from the ground. It was as if it was glued down. Houston pulled and pulled without having success. Then he heard a horn. He looked to his left and saw a bus barreling toward him. His mind told him to run, but his hands continued to tug at the necklace. It would not budge. Frantically he continued to try until the bus collided with him. Pain rushed through his body. It felt like it lasted for an hour as the bus traveled over him.

When the bus cleared his body, he caught a glimpse of daylight and woke feeling startled. Like Fuller, Houston did not go back to sleep.

6:45 a.m.

The sun was beginning to peek through the window of room 421 at The Cheyenne Lodge while Jack Fuller sat at the small desk the hotel provided each room. A standard coffee maker sat on top of the desk. After his early morning shower, Fuller put on a small pot of coffee and took a stroll through the hotel as it brewed. Now he sat reading the local newspaper he had picked up on the stroll, and sipping on his coffee. The blend that had been provided was nothing fancy, and Fuller was not much for the fancy coffee brands anyway. It was a perfect match. It reminded him of the coffee he used to drink at the Vanguard Police Department. Those days seemed like a decade ago.

The news in Cheyenne was not very interesting. Local issues in a town you have no ties to never resonate the same. Regardless, Fuller was on his fifth article of the morning.

With the sight of light from the outside, Fuller walked towards the window. He let out a sigh as he looked out through tired eyes.

"I'm close," he muttered to himself. "I'm oh so close."

12:35 p.m.

The sign hanging on the door to Handy's Hardware listed the hours of operation. Below it there was a second sign that read, "Business Hours Subject to Change Depending on Fishing." Fuller caught a glimpse of it on his way into the store, and laughed it off as a joke. Fuller did not know that for a couple days each summer Wyatt Handy, the store's owner, would shut Handy's Hardware down to go fishing. The fishing usually occurred after a good week of business.

Fuller walked out of the store with two large bags, and tossed them into the trunk of his rented Ford with a thud. Fuller was not sure he was going to be able to stomach why he went to Handy's. It was truly a sinister thought that brought him there. Fuller hoped when the time came, he would be able to change his mind while still appeasing the demon that was haunting him. His stomach felt queasy at the thought of the dark entity he had seen twice in Orchard Park. Perhaps some food would help it settle.

2:15 p.m.

After a quick bite to eat, which calmed his stomach a bit, Fuller walked back into The Cheyenne Lodge and saw Maggie standing behind the counter at the check-in desk. She stared at a computer screen and looked very bored to Fuller.

"Hello, Maggie," Fuller said.

"Hello, it's Mr. Fisher, right?"

"Fuller, but you can call me Jack if you'd like."

She was much younger than him, probably still in her twenties. He did not think she would actually call him Jack, but he threw it out there anyway. He did not like being called Mr. Fuller all that much.

"Okay, Jack. Whatever you say."

Fuller was pleasantly surprised. He was not sure it would stick past this conversation.

"I have a question for you, Maggie. Where do young people live in Cheyenne?"

"Um. Do you mean like where do I live?"

Fuller immediately picked up on the anxiety in her voice.

"No, no. Not you. See, I'm here looking for someone. He's about your age, maybe a little older. He probably doesn't have much money. And I have no idea how to track him down."

She gazed at him for a moment.

"Track him down?" she said. "He didn't give you his information."

"No," Fuller said. "I'm here on business, but this guy, he really doesn't know I'm looking for him."

"Doesn't know?" she hesitated. "What kind of work do you do?"

Fuller tried to remain calm. This was proving far more difficult than he anticipated.

"I'm a private investigator. I can't really say much more than that."

"Oh," Maggie said, and relaxed a little. "There are a few newer developments that are popular with younger people. They are all near the downtown area."

"Are these places pricey?" Fuller asked.

"Most of them are," Maggie said with a nod.

"What about someone who was living on the cheap?"

She thought for a moment.

"I can't say of anything for sure. There are a lot of places to rent in Cheyenne. Some apartments are above storefronts. Some houses have rooms to rent."

"Do you think I'm going to have a tough time with this assignment?"

Maggie smiled and nodded.

"I hate to say so, Mr. Fuller, but you probably are. Cheyenne certainly isn't a big city, but she isn't very small either. People come and people go. It's not like we all notice the new guy in town."

Fuller knew she wouldn't be calling him Jack for a long period of time. It had lasted all of one greeting.

"You know, I could jot down a few places that I know of for you," Maggie said. "At least it would give you a starting point."

"That would be very helpful," Fuller said. "But you don't have to waste any time on this."

"I'm doing nothing right now except looking at celebrity gossip sites. It's no big deal."

Fuller smiled.

"Alright then. I'd appreciate it. Do you guys have a business center here?"

"We do. It's down this hallway," Maggie said while pointing behind Fuller, "on your left side. Your room key will give you access."

Fuller found the business center with ease. There were four out-of-date Dell computers on a large square table. The computers were aligned two to a side, with their backs up against each other. Around the table were four equally out-of-date office chairs. It took nearly three minutes for the computer Fuller sat down at to boot up.

He typed "Cheyenne real estate agents" into Google and it came back with several pages of results. He clicked on all of the results that were listed on the first two pages and printed off the contact information for each of them. Fuller then powered down the computer and headed for the door.

Maggie was still staring at her computer screen when Fuller hit the button for the elevator. He figured she would eventually work on the list she promised, but if she never got one to him Fuller would understand. She looked up and saw him standing there. She smiled at him before turning her focus back to the computer screen.

The up arrow next to the elevator door lit up and the bell dinged as the doors opened. Fuller got in and looked at Maggie again. He smiled to himself at the thought of having her in bed, knowing it would never happen.

When Fuller was back in his room he set the information for the real estate agents on his desk, then went to sit on the bed. He turned the TV on and flipped to CNN. It was a matter of minutes before his head was nuzzled into one of the pillows and his eyes were closed. Fuller napped for nearly two hours before a knock at the door woke him.

4:17 p.m.

The knock roused Fuller. He could not tell how long the person on the other side had been knocking. Was that the first knock? Or the fifteenth? Either way he stumbled from the bed.

He opened the door to find no one standing on the other side. It must have been the fifteenth. Fuller looked down and saw a piece of paper at his feet. He did not notice it poking from under his door before he opened it. He bent down to pick it up, and noticed it was hand written. There was a note on the top that read, "Hope this is helpful! Maggie." The list contained six apartment complexes with the phone numbers for their leasing offices. He set it on the desk next to the contact information for the real estate agents.

While Maggie's list was a nice little jumpstart, Fuller began his search by calling the real estate agents. The first call did not go smoothly. The secretary he was talking to wanted him to come to the office and sign a contract for the services of the agent. After ten minutes of haggling, Fuller thanked her for her time and hung up the phone. The second and third phone calls went unanswered, and Fuller began to think this was a task better suited for the next morning. He made one final call, and reached a secretary.

"Munson Real Estate. How may I help you?"

Fuller glanced down at the piece of paper with the agent's information on it. "Yes, is Barry Munson in?"

"No. He is out for the rest of the day."

"I see."

"Can I take down a number and have him call you tomorrow?"

Fuller wanted to remain as discreet as possible, but he was beginning to think he might have to fake his interest in renting an apartment more than he had originally anticipated.

He gave the secretary his name and cell phone number, and she told him Barry would call him in the morning. Fuller decided to wait to see what Barry Munson had to say before he called another agent. He tidied up the papers on the desk, and threw the contact information for the first agent he called in the trash.

Fuller went down to the lobby, and saw a few other hotel guests milling about. There were also three groups waiting in line to check in. He noticed Maggie hard at work behind the desk as he walked toward The Mountains restaurant. Fuller sat at the bar and ordered chicken wings and a beer. There was a sports highlight show and a sports talk show on the two TVs that hung over the bar, neither of them had the sound on.

There were two other people sitting at the bar, a man and someone who looked to be his son. Fuller noticed they were eating chicken wings as well. The bartender checked in on them, and Fuller saw both of them nod their heads. The bartender then made his way toward Fuller.

"Everything good for you?" the bartender said.

"Yes. Thank you."

"Can I get you another beer?"

"Please," Fuller said. "I'll also put in an order for a cheeseburger with onion rings."

Fuller was surprised at how strong his appetite had come back after his queasy feeling earlier in the day. His dark thoughts had vanished with the queasiness. Fuller thought he might need to take better care of himself physically to shake these thoughts. He made a mental note to make an effort to eat more regularly.

It was a practice that would have no affect on Jack Fuller's dark thoughts.

Fuller downed the last bit of the beer he had in front of him and waited for his second. Before it arrived, he heard a familiar voice behind him. He turned to see Maggie talking to the hostess. She then walked toward the bar.

"Hey there, Jack," she said.

Fuller smiled. "Hi, Maggie."

"I saw you come in here. My shift just ended. I wanted to make sure you got my note."

"I did. Thank you very much."

"Did it help?"

"I think it will help me out. I haven't done much work on it yet. But it should be useful. So thank you again."

"No need to thank me twice. That's for sure," she said with a smile.

"Alright then."

The bartender brought over his beer.

"Your burger will be out in a minute or two," the bartender said.

"Sounds great," Fuller said, and then took a swig.

"Drinking alone?" Maggie asked.

Fuller nodded his head. "It's something that grows on you with age. When you're young, drinking is an event. When you're my age, drinking is a habit."

"Well I can't let you drink too many by yourself," she said. "I'm supposed to meet a friend for dinner, but not for another two hours."

"Is that so?"

"It is," she said with a giggle. "Hey, Tommy, I'll have a beer too."

"What kind?" the bartender, whose name was apparently Tommy, responded.

"Coors Light. Same as my buddy Jack here."

"You know, you don't have to do this," Fuller said. "I'm fine."

"You don't want me to drink with you?" Maggie toyed. "Maybe that father and son over there would want to drink with me."

Fuller smiled. "Sit down."

Maggie laughed.

Tommy brought Maggie's beer and Fuller's cheeseburger. Fuller was happy to have someone sitting next to him while he ate, and really happy it was Maggie. She was short with blonde hair that ran a little past her shoulders. She had blue eyes that looked like the sky on its best days. And what Fuller noticed immediately was that she had a great pair of breasts.

He ate. She drank. And quickly an hour had passed. Maggie ordered another beer.

"Staying for a third?" Fuller asked. He had finished his burger and the side of onion rings. The rings were an order he now regretted. Talking to Maggie with onion and beer breath was not ideal.

"Can't you keep up, Jack?"

Tommy brought her another Coors Light.

"I'll have another too," Fuller said.

"Good man," Maggie said and glanced at her watch. "This is my last one, though."

"Oh, you're hurting my feelings, Maggie."

"I've got to meet my friend. Don't want to make him angry."

"Is he your boyfriend?" Fuller asked.

Maggie was looking at the TV screens. "Um," she said, and then turned her head toward Fuller. "Not yet. But I'd like him to be."

"And yet you are here drinking with me," Fuller said.

"What can I say?" Maggie said. "I'm a charity drinker." She offered her bottle up for a cheers, and Fuller obliged. They both took a large gulp. Maggie's beer was down to a quarter full. Fuller did not want her to go. He looked at her beer like an hourglass with the sand grains slowly slipping away.

"Well, Jack," she said. "I've got to get going. I've got to freshen up a bit before this dinner."

"Okay. Thanks for sitting with me for a bit."

"You're welcome," she said with a smile.

She threw a twenty on the bar for Tommy, and finished her beer.

"Tommy," she shouted to the other end of the bar. He looked her way. "That's for you."

Then Maggie looked at Fuller. "I'll see you around, Jack."

Fuller nodded. "See you, Maggie."

She put on her coat and headed out. Fuller finished his beer and ordered one more. Then he headed back to his room and turned on the TV. His dark thoughts were presently held at bay.

41

November 11, 10:15 a.m.

Barry Munson was not the most reputable real estate agent in the Cheyenne area. He would undercut and bully anyone who would allow him to. He was pretty honest with his clients, but would occasionally charge more than his standard rate if he knew they had some money. Barry Munson was not a particularly hard worker either. He was generally in the office by ten each morning, but there was no guarantee. If he was in the office later than four in the afternoon, something was either very important or very wrong.

Barry Munson was a lazy snake, but somehow he was more successful than most of his competitors. There were plenty of other people who played the same game Barry did. Some of them were flat-out cheats.

Barry liked to drink and he liked to fish. Occasionally he liked to gamble and smoke cigars, especially after sealing a real estate deal with a hefty commission. Drinking was his favorite hobby by far. Barry did not care who his drinking buddy was, or, for that matter, if he had one at all.

He was married for twelve years. His wife, Erin, left him nearly a decade ago. By the time she left, Barry would rather fish and drink than be with his wife. In the immediate aftermath of his divorce Barry developed a habit of hitting the sleaziest strip clubs he could find, and trying to buy the girls into his bed. Occasionally he succeeded, but the failures were usually quite painful. The bouncers were all bigger than Barry, and most of them were looking for any reason to pounce on someone. After one painful exit two years after his divorce, Barry swore off the strip clubs.

When he arrived at his office, Miranda, his secretary, had a list of things to go over. She was two bullet points into the list, and Barry was already uninterested. He mostly just nodded along and said "ok" every couple of points until she was finished. He had not taken his jacket off yet.

"And here are your phone messages," Miranda said while handing him four slips of paper.

Barry shuffled through them quickly, and tossed two in the trash. They were both names he recognized and had no desire to talk to. He picked up the phone to call the first of the other two messages.

"Hello," said the voice on the other end.

"Hello, this is Barry Munson. Is this Jack Fuller?"

"Yes it is," Fuller said.

Barry leaned back in his chair and put his feet on his desk.

"Hi, Jack. I'm returning your call from yesterday."

"Yes, thank you," Fuller said. "I had a little bit of a different request. I'm not looking for property for myself."

Fuller had elected to change his strategy. Instead of trying to backdoor his way into finding "Houston who lives in the West" by pretending he was interested in renting an apartment, Fuller would try to obtain a list from Barry Munson of a set of properties that would fit with what Fuller figured was Houston's small budget. Fuller explained this plan to Barry over the phone.

Barry was intrigued, but did not see the value in helping Fuller. What was in it for Barry? The knowledge that he had helped someone? Barry Munson did not care about helping others. Barry Munson cared about helping Barry Munson.

"Well, Jack, that's an interesting request. It's not really something I do. Have you considered a private eye?"

Fuller rolled his eyes on the other end of the line and sighed. He figured he should stick with the same cover story with Barry as he did with Maggie, so that he did not confuse himself as to whom he had told what.

"I kind of am a private eye," Fuller said.

"Oh," Barry said. "Well I don't know, Jack. There are a lot of places in Cheyenne and the surrounding areas where this guy could be living."

"I asked another person to provide me with a list. I have it here. She was going off the top of her head, but I figured it would be a start. Could I read it to you to see what you think?"

Barry's interest in this call had waned. He wanted it over. Maybe this guy reading his list would end it.

"Sure," Barry said, and closed his eyes.

Fuller read the list and Barry made some notes along the way. All of the places on the list seemed like reasonable options for a young guy without much money to live on.

When Fuller was done reading, Barry said, "I think you've got a decent start there, but this could stretch all over the place. The guy could be renting a room out of someone's house."

"I considered that too," Fuller said. "But that doesn't seem like this guy. He's living on his own. I'd bet on it."

Barry put his feet back on the floor and leaned toward his desk.

"Well good luck in your quest, Jack. I'm sure you'll track him down somehow."

"So there's nothing you can do to help?"

Barry did not want it to come to this, but he laid it out anyway. "Are we talking money here?"

Fuller was not anticipating paying for this service, but he now realized it was foolish to think that. Of course Barry Munson wanted some money.

"Sure we're talking money. What do you think is fair?"

Barry liked that question. Jack Fuller had no idea what to pay. Barry could charge him almost anything and his new friend Jack would likely agree to it.

"Oh, I don't know. Usually I work on commission as part of the sales and purchases. This is different. How does two hundred dollars an hour sound?"

It sounded steep to Fuller. He could see the bill adding up quickly. From his experience with his divorce attorney he knew a little about paying fees in a situation similar to this.

"How about a contingency added to that?"

269

"I'm listening," Barry said.

"Two hundred dollars an hour, but no more than a thousand dollars."

Barry tapped his fingers on the desk. He was hoping for more than a thousand out of the deal.

"What about fifteen hundred?" Barry asked. "I just think I might need more than five hours to put this all together. To do it right."

Barry actually planned on spending less than an hour on this project. He could find a lot of places rather quickly. He guessed that a list of twenty or thirty would probably satisfy Fuller.

Fuller felt a little squeezed. But he supposed fifteen hundred was not that much more than his initial offer of a thousand. He hoped Barry would be able to do it for less than that.

"Okay, Barry. Two hundred an hour, but no more than fifteen hundred total."

Barry smiled. He moved his mouse on the computer and began typing up a list of low-rent places he knew off the top of his head.

"Sounds great, Jack."

"Do I have to come in and sign a contract for this?"

"You know what, let's keep this off the books. I'll give you a buzz in a day or two when this is complete, and you can stop by the office to pay. You want to do cash for this deal?"

Fuller liked the idea of keeping this off the books.

"Cash is good."

"Alright then. I'll be in touch."

"Sounds good," Fuller said.

Barry hung up the phone and continued with his list. It had been less than ten minutes and he already had ten entries. He figured he would do a decent job for Jack Fuller and have Miranda fill in some details about each place.

Fuller was pleased with the deal. He hoped it was a task that would not take much effort on Barry's part. He figured it would not take long to compile a list, but apparently Barry had other ideas. As long as Barry's list eventually led to "Houston who lives in the West," Fuller did not care too much about the fifteen hundred dollars.

12:47 p.m.

Barry's list was complete. He had forty possible places on it. He had even put them in order from what he felt was most likely to what he felt was least likely. He printed it out from his computer and walked to Miranda's desk.

"Miranda, I have a list of apartment complexes here. All I need you to do is add a couple sentence summary about each one as well as the contact information for the complex. Pretty much all of the information you need can be found on the websites for these places. If you can't find it there, don't spend too much time digging deep. I can fill in a blurb about a couple of them. I just e-mailed this to you too. So you don't have to retype it."

"Okay. No problem," Miranda said. "When do you need it by?"

"No rush. Tomorrow or the next day."

Barry went back to his office and grabbed his coat and brief case. Then he headed past Miranda's desk to the front door.

"I'm out for the rest of the day."

"You've got a showing tomorrow at nine thirty a.m.," Miranda said.

"Right. Thanks. I've got it covered."

Barry stopped into a nearby deli and grabbed a sandwich to go. He resisted the temptation to dig into it on his drive home.

1:55 p.m.

Maggie arrived at the main entrance of her apartment building. She was out of breath and sweating from her run. Her iPod was still blaring in her ears. She turned the volume down after opening the door. The apartment she shared with two friends was a second-floor unit of a four-story building. The trio had been living together for a little over a year.

Maggie's two roommates – Ann and Jill – worked standard nine to five jobs. They were off every Saturday and Sunday as well as the standard Federal holidays – not today, Veteran's Day, though, both Ann and Jill were currently at work. Maggie was the roommate who worked the odd hours. Her shifts at The Cheyenne Lodge changed frequently. Maggie liked being the roommate with odd hours. It allowed her to be free from the other two. Jill and Ann did a lot together, but Maggie was able to come and go as she pleased. Often, though, Maggie enjoyed spending her time alone.

After a shower, Maggie opened a kitchen cabinet, grabbed a can of soup, dumped its contents into a bowl, and placed it in the microwave. While she was waiting the two and a half minutes the instructions told her to set the microwave for, she pulled her cell phone from her sweats, and texted a message to Bradley, with whom she had gone to dinner the night before.

Do you have work today?

The microwave dinged, and Maggie grabbed her bowl of soup with an oven mitt covering her hand. As she set it down on the small island counter in the apartment's kitchen, her phone buzzed.

Not until 5. What are you doing?

Maggie read the message and smiled.

Back from a run. About to eat. I'm all alone here. Want to come over and play?

This was another reason she enjoyed her odd work hours. It afforded her the run of the apartment on the days she had off. Maggie spooned some soup into her mouth and waited for a response from Bradley. She did not need to see the message, though, she already knew he would be at her door in less than thirty minutes.

42

November 12, 12:40 p.m.

Munson Real Estate was stenciled in black letters on the large plate glass window of Barry Munson's ground-level storefront office. It was the only storefront of the six in the strip mall without a neon sign affixed to the concrete above the windows. On the whole, the offices of Munson Real Estate did not impress Jack Fuller.

Fuller walked through the door and was greeted by Miranda.

"I'm here to see Barry Munson," Fuller said. "He told me to drop by any time after noon to pick something up."

"Sure, I'll let him know you're here."

Miranda walked toward the back of the office space, and Fuller looked at the pictures on the wall. There were several that showed Barry holding a big catch. There was one that must have been taken on a trip down in Florida. The sun was bright, and Barry and two other men were wearing sunglasses. Each was holding a rod with a large, colorful fish hanging off the end of it. The water that made up the background of the photograph was a beautiful clear blue. Fuller would have liked to have been standing on the boat with these strangers when the camera shutter closed to freeze the moment in time.

"Jack Fuller?"

Fuller turned his head to see Barry standing next to Miranda's desk.

"Yes, nice to meet you," Fuller said.

"Likewise. Did Miranda offer you anything to drink?"

"She did not, but I'm fine," Fuller said.

"Alright."

"You have some nice looking fish here in these photos."

"Oh yeah," Barry said. "It's a nice little hobby."

"It's something we have in common."

"You like to fish?"

"I have since I was a kid with my old man. Most kids hate fishing because it's slow at times. I always loved it."

"I always like doing business with a fisherman," Barry said with a grin. "We tend to have the same line of thinking. Let's head back to my office."

Barry led the way, and Fuller spotted a few more fishing pictures hanging in the hallway that led to the rear of the office. While the general office space was clean and tidy, Barry's personal office was unkempt. There were small stacks of paper on nearly every surface. Somehow Barry had carved out about three square feet of space in the center of his desk to work. Fuller did not know how anything could be found in the clutter.

Amidst the chaos, Fuller spotted a large envelope on top of a stack of papers with his name on it. Barry grabbed the envelope and headed for his chair.

"Have a seat, Jack."

Fuller sat in the only available chair in the office. There were two others with stacks of documents on them.

"Here is your report," Barry said while handing over the envelope. There are about fifty options on there for you to dig through."

From the envelope, Fuller pulled a black binder. He was impressed with the organization of the list, especially after contrasting it to the mess he was surrounded by. Fuller figured Miranda must have been involved in putting it together. Fuller flipped through the pages of the binder at a casual pace.

"Looks good," Fuller said as he flipped the pages back to their original place and closed the cover. "What's the final bill?"

"Fifteen hundred," Barry said while handing over a hand-written invoice. Normally Barry produced bills via the computer to keep everything in order for the taxman at the end of the year. However, he did not want this cash deal going on the books. This was going in his pocket. He might throw a hundred of it Miranda's way, but that depended on whether she pissed him off the rest of the day or not.

Fuller looked at the invoice. Everything seemed in order. He had no disputes about the bill. Fuller produced a bank envelope that contained fifteen one hundred dollar bills. He had made the withdrawal yesterday after locating a branch of his bank in Cheyenne. Barry took the envelope, thumbed through the cash quickly, and set it down on his desk.

"Good doing business with you, Jack."

Fuller nodded. "I appreciate the work you did. I guess I'll be on my way."

"Say, Jack. You in town for long?"

Fuller pondered the question. He was definitely going to be staying in Cheyenne until he found "Houston who lives in the West." He saw no reason to be dishonest with Barry about this issue.

"I don't know how long it will be. The job I am here for doesn't have a set end date. I'm here until it is done, and we'll just see how long it takes."

"I was going to suggest a fishing trip if you had time," Barry said.

Fuller brightened at this idea. The pictures hanging in the hallway flashed through his head.

"That sounds perfect. Give me a call about it."

"Will do," Barry said.

Barry walked Fuller to the door. They made small talk about the potential fishing trip along the way. They did not shake hands at the door. After Fuller walked out, Barry turned to look at Miranda.

"You're going fishing with him?" she said.

"Maybe. He seems like a good guy. Paid in cash. Maybe he'd need more work done before he leaves town."

"I think it just gives you another excuse to fish in the cold. I don't know how you can do that."

"It takes patience," Barry said. He then walked back to his office and decided he would not give Miranda any of the fifteen hundred dollars. Barry grabbed the envelope of cash Fuller had given him, his coat and his briefcase, and headed back toward the front door.

"I'm gone for the rest of the day, Miranda."

"Have a good one," she said.

Barry barely heard it. He was already out the door.

1:30 p.m.

Fuller sat on the side of the road in his rented Ford. He was examining the map he had purchased at a gas station ten minutes ago, and attempting to locate the first apartment complex on Barry's list. Cars rolled by him at thirty miles per hour. Fuller found the street he was looking for, but decided it was too far away for this trip. He wanted something that was near The Cheyenne Lodge so he could check it out on his way back. His stomach rumbled with hunger, and his mind pulsed with evil thoughts. Fuller was alarmed that they rushed through his mind so frequently. He could feel himself falling deeper into the dark.

Fuller searched for the next listing, and found it to be much closer to The Cheyenne Lodge. He put the Ford in gear and swung a U-turn on the side street he was parked on. He got back on the main road and headed toward Fifth Street, where an apartment complex named Dillard Apartments was located.

After two wrong turns, Fuller found Dillard Apartments and parked in one of the four spaces reserved for visitors. From what Fuller could see there were four buildings that were each five stories tall. The four buildings, where Fuller assumed the apartments were, surrounded a smaller one-story building with a sign reading Dillard Apartments in all capital letters. Fuller figured that building was home to the leasing office, some kind of common room, and a small workout facility. The complex did not look like the one the demon spirit in Orchard Park had showed him. Fuller was not going to disregard Dillard Apartments on that alone. He was going to do his diligence and check every apartment on his list in his attempt to find "Houston who lives in the West."

Fuller estimated the apartment complex was not more than ten years old. He grabbed the black binder that Barry Munson had made for him from its spot on the passenger seat. It was still open to the page with Dillard Apartments listed on it. There was a small paragraph for each entry, which was listed below the address, phone number and rent each facility charged for a one-bedroom apartment. The summary paragraph made no mention of how old Dillard Apartments was.

The front door to the clubhouse looked like it was made out of three large wooden logs. Fuller could tell they were some kind of synthetic material made to look like wood. It gave Fuller a little less respect for the place.

A fireplace, which was not lit, greeted Fuller upon entry. Fuller could walk either to the right or the left around the fireplace; both options led to large room with a vaulted ceiling that had an atrium at the top. The peak of the atrium had windows on all sides of it. The light was shining through brightly.

To his left, Fuller saw a room with two couches, a pool table and a big screen TV mounted on the wall. To his right, he saw a small weight room. Both rooms had floor-to-ceiling glass separating them from the open area where Fuller stood. The interior made him forget all about the fake wood door he had entered through. He liked Dillard Apartments. If he were twenty-five, he would have enjoyed living here.

What Fuller did not see was a leasing office. There was a hallway to his left, and he thought he heard voices. He headed that way. Once he reached the hallway, he saw signs for a men's room and a woman's room on his left, and another sign for the leasing office on his right. The door was open and the voices were becoming clearer.

"I can't believe it ended that way," a female voice said.

"I know. I can't wait for next week's show," another, slightly higher pitched female voice said.

"This season is so good. So, so good."

"It is. It's the best season yet."

"Better than the first season?"

"I think so."

"Wow. I'm not sure. They are both so good. I didn't like season two nearly as much as season one, but season three is amazing."

Fuller tapped on the doorframe.

"Hi," the woman who belonged to the first voice said. "Can I help you?"

Both women remained seated. The office contained four desks, and looked very cramped because of it.

"Yes," Fuller said. On his ride over he debated if he would use a cover and claim he was looking for an apartment, or be up front with his request. He figured using a cover would do him no good. The only way to find "Houston who lives in the West" was to be direct. "I'm not interested in looking for an apartment, though."

"Oh," the first woman said. The woman with the higher pitched voice was looking at her computer screen. She had turned to it shortly after Fuller had knocked on the doorframe.

"I'm looking for someone, and he might live here. I was wondering if you could tell me if he does."

"Oh. I see. Well, I don't really feel comfortable giving that information out. I really don't know if I'm supposed to."

"What's your name, miss?"

"I'm Viv, and this is Michelle," she said while gesturing at the woman with the slightly higher pitched voice. Michelle peered over her computer screen at Fuller and smiled. Then she went back to looking at the webpage she was on.

The Mother Who Loved Halloween

"Well it's nice to meet both of you," Fuller said. "My name is Jack Fuller, and I'm a police officer from Massachusetts." He pulled his police ID out of his wallet. He did not bring his badge with him on the trip to Cheyenne, at this moment he wished he had.

Viv stood up and walked toward Fuller. She took the ID from his hand and examined it. She looked back up at Fuller.

"Why aren't you in uniform if you are here on police business?" she asked.

Michelle's ears perked up as she sat at her desk. She continued to look at her computer screen, so as not to stare. The conversation between Fuller and Viv had her full attention.

"I'm a detective," Fuller said. "I haven't worn a uniform in years."

She glanced down at the ID again. It was at that moment Fuller knew Viv would give in to his request.

"Ok, Mr. Fuller," Viv said. "Or, I mean Detective Fuller."

"You can call me Jack," Fuller said while taking his ID back from Viv.

"Ok, Jack, how can I help you?"

"The person I'm looking for is named Houston. I was just wondering if you could tell me if he rents an apartment here. My guess is he would live alone."

Viv pulled up a program on her computer, and Fuller could see her type Houston's name into a search function.

"Nope," she said. "There is no one here by that name. No one that's here officially at least. Sometimes people sublease their apartments without telling us. They aren't supposed to do that. They are supposed to go through us, but it happens from time to time."

Fuller immediately thought Houston could have signed up under an alias as well.

"Let me ask you this," Fuller said. "Is there anyway this person I'm looking for could have signed up with a phony name?"

"I mean, maybe," Viv said. "But it's doubtful. We require a driver's license and then a second form of ID."

"So he'd need two fake forms of ID to sign up under a phony name?"

"That's right."

Fuller knew Houston was smart, he had to be to pull off a crime like he did, but he did not think he would arrange for two fake IDs.

"I appreciate your time," Fuller said. "Thank you very much."

Viv smiled. "Anything else I can do for you?"

"Nope. That will be all. Thanks. It was nice meeting both of you."

Fuller headed back down the hallway toward the fireplace. He exited the building, and got into his rented Ford. It would have been pure luck to find "Houston who lives in the West" on his first stop. He took out a pen and made an X over Dillard Apartments in the binder Barry Munson had given him. He looked straight ahead and exhaled loudly.

Fuller started the car and drove straight to The Cheyenne Lodge. Once inside, he headed directly for The Mountains restaurant. To his dismay, Maggie was nowhere to been seen. He sat down at the bar and ordered a turkey club and a beer from a bartender who was not Tommy. His sandwich arrived quickly and he devoured it in less than five minutes time. The bartender came back over to check on him. Fuller ordered boneless Buffalo wings and a second beer. He finished those items at a more reasonably pace.

"You shouldn't have done that," Michelle said after she saw Fuller's car drive away through the window of the leasing office.

"Why not?" Viv said. "He was a cop."

"I think they need a warrant or something for stuff like that."

"Oh, no big deal. The guy doesn't even live here."

Michelle popped two Doritos into her mouth. "That's true. Megan would have gone nuts, though."

"Screw Megan," Viv said with a laugh.

Michelle nodded with a smile, and went back to surfing the Internet.

4:55 p.m.

"Got one," a man in a yellow University of Wyoming shirt called out.

"No way," the man who stood closest to him said. This man was wearing no shirt at all.

"That's not a foul," another shirtless man said as he walked over to the man in yellow.

"I got one," the man in yellow said. "He got me on the arm."

"Whatever. Ball up," the first shirtless man said.

Houston West stood at the entrance to the basketball court watching the game take place. He was dressed in a black shirt and grey sweats. A nametag was affixed to his shirt slightly above his chest. Houston had not been working at Elite Fitness for long, but he already knew the man in the yellow shirt – a member by the name of Ronald Field – was always on the basketball court. Ronald usually rubbed other members the wrong way. It did not take Houston much time to figure that out.

Houston looked at the clock on the wall, and began making his way back to the fitness floor. He walked down a hallway that held a racquetball court and two group exercise rooms. On his way, he looked through the window of a group exercise room that was getting ready to hold a high-tempo dance class. There were always a dozen or so attractive women who took that class. Houston caught a glimpse of two of his favorites as he walked by.

He made a right turn at the end of the hallway, and followed it the rest of the way to the fitness floor. Houston had his head on a swivel, looking for another black shirt to show up. After a quick lap around the exercise machines, Houston saw Katie walking toward him.

"There you are," she said.

"Ready for another closing shift?" Houston asked.

"No. I hate closing. Some of these people never get out of here on time."

"I know what you mean."

"I'm tired, and I don't feel well," Katie said. "I went out drinking last night. Overdid it a bit."

"Never a good thing," Houston said.

Katie shrugged her shoulders, "It was fun while it lasted," she said with a laugh.

"Well, I'm out of here," Houston said. He unclipped a walkie-talkie from his pants and handed it to Katie. "Have a good night."

"Thanks. You too."

Houston went to the fitness office to punch out and gather his things. He enjoyed working at the gym. It paid well and there were always people around to talk to. His co-workers were really nice, too. He had become friendly with a few of them, but not friendly enough to see any of them outside of work. Every once in a while Katie would flirt with him. Houston was not sure if she was dating anyone or not. He knew Samantha, another co-worker was dating someone, yet she flirted with Houston more than Katie did. If Houston had his choice, he would spend a night with Samantha before he would with Katie.

Houston stopped for fast food on his drive home from work. He grabbed two burgers and an order of fries at the drive-thru window, and began snacking on the fries immediately. The salty deliciousness combined with the warm aroma the fries gave off was too much for Houston to resist. By the time he reached his apartment, the fries were more than halfway gone. Houston ate his dinner while watching a re-run of a comedy show on cable. When he finished, he showered and changed into a different pair of sweats and a different t-shirt. Even though he worked in sweats and a t-shirt, they were still his work clothes. When work was done he desired nothing more than to take them off.

He sat on his couch flipping through channels. He thought of Lauren, and Samantha, and a little bit of Katie too. He was lonely in Wyoming. Houston wanted to meet people, and really wanted to date someone. He made a mental note to try a little harder with Katie and Samantha at work. Still, he had been in Wyoming for a little over two months, and was enjoying it far more than the home he had left, especially after what happened aboard the *Catiana*. Until his dream two nights ago, Houston thought he had escaped the dark demon that had been chasing him. He now feared it had tracked him to Cheyenne, and that perhaps he would never truly shake it.

-43-

November 14, 10:46 a.m.

Fuller's cellphone danced to life on the desk in his room at The Cheyenne Lodge, but he did not hear it. He was in the shower, and thinking about Joan, his fling from the Farnelli Bakery and Pastry Shop. With his mind and body elsewhere, the call went to his voicemail, where the caller left a detailed message. When Fuller stepped out of the shower he was still thinking about Joan and how good her naked body had felt against his as he draped a towel over his shoulders and wrapped another around his waist. It took Fuller a little while to check his phone as he daydreamed on the bed. When he finally did check his voicemail, he smiled, and returned the call at once.

"Barry, it's Jack," Fuller said.

"Hey, Jack. I'm figuring you got my voicemail."

"I did. I did. Fishing sounds fantastic. I don't have any gear or anything with me, though."

"Don't worry about any of that," Barry said. "I've got plenty of stuff. You can borrow it."

"Is this ice fishing?" Fuller asked.

"No, it's kind of like pre-ice fishing. There is this river I like to fish. It is not frozen over, but the water is damn cold. There are still good fish to be caught."

"Sounds great to me. When were you thinking?"

"Tomorrow if it works for you."

"Tomorrow it is," Fuller said.

"Great, just meet me at my office at seven in the morning."

"I'll see you there."

"Alright, Jack. Have a good one."

Barry hung up the phone and smiled. He took fifteen

hundred dollars from the guy. The least he could do was go fishing with him. Barry hit the intercom button on his phone.

"Hey Miranda," he said.

"Yes," Miranda responded.

"I'm going fishing tomorrow."

"Okay, will you be in at all?"

"Probably not. Don't let the place burn down."

"I won't," she said.

11:42 p.m.

Total blackness surrounded Houston. He began to walk in an unknown direction. His feet made no sound when they touched the ground below.

Before waking up from the black box of a dream, Houston saw the slightest glimmer of light on the horizon. A sentenced echoed in his head.

I'm coming for you.

44

November 15, 6:51 a.m.

Fuller stood outside of Barry Munson's office. He was wearing jeans, a sweater, and his winter coat. It was a warm day for November, and he wished he had a lighter jacket. He had not been at Barry's office long, and it was no time to be irritated, since Barry had told him to meet at seven. Still, Fuller was impatient. He had figured Barry would have arrived first. What Fuller did not know was that if Barry Munson arrived first for something, then the other people were running extremely late.

A large SUV pulled into the parking lot for the strip mall where Barry's office was, and headed toward Fuller's parked car. When it was about fifteen feet away, Fuller could see Barry behind the wheel. Fuller waved, and saw Barry raise his hand in recognition. Barry parked the car, and got out.

"How's it going this morning, Jack?" Barry said while extending his hand for a handshake.

"I'm doing alright, Barry," Fuller said while taking his hand.

"Good, good. Haven't been waiting long, right?"

"Oh not at all," Fuller said. "Maybe ten minutes."

"Good. I've got all the gear loaded up in the truck. Did you need something different to wear?"

Fuller looked down at what he was wearing, and then back up at Barry.

"I'm fine with the clothes. Do you have a lighter jacket? And maybe some boots?"

"I'm afraid I don't have any boots. I've got a set of wading boots at home, but we aren't going to be wading. We'll be in my boat. Plus home's about a twenty-minute drive in the wrong direction. As for the jacket, you're in luck. I've got a nice windbreaker in the back seat."

"Nice," Fuller said. He noticed there was no boat attached to the trailer hitch of Barry's SUV. "So where's the boat?"

"I keep it docked on the river. It's about thirty minutes from here."

Fuller nodded.

"Well, hop in," Barry said. "We'll get moving. You hungry?"

"No, I'm fine."

"Alright."

Barry surprised himself with how nice he was being to Fuller. He was not this nice to his actual friends. Barry was a crafty manipulator, and he knew it. It was not something he tried to hide. Maybe there were a couple of days a month when he seemed genuinely generous, but the people who knew Barry also knew he would scam anyone for an extra few bucks if he was given the chance. Yet on this morning, Barry found himself excited to enjoy a day of fishing with a total stranger. He was not sure why.

Barry hated fishing alone, and most of his fishing buddies had jobs they had to report to during the week. Barry had flexibility with his work time. With nothing scheduled for today, he figured it was the perfect opportunity to feed his fishing craving. Real estate could wait. With Barry Munson, real estate could always wait.

"So, Jack," Barry said, breaking a three minute span where the duo listened to Jimi Hendrix wail on his guitar through the SUV's speakers, "how long have you been in Cheyenne?"

"Today makes a week," Fuller said.

"How do you like it?"

Fuller liked it fine. He was a little frustrated that he had not found Houston yet, but he felt he was getting close.

"It's very nice," Fuller said. "I'm enjoying the people I have met so far."

"And your search? How's that coming along?"

"Empty so far, but I feel like I'm getting closer," Fuller said truthfully. "I've crossed quite a few places off of your list. It's been very helpful."

Barry had not wanted to talk about the list this early in the journey. He wanted to be out on the river with a few fish in the boat before he tried to ask Fuller for more work. Barry decided now was as good a time as any, though. The subject had been brought up.

"Anything else you need? I could provide more detail on what you have left. Maybe it will help you narrow your search."

"Thanks," Fuller said. "But I'll stick with the original. I do not think anything will narrow it now. I just have to keep knocking on doors. If nothing hits, and I run out of places to search, I'll definitely be getting in touch with you."

Barry was disappointed, but he still held out hope for Jack to contract him into more work.

"How long have you been out here, Barry?"

"I was born here, Jack. Lived almost my entire life in Cheyenne. I went to college at the University of Colorado, and I spent a three-year stint after college living in Arizona. After that I came back here."

"What brought you back?

"A woman."

Fuller smiled. Wasn't that always the case?

"Why'd you go to Arizona?"

"Same woman," Barry said with a laugh. "I chased her from college to Arizona, and when things were over I bailed back to Cheyenne. I was a real estate agent down in 'Zona too. When I quit, I came back here and opened up my own shop. Been doing it by myself ever since. And you? What's your story?"

"I grew up in a town called Hazelton, Pennsylvania. I went to college at Pitt, tried to walk-on to the football team there without much success. When I finished, I moved to Boston and went through the steps to become a cop. Eventually, I became a detective, and that's what brought me here."

"So you're here on police business?"

Fuller had told enough lies during his time in Cheyenne. He was ready to tell Barry some truth.

"Not really. I quit a few months back."

"Oh," Barry said.

"It was about a case. My Captain said we were not going to pursue it anymore. I disagreed with that idea. We had a blow up. He suspended me, and I never went back. I threw my life into the case. And, well, it's brought me here."

Fuller knew he could not explain exactly why he was here. He could not talk about the nightmares, and seeing the dark phantom in Orchard Park. He could not mention Joan and their night together. Fuller did not know how Barry would react. Fuller also knew he could not tell Barry about his thoughts of murder and vengeance. Barry would likely frown upon such ideas.

"I hope you find what you are looking for out here," Barry said. "And maybe you'll stay. I could show you a couple of places."

"Thanks, Barry, but as nice as this town has been to me, I don't think I am going to be staying in Cheyenne."

They reached the river, and Fuller saw about a dozen small boats in their slips at the dock. A small building stood in front of the dock. It had no identifying marks of any kind. It was white, and had windows. Otherwise Fuller thought it was the most unimpressive building he had seen. It was certainly blander than any warehouse or industrial storage building he had ever been to for an investigation. Fuller was actually impressed with its simplicity – it stuck in his mind.

Barry and Fuller walked around the building and out onto the dock. Once there, Fuller could see the dock was located in an inlet off the main river. The inlet was small, but easy enough to maneuver a boat in. Fuller followed Barry to the very end of the dock, where he stopped in front of a small, twelve-foot fishing boat.

"Here she is," Barry said.

There was not much to the boat, but Fuller thought she looked perfect. Big enough for four guys to fit and fish comfortably. It was free of clutter and well maintained, the complete opposite of Barry's personal office at his real estate agency.

"Very nice," Fuller said.

"She's great at what she does."

"It looks like it."

They loaded the gear into the boat – which had no name because Barry did not believe in naming small fishing vessels – and headed off. The fish were biting at an impressive rate, and within an hour the pair had landed fifteen fish. They released them all, having no plans to clean or cook any of them. Fuller felt himself relax for the first time since coming to Cheyenne. Slowly his mind drifted to thoughts of Alicia Martin. He pictured her crying on the first day he met her, and imagined the horror of her last day on Earth. He tried to shake the image he created of her daughter finding Alicia, but it held in his head for a while. It was as though the image was being forced upon him. Fuller felt his heartbeat increase, and his tension level rise. Thoughts of vengeance followed.

He took two deep breaths in an attempt to gain control of himself. Fuller felt tension on his line and began to reel it in. After a brief battle he pulled the fish into the boat. It was good-sized, his biggest of the morning. This calmed his building anxiety.

"Nice," Barry said. "They are really biting today."

Fuller was a little more at ease. Alicia Martin was no longer displayed in his mind's eye.

"They really are," Fuller said. "It's been a great morning."

The pair fished for another three hours before calling it a day. Fuller felt good, even though he knew the dark demon was still haunting him. Still taunting him. Once they were back outside of Barry's office they shook hands, and parted ways.

Fuller went back to The Cheyenne Lodge to take a nap. He was not sure if he would resume his quest for "Houston who lives in the West" today. The fresh air and fishing had exhausted him.

45

November 18, 12:45 p.m.

The Dunes apartment complex looked similar to nearly every apartment complex Fuller had been to in the last few days. Even though his list was dwindling, he felt no closer to his target than when he had started. In fact, he felt no closer to solving the disappearance of Josh Martin than he did nearly a year ago, despite all the metaphysical magic. This feeling of incompleteness only added to Fuller's simmering rage. He struggled to keep his dark feelings buried. Fuller feared they would come out when he found "Houston who lives in the West."

"May I help you?" came a female voice from Fuller's left just moments after he entered the main building of The Dunes apartment complex. Fuller had come to appreciate a well-located leasing office. He was already undertaking one miserable search; he did not need several tiny miserable searches living inside of his grand mission.

"Yes, thank you," he said. "I'm Jack Fuller, a detective from Massachusetts." Fuller took out his ID card as he said this and handed it to the woman. "I'm here because I am looking for someone, and there is a chance he lives in this apartment complex. I was hoping to search your records, or if you would prefer, have you search your records, to see if he does indeed live here."

Fuller had worked out this little speech after his third or fourth visit. There were often little variations, but the gist of the speech was the same for every stop. None of the employees Fuller had encountered had given him much trouble since he mastered his approach.

The woman looked at Fuller's ID, and then handed it back to him.

"I suppose that won't be a problem, but I would rather search the records myself," she said.

This was always the case. Fuller had not looked at a single lease with his own eyes, nor did he really want to. He only said it to give them a choice. To make them feel like they had some sort of power. It also implied that if they did not search their own records, Fuller would search them no matter what. If he was denied – which he had not been – Fuller would attempt to further persuade the employee he was in contact with. He knew he had no jurisdiction to obtain a search warrant, and no grounds to force a search. He might hint at it, and get their minds dancing with thoughts of the detectives on *Law & Order*, but he would never say he was going to get a warrant when it was something he could not do. Hell, Fuller was not officially a detective anymore. He was doing his best not to tell outright lies during his search – the fact that he was no longer employed by a police department notwithstanding. If the people he met in Wyoming assumed something that was untrue, that was their problem.

"Wonderful," Fuller said. "Thank you very much. Your name is?"

"It's Amy," she said.

"Thank you, Amy."

"Follow me," she said.

Amy appeared to be in her late thirties, and Fuller admired her shapely backside as she walked in front of him. She was short and fit. Fuller guessed she was married. She had the type of look any man would find attractive. She had short brown hair, brown eyes, and clear skin. Amy was sharply dressed, and wearing a form-fitting skirt.

The leasing office was just steps away, and Amy slid into her chair before Fuller entered. Fuller glanced at a framed picture on her desk, and sure enough, it was of Amy, a man, and a small child.

"Is that your son?" Fuller asked while pointing at the picture.

"Yup," Amy said. "His name is Alex. He's adorable, isn't he?"

"He is," Fuller said with a smile.

"So who is it you are looking for?" Amy said.

"His name is Houston. I'm honestly not sure of his last name, or maybe Houston is his last name. Is it possible to just search for Houston?"

Fuller had said the name so many times at so many different apartment complexes that he expected nothing but rejection at this one as well. He felt destined to chase "Houston who lives in the West" forever.

Amy clicked her mouse a few times, and pressed a few keys on the keyboard.

"You're in luck," she said. "We have a Houston who lives here. Houston West."

Fuller's eyes widened in disbelief. "Houston who lives in the West" is named Houston West? Could it be?

"You do? Um, which apartment?"

"Apartment 32B. That means building three, second floor, apartment B."

Fuller felt as though he were high. It seemed like Amy's words were floating into his ears from some fantastical dream. He did not think this could be real.

"Could you write that down for me," Fuller heard himself say. His brain was working on autopilot. Fuller was barely aware of what he was saying. The words "You're in luck. We have a Houston who lives here. Houston West," were still echoing in his ears.

Amy jotted the apartment number down on a slip of paper and held it out for Fuller to take. It took Fuller a few seconds to react to the simple task. A puzzled look crossed Amy's face.

"Are you ok?" she said.

Again it took Fuller a few seconds to react.

"Yes," he said. "Yes, I'm fine."

"You sure don't seem fine," she said.

Fuller nodded. "I'm alright," he said in a more convincing tone. He wanted to shout, and spill everything he had gone through to this point to Amy. He wanted to hug her and dance around the leasing office. He knew these actions would not go over well, and was able to control the urges.

Fuller tried to focus, and remain in the present. He still felt his mind drift. The entire case was suddenly laid before him, spilling out of his memory banks like spaghetti noodles crashing to the floor from a dropped pot. He saw Orchard Park. He saw Officer Jim Warner. He saw McAvoy. Alicia Martin's tearful face came next. There were flashes of his interviews with Josh Martin's friends, and moments working late in his office. All the images vanished in a heartbeat. They were consumed by a black image. It was all Fuller saw. The room was gone. It was only darkness.

"It is here," Fuller mumbled.

"What was that?" Amy said. Fuller could barely hear her, and could not see her. It sounded like Amy was talking into a pillow.

Amy was dumbfounded. This stranger was standing in front of her desk, staring off into the distance. He was nearly unresponsive. She was tempted to call the police, or perhaps an ambulance. She wanted to call someone. Or for him to come around. Amy now regretted giving in to his request. She looked at the picture of her husband and son on her desk, and felt fear rise up from her belly.

"Mr. Fuller?" she said in a loud tone.

Fuller heard that more clearly. When the words reached his ears, a shimmering light briefly punched through the darkness. It was like the picture coming into focus on a 1960s TV set. Fuller saw the outlines of the objects in the room. A desk, the windows, and Amy. Then the images quickly vanished back into the black abyss. The dark force that had led Fuller here was surrounding him on all sides. The evil thoughts that had been with him for weeks began to rise to the surface. Fuller fought to bury them again.

"Yes," he said. His response had taken thirty seconds to form.

"What did you just say? And are you okay?"

Theses words pulled Fuller out of the dark haze a little. They were stronger. The shimmering image stuck this time. The knobs were being adjusted correctly.

"What do you mean?" he said. "I'm fine."

Amy stood up and walked over to Fuller. He did not react to her movements. He did not look at her at all. She grabbed his left arm with her right hand, and he turned his head toward her.

Suddenly, the room came into view. The darkness vanished when Amy touched him. It faded in an instant, as if it had never been there. Fuller saw no remnants, and he felt fine. Physically it was as if nothing happened.

"You said, 'It is here.'" Amy said.

"No, no. I think I said 'He is here,'" Fuller paused and looked into Amy's doubting eyes. "Houston is here."

"Well he is, but that's not what you said."

"My mistake," Fuller said.

"Are you sure you are alright? You were kind of in a daze there for a second or two. I think I should call an ambulance."

Fuller could not imagine what he looked like standing in the middle of the room, and not responding to Amy in a normal way. He was fully aware that something had not been right.

"It was just surprise," he said. "That's all. It's been a long journey to this point. It was surprising to hear that he is here. No need to call an ambulance."

Amy seemed to buy his explanation, but Fuller could tell there was still a lot of doubt. She had a puzzled look on her face as she slowly sat down in her chair again.

"How do you know this is the Houston you are looking for?" Amy said.

Fuller had his doubts when she first said the name, because he did not have a last name to go on. It was the first Houston he had discovered, though, and excitement came with that discovery. The fact that the darkness had arrived shortly after the excitement confirmed in Fuller's mind that the Houston of his nightmares is Houston West.

"I just know. I feel it," Fuller said.

Amy shrugged her shoulders. If it meant that this Fuller character was going to be leaving her soon, then she was pleased. Amy did not care if Houston West of apartment 32B was the Houston this man was looking for. She just wanted Fuller away from her after his little episode. The fear that had risen from her belly was very real. She did not like this situation.

"Ok. Well is there anything else I can do?" Amy said. The second sentence impulsively jumped from her lips.

"No, thank you very much for your help," Fuller said. "I appreciate it."

"You are welcome," she said with relief.

Fuller walked from Amy's office toward the front door. He resisted every temptation to immediately sprint to the door of apartment 32B, and barge through it. He resisted the urge, knowing he needed some planning first.

After all of his searching, Jack Fuller had finally found his target. There was no magical force, no wonderfully insightful nightmare that led him to The Dunes. When he arrived, though, the dark demon revealed itself at the most shocking of times.

Fuller's detective instincts were telling him that he was close to finding out everything he wanted to know about the Josh Martin case. This made him smile. When he began he did not have a clue. He had quit his job and been led to Cheyenne by following something he could not define. If Fuller were forced to explain why he had been looking and, ultimately, how he had found Houston, he was not sure he could. But Fuller had found him, and he was ready for his saga to be over.

2:13 p.m.

As Jack Fuller walked into The Cheyenne Lodge he thought about his drive from The Dunes apartment complex to the hotel. He could not remember exactly how he got to where he was. The entire drive was hazy. His memory was failing him. His emotions were not where he thought they would be. Originally, he thought he would be euphoric upon discovering where Houston West lived. Instead he felt, surprisingly, nothing. He felt empty inside.

Maggie was not at the front desk, which disappointed Fuller as he walked by. He had not seen her much around the hotel recently. She was a good ally, even if The Dunes apartment complex was not on the short list she had provided. The elevator dinged, and a couple about Fuller's age walked out. Fuller smiled at them as he walked into the elevator.

The maid was walking out of Fuller's room as he arrived. Fuller smiled and nodded at her. She nodded in return. As he sat at the desk inside his room, Fuller was amazed that he had no urge to bang on the door of apartment 32B this very instant. It felt as though simply knowing Houston was out there was success enough. He had thoughts of packing up his belongings and flying home. It felt like the job was over.

It was fear that was driving him to think this way. The discovery that the darkness had followed him to Wyoming had shaken him. His episode in Amy's office was alarming. He was not sure what would happen if he went to Houston's door. Fuller feared another episode, and if he could not see – like what he experienced earlier in the day – then he would be defenseless against a cold-blooded killer.

At the crux of it, death was not what frightened Fuller. It was what would happen after death that worried him. He felt bound to this dark force, which he assumed was pure evil manifesting itself in this realm. Fuller feared it would claim him for its own once he died, and he would be trapped in a brutal eternity of torment.

While he pondered his death, another memory crossed his mind. It was of him being forced down to the ground in Orchard Park, with the sensation that his spine would be crushed inside his body. Fuller's body shook with fear as he recalled that night. The dark entity had commanded him to come here to find Houston, and to kill him. He had been told the act would be his release. With Houston's death, Fuller's purpose will be served.

Despite his reservations, and a persistent urge to flee, Fuller decided he would complete his quest. He would go to apartment 32B, and he would kill Houston West. The rage Fuller had been able to bury for so long rose up again, and he did not try to suppress the feeling this time. He knew he would need it to complete his final task. Fuller decided to rest for the remainder of the day and night. He knew he would need to be at his mental peak for the task that lay ahead.

Fuller got up from the chair in front of the desk, and lay down on the bed. He decided against turning on the TV at that moment. Instead, Fuller closed his eyes and tried to picture Alicia Martin. With some effort, her face came to him.

46

November 19, 3:10 a.m.

Houston West had been awake for a little more than an hour. He was sitting in his bed with his knees drawn up to his chest. His arms were wrapped around his shins. If he stretched with all of his might, the tips of his fingers could touch his sides. His chin rested on his knees. Ever so slightly he was rocking from side to side.

Houston was having a nightmare before he woke up. It was the most terrifyingly real dream he had ever had. He had been standing in a dark dimension. There were no walls, or buildings, or people. Even the ground was a deep black void. Houston had looked down, and could see his feet, but he had no idea how he was standing up on what appeared to be nothing. There was a sliver of light to mark the horizon. It was a thin ribbon amidst the darkness. It was as bright as any light Houston had ever seen.

He had dreamed of this place once before.

I'm coming for you.

As soon as he had seen it on the horizon, Houston sprinted toward light. It grew no closer, though. The light was frozen in its position on the horizon, as though Houston was running on a treadmill. He stopped and looked back over his shoulder. There were no discernable markings as a reference point to see how far he had run. Other than the burning in his lungs and legs, there was no way to tell Houston had gone anywhere at all.

In his dream, Houston decided to sit and think. He sat cross-legged in the nothingness and stared at the light. He was not sure how long he had sat there, it felt like hours. He was mesmerized by the sliver of light.

He attempted to run toward the light again, but for the second time had no success. It stayed on the horizon, despite his best effort. With this second failure, Houston decided the light was not what he wanted. He turned around and stared into the pure darkness that was behind him. Houston began to walk in that direction, and, after what felt like a good amount of time, he glanced over his shoulder to look at the light. It appeared to be fading. Houston could not be certain, but it did not seem as bright as it did before his about face. Houston continued to walk into the dark.

He stayed this course for what felt like an hour before looking over his shoulder once again. When he did this time, the light was nearly gone. He thought there was no way he had traveled farther into the darkness than he had during his runs toward the light, but apparently he had. He pressed on. After another unidentifiable amount of time and distance, Houston took a step and the ground seemed to fall out from beneath his foot, as if he had walked over a cliff. He lost his balance temporarily, but regained it in time to scramble backward. As he did so, he noticed the light on the horizon was completely gone. All Houston saw was black.

Houston got to his knees and began to crawl in the direction he thought the cliff was. His right hand was extended, patting the ground as he went. After some searching, he found the cliff's edge. Houston leaned forward to dangle his arm over the edge in an attempt to see how far the drop was. He felt nothing. There was no surface within arms reach. Houston inched his knees directly up to the edge of the cliff, kicked his feet out, and sat down with his feet hanging over the edge. He stretched his legs as far as they would go, but again felt no bottom. Houston pulled his feet up and sat at the edge of the unseen cliff.

He decided to try to find away around the cliff. Houston was thinking perhaps it was not a cliff at all and instead a large hole in the ground. Houston began to crawl to his right. He kept his left hand cupped over the edge of the cliff as he went. His palm remained flat against the ground while his fingers wrapped over the edge. This would be his reference point. As he crawled, he noticed that the edge of the cliff was completely flat, and it did not waver in angle. His hand and knees began to hurt from crawling. When he stopped to look at his hands, there were no marks or scrapes on them that he could see in the dark. It was as though he was crawling on a cushion. Houston started on his way again, and then heard a boom in the distance. It sounded like it came from miles away. Houston saw nothing in the direction of the boom. He desperately wanted to know what it was.

Before he started to crawl again, another boom rattled off to his right. It sounded closer than the last, but still he could see nothing. He stood and looked in that direction, wondering what the darkness held. Another boom struck a little more to his left. He felt the ground shake. It was much closer. Then came two more back-to-back, one closer than the last. The ground shook so much on the second one that Houston dropped to a knee to maintain his balance.

The next boom was right in front of him. It was tremendously loud. Houston covered his ears, but still found them ringing when he removed his hands. Then a bright light appeared. It was as if the brightest spotlight in history had been turned on, and it was pointed directly into Houston's face. He could not help but feel like a prison escapee in one of those old movies when the spotlight trapped him against the wall. Houston shielded his eyes with his right arm, and tried to give them time to adjust. More spotlights began to flick on from all around him, until every piece of dark space was covered in light. Black gridlines lined the ground as well as distant walls. Houston looked up and saw that what he presumed to be infinite space above him was now a ceiling maybe forty feet high. He looked back and saw there was indeed a deep drop behind him. A fall over the edge looked like it would have been more than a hundred feet.

Houston could see no evidence of explosions from the booms that had sounded. He spun around in a circle, taking in the light. When he got all the way around, he saw something in the distance. He began to walk toward it and saw that it was coming toward him as well. He glanced to his left, and saw something similar coming toward him from that direction. And then to his right he saw something similar as well. He stopped walking. The edge of the cliff was now about two hundred feet behind him. As these distant figures grew closer, Houston could see they were walking on four legs. They continued to come toward him.

As they drew nearer, Houston saw they were three of the most retched beasts he could have imagined. They were scaly, almost like a crocodile, but stood taller, similar to a lion. They had large jaws, and Houston could see sharp teeth protruding out past their lips. Tails hung from their backsides, with what looked liked giant stingers pointing out from their ends. Even though Houston was dreaming, his mind flashed to the night he killed Josh Martin. These beasts were the same he had seen moments before he snapped back into reality and saw himself pulling a knife from Josh's back. Fear brewed inside of him now, and began to drip into his veins. Houston tried to run to his right, hoping to out flank them, but saw the trio move with remarkable speed to keep him trapped in a triangle. They continued to close in.

He tried to run to his right again with no luck. The beasts were inside one hundred yards now. It was only a matter of time before they got to him. When they were about fifty yards away, Houston could see silver necklaces with a heart-shaped pendant dangling from each of their necks. When he saw the necklaces, he suddenly could not move at all. It was then that the lights went out, and total darkness returned. Houston screamed. It was not just in his dream that this scream was audible. He had unknowingly woken one of his neighbors with it.

When Houston stopped screaming, he could hear the beasts snarling as they marched toward him. The razor-sharp nails on their feet clicked on the ground with each step. Houston was still frozen in place. As much as he wanted to run and jump over the cliff, he could not move. Their pace quickened, the beasts must have smelled him now. He thought it was as though they could sense his fear. He tried to suppress it, and bury it deep inside. Houston thought that hiding his fear could somehow change his fate.

The beast to his left broke into a run. It grunted as it did. Houston then heard the other two quicken their paces. None of them wanted to be last to the feast. Houston felt a hot puff of air on his left leg as the first one came upon him. He shivered as the sensation drifted up his leg. The beast sunk its teeth in quickly, and the long, protruding fangs were driven deep into Houston's lower leg. Houston howled in pain and doubled over. His hands now touched the ground. His feet were still glued in place. The beast continued to chomp and pull at his left leg. Houston swung wildly at it. His hands were met with pain as they connected on its armored, crocodile-like skin.

Houston heard the other two beasts nearing him now. He screamed as the one attached to him continued to work at his leg. He could feel his flesh and muscle being ripped away. The beast from the middle arrived second. Houston's eyes had adjusted enough to the dark to see it from a few feet away. It leapt, and landed with its front feet on Houston's shoulders. He fell backward, and crashed to the ground with a thud. His head smacked firmly as he landed, and the pain rushed through his body immediately. For a moment it hurt so much he could not feel his leg being devoured.

Then, the lights snapped on again. For some reason they did not blind his vision this time. It was just enough time for him to see the awful jowls of the beast that had him pinned. His last image before waking was that of the sinister tail with the stinger on the end of it descending toward his chest. When Houston woke he was screaming, and nearly panting. He immediately clutched at his lower leg and breathed relief when he found it intact.

The image of the stinger on the end of the tail was still stuck in Houston's head, as well as the ferocious jaws that hung above him. Even though he was awake, his mind continued to play out the rest of the nightmare. He saw the horrific beasts feast on his helpless body. He could not shake the images, despite how much he rocked.

I'm coming for you.

*　　　*　　　*　　　*　　　*

Jack Fuller was awake in his bed on the same night. He too had been dreaming. There were no monsters or evil in Fuller's dream. He dreamed of a splendid open wilderness. Fuller was on an isolated lake, with a bright blue sky. The sun was shining, and it reflected off the lake in an array of colors that did not seem possible.

Fuller was in a boat by himself, peacefully fishing. The fish were biting and he felt no need to move the boat to another spot. Fuller kept every fish, and within a short time, his small boat was nearly filled. He smiled when he noticed how much success he was having.

He woke from the dream when he was in the middle of casting a line. His eyes had peacefully opened. Instead of staring at the beautiful blue water, he was starting at a wall in The Cheyenne Lodge. It was the first good dream Fuller had in months. He hoped it would be the first of many more.

For Jack Fuller the dreams had become peaceful, it would be reality that would bring the nightmares.

9:50 a.m.

Jack Fuller sat at the bar area of The Mountains restaurant eating eggs. He felt completely relaxed. One of the TVs suspended above the bar was tuned to a local newscast. Fuller did not hear the words the young female anchor was saying. It was not because the volume was too low. He was in a daze of euphoria. The outside world was but scenery to Fuller.

Peacefulness had become a foreign feeling for him during the last few months. No matter what he had tried to do, nothing could end the war in his head. Nothing, that is, until Amy spoke those beautiful words. *You're in luck. We have a Houston who lives here. Houston West.* Fuller heard them echo time and again in his head. Each time it seemed as though they were said more sweetly.

Those twelve simple words had wiped away over a year of frustration and self-destruction. Fuller had experienced a rebirth of some kind since hearing them. Everything around him seemed brighter on this morning, as though everything dark had been removed.

"You seem happy today," a voice from behind him said. It broke through the muted scenery, and woke Fuller up to the world around him. Fuller recognized the voice as Maggie's. He turned to look at her. A smile formed on his face.

"Now how could you tell that without seeing my face?" he said.

"It's in your shoulders," she said. "They're not slouched. You've been walking around here slouched since you checked in. And look at you, is that a smile I see?"

Fuller laughed and nodded.

"You sure know a lot about body language. I'm feeling great this morning."

"Good," she said, taking a seat next to him. "I made up the bit about the shoulders. Jilly, the hostess over there, said you smiled at her and actually said 'good morning,' earlier. That's unusual behavior from Mr. Jack Fuller."

"So you had an informer? You are not an expert?" Fuller said with a grin.

"Well," Maggie said. "I'd call myself an expert. Just not when viewing my subject from behind. I need to see their face."

"Either way, you were right. I feel great."

"Does this mean you found who you were looking for?"

Fuller took a sip of coffee and nodded.

"My time in Cheyenne is nearly done."

Maggie noticed an alarming difference in Fuller's eyes. They were absent of any red. No matter what time of day she had seen him during his stay, Fuller always looked tired to Maggie. His eyes were often bloodshot, and routinely had bags under them. Looking into his face now, Jack Fuller looked like he was ten years younger than the last time she had seen him.

"I've got to get up to the desk," she said. "My shift starts at ten."

She smiled and touched his arm as she got up from the stool next to him and began walking toward the restaurant's exit.

"It was good seeing you this morning, Maggie," Fuller said.

"Likewise," Maggie replied.

Fuller turned back to his meal. His expression soured slightly as he took a bite. His eggs were now cold.

11:44 a.m.

Sunbeams had been shining through Houston West's bedroom window for nearly four hours, but it was only now that he became too hot to sleep. He woke up with small beads of sweat forming on his brow, and his t-shirt sticking to his chest and armpits. He made his way to his shower immediately. As he turned the water on, he noticed some water stains forming on the bathtub basin at the bottom of his shower. He made a mental note to scrub those away at some point during the day.

His nightmare from the night before was still with him, but he did not feel nearly as shaken with the morning sun now around him. He found it silly now that he felt so scared the night before. The vividness of the dream was passing with each moment, and in a week or so Houston knew he would barely remember it.

When he stepped out of his bathroom, he felt cold immediately. He quickly toweled off and put on sweats and a t-shirt. He sat down at his computer, and pulled up his photo library. He clicked through pictures of his life back east. There were images from parties, and ballgames. He smiled as he scrolled through the digital memories. Houston lingered longer as a section of pictures of him and Lauren Funst came up. They were from a party nearly three years ago. Houston thought he looked so young in the photos, and that Lauren looked beautiful. She always looked beautiful to him.

His mind drifted to the night they had sex. He wished he could live in that moment forever. It was the happiest night of his life, regardless of what had infected his life afterward. He remembered the way she looked at him when he was removing her bra. She had a wry smile on her face as he did; it had escalated his excitement exponentially. He pictured her naked body pressed up against his. He tried his hardest to remember every detail, but some had faded with time. He could not recall what it felt like to kiss her, nor could he recall the scent of her perfume. He did remember the firm but soft feeling of her skin, though. The only way he could describe it was perfect. He wished he could have her just one more time. Just once more would be enough.

Houston found his phone and pulled up his contacts. He stared at her name for two minutes while lying on his bed. He typed a text message to Lauren. *Hey, I'm just texting because I miss you. I hope everything is going well.* He read it over and over, but eventually felt it would not change his mood. He deleted the message before sending it, and put his phone in the pocket of his sweats. His stomach grumbled, and he obeyed the urge by going to the kitchen to scrounge up something to eat.

3:39 p.m.

Maggie looked at the clock that hung near the front desk of The Cheyenne Lodge. She tossed the idea back and forth in her head once again. She told herself it was foolish, and she should let things run their natural course. Something inside of her was making her do nothing. She chalked it up to fear.

What is there to fear? He'll be leaving soon.

After another few minutes, she decided that indecision be

damned, she was going to do it. She walked toward the back office, and knocked on a half closed door.

"Mike," she said as she pushed the door open. "Can you cover me for just a moment. I have to run something to a guest."

Mike was one of the managers of The Cheyenne Lodge. He was in his late 40s, divorced, with no kids. He hated the way his life had turned out, and had developed a mild drug habit. One time he had feebly attempted to hit on Maggie. She did not even realize he was hitting on her.

"Sure," he said. "Give me a minute."

She walked back up to the desk and grabbed the envelope that was sitting next to her keyboard. She stuck out her tongue, and licked the seal. Mike came up to stand at the desk, and Maggie left without saying a word. He stared at her butt as she walked away. It was a habit he was trying to break without much success.

The walk to Fuller's room took a lot less time than Maggie anticipated. The final moment to back out was upon her too quickly. She stood in front of Fuller's door, and exhaled. She decided to knock.

At first she heard nothing on the other side. She knocked again. The handle moved practically at the same instant. Fuller opened the door. He was wearing jeans, but no shirt.

"Geez, Maggie, I didn't realize it was you. I was just coming out of the bathroom and I heard the knock. Let me grab a shirt."

He was talking fast. Faster than Maggie had ever heard him talk. He must have been embarrassed. She immediately thought he should not be. He looked good without a shirt on.

Maggie stood one step inside Fuller's room as he finished buttoning his shirt.

"So, what's up, Maggie?"

"I wanted to drop this off for you is all," she said while holding out the envelope. Fuller walked over to take it from her. "Open it after I leave."

"I will do that," Fuller said, and then tucked the envelope into one of the back pockets of his jeans.

"Thanks," Maggie said. She took a quick look around the room and saw nothing of interest. "Well, have a nice rest of your day." She was tempted to lean in and kiss him on the cheek. She resisted the temptation.

"I will do that," Fuller said. "You too."

Maggie nodded, and left the room.

Fuller pulled the envelope from his pants pocket and examined it. He decided against opening it right now. He put it on his desk, and made a mental note to open it later.

4:04 p.m.

Houston West looked at his cell phone again. There was still no activity. He set it down, and looked back at the TV. A minute later, he checked his phone again. There was still nothing. After drafting several messages only to delete them before sending, Houston had texted Lauren Funst about an hour ago. The message read, *Hey, I've been thinking about you a lot today. I just wanted to say I miss you. It's been a while since we spoke. I hope you are doing great.* He had tried to sound casual yet sincere. When he reread the message thirty minutes after sending it, he did not feel it put forward the tone he was looking for.

When he sent it, Houston figured Lauren would be getting out of work since it was five o'clock in the Eastern Time Zone. He figured a response would be almost immediate. He should have known better. His success rate of getting in touch with Lauren was not very high. He thought perhaps she had gotten a new cell phone and the number had changed. He contemplated sending her an e-mail, but then thought that would look like he was desperate. Houston checked his phone again, and there was still nothing. He did not know why he continued to check. The phone was set to vibrate, and was sitting right next to him. He continued to wait.

4:50 p.m.

The content of Maggie's envelope was a two-page, handwritten note.

Jack, it read.

With your time in Cheyenne coming to an end, I just wanted to tell you that it was a pleasure having you as a guest at The Cheyenne Lodge. I feel a bit funny saying this, but you were definitely more than just another customer. Sitting at the bar in The Mountains and drinking with a guest is something I never do, yet I had a blast doing it with you. I feel like we have truly become friends, and I hope you feel the same way. Because otherwise I'm going to feel real dumb if I see you before you check out and you have read this.

Take care, Jack. And if you ever find your way to Cheyenne again, I hope I will see you.

The note was signed at the bottom, and Maggie listed her cell phone and e-mail address. Fuller smiled while he read it. He wished he would be able to contact her. Whatever was going to happen after he killed Houston West might get in the way of his wish.

8:21 p.m.

The day had slipped away. Houston had not done much besides watch TV and think about Lauren. He had just finished a dinner of spaghetti and garlic bread, and he was feeling regret over accomplishing nothing. Lauren had still not responded to his message, and he stopped checking his phone after two and a half hours of worry.

He went into the bathroom to look in the mirror and noticed the water stains in the bottom of the bathtub again. He had not even attempted to clean them. Out of frustration, he walked out of the bathroom toward the kitchen. Beneath the kitchen sink he found his cleaning supplies, which included a couple of rags. Upon returning to the bathroom, he sprinkled bleach on the bottom of the tub. He dabbed one of the rags with water from the sink, and began scrubbing at the water stains. A short time passed and Houston noticed the stains were not coming out very easily. He scrubbed furiously, and found some success. Elbow grease had a way of prevailing given enough time. After about ten minutes of work, the tub looked noticeably cleaner. You could still see the stains if you looked closely, but Houston was satisfied with his work.

He put the cleaning supplies back underneath the kitchen sink, and sat back down in the living room. He felt a little tired, and the smell of bleach hung in his nostrils. He thought he might have inhaled some of the fumes. For the first time in an hour he checked his cell phone to find no messages or missed calls. Houston sulked on the couch and wondered what Lauren could be doing. Immediately he thought she was with some other guy. Jealousy bounced through his body, even though he was not sure he had anything to be jealous of. He felt a bit angry too, but knew he had no reason for that either. He and Lauren had not had any contact since he moved to Wyoming. He simply hoped for a reply. A response from her would calm his nerves.

A knock came at the door. Houston was puzzled. He was not expecting anyone. He did not know many people in Cheyenne, and very few of the very few he knew were aware of where he lived. He figured it was a neighbor of his asking for help with something.

Houston West walked toward the door, and grabbed the handle.

8:48 p.m.

Jack Fuller walked up to building three of The Dunes apartment complex with a slight tremble in his hand; like a leaf in the breeze. This was a moment Fuller had been itching for, a moment that he had dreamed of on many nights. He was surprised at how clear his head felt in this moment. There was no hint of darkness. The force that had brought him here was not present. He reached the door and knocked. Fuller heard a shuffle inside, and footsteps approaching. His pulse started to quicken.

The door swung open and there was a slender man on the other side. He was such a young kid. His hair was longer now than it was in the last image Fuller had seen of him, and his facial hair was not clean cut. He looked ravaged mentally, and perhaps high at the moment.

"My name is Jack Fuller, may I come in?"

"What is this about?"

"I have some questions to ask of you. And a story to tell to you, as well. It involves you very much, Houston."

Houston's eyes widened.

"How do you know my name?" Houston said.

"Well, I can't really say that. It was in some information I found. But it is you I am looking for. I am certain of that. So what do you say? Do you want to know this story or not? It is important, Houston. It is very important."

Houston was intrigued. He wanted to know what this stranger had to say.

"Yeah man, come on in."

"Thank you."

They walked into the living room. The TV was blaring something ridiculous. Thankfully Houston turned it down. Houston took a seat on his couch. Fuller sat in an easy chair.

"So who are you, and what's this all about?" Houston asked.

"How long have you been living in this apartment?" Fuller asked, ignoring Houston's question.

"Um, I don't know, a couple months. I moved in over the summer, so, like, six months."

"What pressed you to move? Are you new to the area?"

The detective who still lived inside Jack Fuller wanted to be sure he had the right man before doing anything else. Fuller would not need a full confession; circumstantial evidence was enough in Fuller's personal court of law.

"Um, yeah bro. I used to live out east but it is just so much more peaceful here in the mountains. I always wanted to live in Wyoming, and I just went with the opportunity."

Houston was not sure why he was answering this stranger's question. Perhaps it was boredom. Perhaps it was loneliness. Perhaps it was curiosity.

"Opportunity?" Fuller asked. "Did you get offered a job out here?"

"No, man, no. I quit my old job back east, bummed around there for about six months and then decided that nothing was working out, might as well try to change the scenery, ya know?"

Houston did not mention the *Catiana*. He figured his background went smoother without it. He still did not have any idea of how to explain his survival of the boat's sinking. Or how to explain what he had seen on the *Catiana*'s final night. He still shuddered at the thought of the dark form he had seen.

"I understand that," Fuller said, bringing Houston's focus back into the room. "I'm begging for a change myself. The last year I've just been worn down. I can't focus on a thing. Well, I can focus on one thing."

"What's that, man? That one thing?"

"Oh, I'll get to that. I'll get to that," Fuller said as he gazed around the room. The kid did not have much money, that much was obvious. Fuller's hunch had been correct. "About you moving out here. Let's go back to that," Fuller said. "You weren't running from something were you?"

Houston paused for a good thirty seconds, and stared at the wall. Fuller could see the wheels turning; Fuller had brought him back to something. For some reason Houston wanted to answer truthfully. He wanted to bare his soul to this stranger. At the last minute, he changed his mind and tossed out a cryptic answer.

"I guess we're all running from something, Mr. Fuller. I'm running from my past. Who isn't?"

Fuller pondered this for a moment. He actually agreed with it. Fuller would not hint at it, but it was a notion he understood.

"Okay kid, I think you are ready to hear what I came here to say."

With a deep breath, Houston turned and stared into Fuller's eyes. Fuller had his complete attention now. Fuller leaned back in his chair before beginning his tale. Houston was genuinely gripped by his visitor's actions.

"First I need something to drink, you got anything?" Fuller said. "Something hard. Scotch, brandy, anything like that."

Houston startled. His concentration broke.

"Oh, sure. I have some scotch over here. It might not be the best, but it gets the job done."

"That's fine, Houston. That's fine."

Houston poured two large glasses and returned to his seat, handing one to Fuller on his way. Fuller took a large gulp out of it, helping to calm his nerves. Fuller was not sure he could go through with killing Houston. He did not feel the dark demon inside of him. Murder was not on his mind.

"Alright, kid. Here goes. This story is about a woman, a mother, really. A mother who loved her children more than anything in the world. A mother who loved holidays and would decorate the house up beautifully on Christmas, Easter, Halloween, Thanksgiving, any holiday. She was an involved woman, a woman who was really part of her kid's lives. She wanted to be there every step of the way."

Houston's eyes were fixed on Fuller; his ears focused on every word.

"This woman is all I have thought about for almost the past year, kid. All day. Every day. She is a woman who I sympathized with because she went through something terrible." Fuller was exaggerating a bit. Alicia Martin had been on his mind often, but really it was Houston West, and the dark demon he brought with him, who had constantly been on Fuller's mind. Fuller felt his rage begin to form as he told the story of Alicia Martin to Houston. It was like an old wound slowly being ripped open.

Houston was engrossed. He did not know why. He was wrapped up in this story. He felt drawn to it. It was a feeling he could not fully explain, but it was something he could not deny.

"She lost a son. Her first born. He was taken from her on the holiday that she loved the most. Halloween."

That sentence hit home for Houston. He knew immediately what Fuller was talking about. Houston knew he was in trouble. He needed to buy some time to come up with a plan. His focus was still on Fuller, but panic had risen inside of him. How had he been found? What had happened to his dark protector?

"Was it an accident?" Houston said without any waver in his voice.

"No, kid. It was no accident. Her boy was murdered. And the worst part was the guy who did it came to her house and told her what happened. Only he came dressed as a cop. The mom came to the station the next morning, looking to claim her son's body and there was no body to be found. She was devastated. She did not know what to think. She thought it might be a prank. She thought it might be real. She found out that the only thing worse than discovering your first-born is dead is discovering that he might still be alive. You see, she had no closure. Which is what you need with death. You need it to be over. You need it to be complete. You need closure so you can begin grieving, begin to move forward."

Fuller paused to take a swig of his drink. His voice had been growing louder with each sentence. Houston must have heard the anger growing in Fuller's voice because the detective could tell the young man seated across from him was nervous. Fuller figured Houston had to have known what was going on by now.

"Wow, man. That is an intense story."

This would have been an opportune time for Fuller to draw his gun on Houston. Instead, Fuller felt the need to push forward with his story. He wanted Houston to understand all that he had done to the Martin family.

"Oh, it's not over yet. You see I was a detective at the station at the time. I was actually the one who walked this woman to the officer she thought came to her house that night. The officer's name was Jim Warner. The look on her face when Warner turned around nearly brought me to my knees. It was a look of confusion and there was no sign of recognition. After all, I told you it was not Warner who went to her house. Warner did not kill her kid. Anyway, I became enthralled with this woman. Infatuated, actually. I was obsessing over everything she was doing or not doing. You know anything about obsession, kid?"

Fuller was staring at Houston. Houston's eyes did not return Fuller's stare. The young man's head was down. Houston was trying to think. He needed to figure out a way out of this.

"I suppose we all know something about that," Houston said without lifting his head.

"Anyway, as I obsessed over her I also obsessed over her son's killer. We never found a body, but I always assumed that the guy who came to her house dressed as a cop had really killed her son. And I knew that guy was out there somewhere, and it drove me nuts. Sleepless nights, hours upon hours of researching clues. You see it got so bad that my superior told me I had to drop the case or leave the force. I told him I would drop the case, but when he caught me still snooping around a few weeks later, he fired me. Technically, I guess I never returned from time off. Same difference. The point is I don't work there anymore."

Fuller was racing now. He knew he did not need to say anything else to Houston. The story continued to spew from his lips. Fuller felt the dark force growing inside of him. It pushed him to keep talking.

"That's crazy, man. Crazy."

Houston was starting to fidget. He did not have the same calm demeanor and dazed look in his eyes as he had when Fuller first came through his door. Fuller could see Houston's thoughts spinning as the words reached his ears.

"That isn't the worst part of the story, though. Me getting fired is no big deal compared to the mother killing herself."

"What?" Houston said. His shoulders shook while he picked his head up to look at Fuller.

It was the first major reaction Houston had to the story. Fuller had surprised him. Houston's mind was spinning. The consequences of his actions were unraveling before his eyes. He wanted to blurt out that it was not his fault, but instead he tried to keep calm. Tried to think of a way out. Tried to think of a way to survive. The fight or flight trigger had been pushed in his brain. For a moment he saw a 1970's-style game show stage with two doors on it. They were painted red with black lettering. One said "Fight" the other said "Flight." Houston needed to make a decision in a hurry.

"Yeah. Her second oldest found her in her bed. Two bottles of pills that aren't supposed to be mixed were on the table beside her. The darkness consumed her."

The word *darkness* made Houston twitch. An image of the *Catiana* flashed in his mind. The terror of his nightmare from last night caused him to shudder. Fuller noticed Houston's reaction to the word *darkness*, and knew the young man had been affected too.

"What happened to her other kid?" Houston asked.

Houston knew there was more than one other child, but he could not say as much to his new friend. He would be caught in an instant. He figured there was still a way out of this. There must be.

"Kids, actually. She had three others."

321

"They go live with their dad?"

"No. Alicia Martin was a widow," Fuller said. "The kids live with the grandparents now. It's going to be tough. They're orphans."

Houston was silent for a moment. Fuller could tell he was thinking of what to do next. Fight or flight was still rattling around in Houston's head. He was trying to buy time for a decision.

"That's one sad story, man. One sad story. Hey, can I get you a refill on that drink and you can explain where I fit in to all this. Am I some kind of relative for these kids to come live with for a while?"

Nice try, Houston, Fuller thought. He was trying to worm his way out.

"You're something like that, kid. But yeah, get me another drink if you would."

Houston jumped up off the couch. A surprising spring in his step after such a sad story.

"Hey, Fuller, I gotta hit the can real quick, back in a flash."

With that, Fuller stood up and began to walk around the apartment, looking at the CD rack, checking out the kid's DVDs. Houston came back awfully quick, even for taking a piss. Houston had made his choice. He had opened his game-show stage door. He was unsure what prize stood on the other side.

"Alright, man, just gotta make your drink here." Houston bent down to grab the bottle of scotch and when he popped up he was dropped backwards by a bullet.

Fuller stood in the middle of the living room, staring into the kitchen, with his gun still raised; a silencer was attached to the end of it. Fuller walked into the kitchen, bent down and kicked the 9mm out of Houston West's hand.

"The scotch is on the top shelf, Houston."

Houston was not breathing well, the bullet was lodged directly below his heart. To be safe, Fuller put the gun to Houston's right knee, and pulled the trigger. A scream followed. He then put the gun to Houston left knee and pulled the trigger. That scream was not as loud as the first. Shock must have already been settling in.

"Now, we can be sure that you are not going anywhere, Houston. If you promise to be a good little boy, I promise I won't shoot you in the elbows and hands."

All Houston could muster up was a nod.

Fuller felt a strength he did not imagine he had. He felt a power pulse inside him as strong as the power of a nuclear bomb. He felt invincible. Fuller knew it was the dark demon he felt. For the first time, Fuller embraced the darkness, and let it drive him. He knew this force would lead him the rest of the way. It led him here, and it would give him the strength to do what was needed.

"Okay, then. I have one last question. What did you do with the body of Josh Martin?"

"Why?"

"Why what, Houston?"

Houston could barely speak. His voice was slightly above a whisper. His body was attempting to conserve its precious energy.

"Why did you ... tell me that story?"

"That's easy, Houston. I wanted you to understand what you had done. I wanted you to understand how your selfish, sadistic behavior ruined the lives of more than just one person. Another woman died, a good woman. Three children have had their lives ruined. And I might as well be dead. That's why Houston."

A nod of understanding is all the kid could manage while dealing with the pain. Fuller had always thought that Josh Martin's killer was full of cold blood. Fuller realized now that he was not. Houston seemed distraught, scared, and remorseful. In that moment, Fuller did not think Houston would have been capable of killing Josh Martin.

"Now, what did you do with the body of Josh Martin?"

Houston screamed. It was a horrifying scream of terror. His eyes were wide and twitching from side to side. The scream continued.

Houston did not see Fuller anymore. He saw a dark shadow in front of him. It looked like a person with no limbs. There was no head either. The only thing Houston could see that was not blacker than the blackest of night was a silver necklace hanging off what would be the shoulders of this dark shadow. From the necklace hung a heart-shaped pendant. It was a bright, almost neon, red. Slowly the red turned to black, then back to red again. Houston let out another scream.

Fuller thought maybe the pain had gotten to Houston. He could not think of any other reason why Houston had suddenly started to scream. Fuller could not see his own transformation take place. He did not know that what he felt inside of him was being projected on the outside.

"What did you do with Josh Martin's body?" Fuller asked again.

Houston's head turned to the side. He looked at the dark form that had asked him a question out of the corner of his left eye. He felt compelled to answer. It was as if he had no choice.

"I ... I ... chopped him up," Houston whispered. "Arms ... legs ... everything," the words were barely audible now, Houston was dying rather quickly. A large pool of blood was forming on the floor. It would not be long now. "Why are you asking me this? You know what I did. You were there. You made me do it."

Fuller disregarded Houston's ramblings. Perhaps Houston would not make it to the end of his interrogation.

"What did you do with the body? Confess to me," Fuller said.

"I ... distributed those ... parts all over the city. Landfills ... the rivers ... lakes ... buried some. It took a while. I ... kept him in ... this large hockey bag ... in my house. Loaded it up ... with deodorants ... the smell was ... awful. I took the last parts aboard a ship with me. The *Catiana*. I ... threw it ... overboard. The boat sank after that. You ... you sank it."

"Is that all, Houston?"

"Yes ... that's all I did. Why?"

"Because that is exactly what I'm going to do to you. Only you won't be so lucky as to be dead when I begin. You will die somewhere along the way."

Horror struck the eyes of Houston as he tried to squirm out of the kitchen. Fuller shot him in the right shin.

That scream was grotesque.

"Houston, I have to do this because it is the only way for you to feel the pain that you caused. It is your punishment."

With that, Fuller picked Houston up and set him on the kitchen table. He went down to his rented Ford and grabbed the bag of tools he had purchased from Handy's Hardware store shortly after arriving in Cheyenne. They had been stashed in the trunk. When he returned Houston had rolled off the table and crawled into the bathroom. Fuller followed the trail of blood.

Perhaps the bathroom was better, Houston. Fuller thought. *Thank you.*

Houston screamed when Fuller entered the bathroom. He still did not see Fuller. He saw only the dark shadow. Fuller placed Houston in the tub and shot him in the left elbow to ensure Houston would not be climbing out. The screams that followed were sickening enough to satisfy justice in Fuller's mind.

Houston did not see any weapons or tools. He did not hear any sounds. There was no gunshot; he suddenly felt a pain in his elbow. He felt pain everywhere, but he could not see what was going on. He only saw the dark entity. It hovered above him for ten minutes before Houston saw it grow in size and envelop the room. His bathroom had ceased to exist. Everything around him was dark. Houston felt cold on the inside. When the room ceased to exist, and only darkness remained, Houston heard the snarl of something off in the distance. All he could think of was the horrible beasts that had come for him in his nightmare. They were going to come for him again.

Fuller felt nothing but strength during his effort to kill Houston. At times, it did not feel like he was in his own body. It felt like he was high above the scene, looking down as Houston died in the bathtub. Fuller did not care if Houston's neighbors heard the screams. They did not last long. Fuller's life had ended long before this act. His sole purpose was to find Houston West and get justice or revenge or whatever it is that he needed to call it to justify killing for Alicia Martin and her son, Josh. He had been driven to this moment by a force he did not fully understand. When Fuller did not think he could go on, it pushed him, with its dark and formidable power. No one would ever understand it. Fuller knew he could not speak a word of it.

Fuller disposed of the parts in the same way Houston had disposed of Josh Martin's, with the exception of going out to sea. Fuller's final stop was at the Cheyenne Police Department, where he claimed responsibility for the death of Houston West.

47

November 21, 6:20 a.m.

After Jack Fuller walked into the Cheyenne Police Department and confessed to the grisly murder of Houston West, Sergeant Willie Pendleton had driven to Houston's apartment to collect evidence. Two other officers accompanied Pendleton – Cheryl Hansen and Ryan Hargrove. Hansen was an experienced officer. Hargrove was a rookie.

The confession would hold up in court, but every police officer knew they had to cover all their bases. Allowing evidence to become stale was a bad idea. Houston's apartment was unlocked, and immediately Pendleton could tell Fuller had not tried to clean up. There were dark stains of blood on the carpet leading to the bathroom. They led to the tub, where Fuller admitted to doing most of the damage. Dried blood lined the shower basin. Hansen entered the bathroom with a camera. She took several photographs before moving on to the next room.

Hargrove tried his best to keep his stomach under control. This was his first homicide investigation. The amount of blood on the carpet was alarming.

Pendleton stood in the bathroom and felt an odd sensation cascade over him. It was a sense of evil. He felt dread and apprehension. Pendleton tried to shake it off, yet it stuck with him for the duration of that night.

The trio collected as much evidence as they could, along with as many personal effects as they could find. One of the items was Houston's cell phone, which proved useful in contacting his parents to inform them what happened. Pendleton had made the call, and Houston's mother – Ginny – handled the news pretty well on the phone. Pendleton could hear some wavering in her voice from time to time, but she did not cry while he spoke to her.

Houston's personal effects were being kept in a small storage closet at the Cheyenne police station. Ginny had told Pendleton she was unsure if she wanted the items shipped back to her or if she was going to make the trip to Wyoming to retrieve them.

No one at the police station heard the buzz of Houston's cell phone from inside the storage closet on this morning. Lauren had responded to Houston's text message. Her message read: *Hey! I'm so sorry I haven't gotten back to you sooner. I miss you too! How are you? How's Wyoming? Are you coming home for Thanksgiving? I want to see you.*

48

June 9 of the following year, 4:30 p.m.

The day had been strange. None of the children knew how to act. They were still kids, and school had just let out a week ago. They wanted to have fun, but Macy did not feel it was right to smile and laugh. Each of them had grown used to their new routines. They moved in with their grandparents, and, with their loving support, adjusted to a new school.

Macy felt the most pain. She was on the cusp of fully understanding death when her dad had died, and this time around it was much worse. She knew growing up without parents would be tough. She knew the word that now defined her and her siblings: orphans.

Sam could not fully explain how much he missed his mother. He internalized his emotions, and tried his best to be strong. Sam kept telling everyone that he was ok. Over and over again. He figured if he said it enough, it would become true. He did not realize no one would think less of him if he shared his feelings and cried about it.

Angel cried a lot during the first few weeks after Alicia took her own life. Angel was the baby of the family, and Alicia had smothered heaps of attention on her. Angel was still very young when their father died. She did not even know him. All she knew was Alicia, her mother. After several months had passed since Alicia's death, Angel began to grow stronger. It was more out of ignorance. She had no real idea what she was missing with her mother gone. Her grandparents filled the hole Alicia left. Many times when Macy cried, she cried for Angel.

It was their grandmother's idea to visit the gravesite, a place none of the children had been to since Alicia was buried a year ago. The cemetery was a forty-minute drive from the home Cynthia and Herbert had moved into after Alicia's death. They felt it would be good to move the children to a new area, away from Vanguard. As much as they had loved their retirement in California, Cynthia and Herbert were happy to come back to Massachusetts to take care of their grandchildren. The children sat quietly in the car during the drive to the cemetery.

"We just have to go," Cynthia had said when they protested. Cynthia understood that it might be painful, but also knew it was something that needed to be done. They were still young kids. They still had much to learn about death and moving on with life.

The sun was shining brightly during the drive, and it was cooler than usual for June. Cynthia drove with all of the windows down, and the wind rushed through the shoulder-length hair of both Macy and Angel. Herbert sat in the passenger seat.

The drive seemed to go fast for Macy. She envisioned a long haul where she would think of nothing but her mother. Instead, she thought about how happy she was that it was summer time, and also about Brandon Bakes, the boy she had a crush on. When she saw the gates to the cemetery her thoughts shifted. Immediately they went back to her only other visit to this place. She felt her breath catch in her throat, and her eyes begin to well up with tears.

A road meandered through the cemetery like a perfect country stream. Cars drove slowly on it, with the passengers looking for their loved ones. It only took a few turns after passing through the gates to reach Alicia Martin's grave. Macy and Sam quickly got out of the car. Angel did not want to get out.

"Come on, sweetie," Cynthia said. "We have come all this way. Do you really want to stay in the car?"

Angel nodded that she did. Her eyes filling with tears. Cynthia leaned in and hugged her.

"It's okay, sweetie. Grandma's here. It will be ok."

Cynthia unbuckled Angel, and led her to Alicia's grave. Cynthia had spent so much time worrying about how her grandchildren would react that she had not prepared to temper her own emotions. When Cynthia looked at Alicia's gravestone she began to cry.

"Are you sad, Grandma?" Angel said.

"Yes. Grandma is sad. But Grandma is going to be ok."

Herbert grabbed Cynthia's hand and looked into her eyes. He did not say anything. He did not need to. Cynthia gained control of herself, and wiped the tears from her eyes with the back of her hand.

Each member of the family had brought something to leave at the gravesite. Cynthia and Herbert each brought a bouquet of fresh roses – one for each side of the gravestone. Angel brought her school photo, and Sam brought a ribbon he had won for first place in the high jump in his school's track and field meet.

Macy held two pieces of paper that were stapled together. It was an essay she had written for her English class. The assignment was for each student to describe the most memorable moment in his or her life. Most of the children wrote about a favorite vacation or a great gift. Macy wrote about her mother and brother.

I have two "most memorable moments" Macy wrote. *I cannot separate one from the other. It is not possible. The first is the day my mother told me my brother was dead. And the second is the day I found my mother dead in her room.*

I know when I write those words they are different from what everyone else is going to write, but it is what has happened to me. Both days were very sad. Almost every day since then has been sad. Every day I think about my brother Josh and my mom. I would like to say I remember every detail, like the weather or what I was wearing, but I do not. What I remember is how sad my mom looked when she told us, even though she was pretending everything was going to be fine.

She pretended for the rest of her life. Right up until the day she died. Some days she pretended better than others, but I could still tell she was pretending. I miss Mom and Josh so much. I miss how Josh would look out for me, and also how he teased me. He would protect me, and then make me laugh. I miss the food my mom made us, and when she would take my sister and I shopping for new clothes at the start of every school year. It was always my favorite day.

I also miss Halloween. My mom loved Halloween. That was the day Josh was murdered. This year when Halloween came up, I did not want anything to do with it. I probably will not want anything to do with it again. It used to be my favorite holiday too. Just because of how fun Mom made it. Grandma tried hard this year to make it fun, but it was not.

I wish I had something nice to say about a vacation, but it is not my most memorable moment. My most memorable moment is a tie between the days I found out Josh and my mom were dead. They were sad days, and I cried a lot on both of them. I wish I could change both of those days into something else. If I could do that everything would be ok, and two of the people I love would still be here.

Macy received an A-plus on the essay. She knew her mom would be proud of her.

She set it down next to her mother's grave. The stone read *The Mother Who Loved Halloween*, it was something Macy, Sam, and Angel had decided on. Macy kissed her fingers and touched her mother's gravestone. She would never return to it. It hurt too much.

Epilogue
The Bait and Tackle Shop

October 30, 9:30 a.m.

Fourteen years after the murder of Houston West

The cabin had cost forty-five thousand dollars. It had two rooms. One contained the kitchen, a twin bed, a small table with four chairs, the fireplace, a TV set with a satellite hookup so the owner could watch his beloved NBA games, and a couch. The other room was the bathroom. It took a little over half of Jack Fuller's savings to buy it.

The cabin was located in Barnstead, New Hampshire. He was finished with Vanguard, figuring word of murdering Houston West would follow him until his final days if he chose to move back there. Fuller planned to have fresh beginnings in Barnstead.

Fuller served twelve years and eight months of a thirty-year sentence after confessing his crime. Some days while he sat in his cell, Fuller thought he could have gotten away with killing Houston. If he had driven to the airport instead of to the Cheyenne Police Department, he likely would have been a free man. He knew freedom could mean many things. While Fuller's body would have been outside of a jail cell if he had fled to the airport, he had a feeling the dark demon that led him to Houston would still haunt his mind if he did not atone for his actions.

Once in New Hampshire, Fuller spent the first year of his regained freedom getting reacquainted with his favorite hobby – fishing. His cabin was a short walk from Half Moon Lake. There was a small bait and tackle shop with a community slip where Fuller could store his small fishing boat, another purchase he had made with his savings account. Each morning until winter crept in, Fuller would walk to the bait and tackle shop, which was named Harry's, buy some bait, and then board his boat to fish for his dinner. While not much of a cook in his previous life, Fuller quickly learned that cooking fish is not very difficult once you gut them.

Fuller had become friendly with Harry, the owner of the bait and tackle shop, and, in time, Harry extended him some hours to work in the store. Fuller did not tell his new boss about being a confessed murderer and that he was trying to start a new life in New Hampshire. Instead, Fuller said he had retired to Barnstead after being a detective in Massachusetts.

Harry caught pneumonia during the first winter Fuller was in New Hampshire. When people Harry's age get pneumonia, it is a death sentence. He died alone in his home. No one in Harry's family wanted anything to do with moving to Barnstead to run the bait and tackle shop. The profits barely covered the overhead. Fuller assumed ownership for the small fee of three thousand dollars.

Expenses living in Barnstead were small, and Fuller carved out a little slice of heaven. Peace had settled into his soul. The dark demon had not haunted him since the night he murdered Houston.

This morning, October 30, felt different for Fuller. Peace was not in him. He woke up with a creeping feeling of despair. His morning walk to the bait and tackle shop did not relieve it. Fuller's attempts to occupy his mind by taking an inventory of the items in the store did not ease this feeling either.

The bell that hung above the front door of Harry's Bait and Tackle Shop jingled to signal a customer walking in. It was Fuller's first customer of the day.

"Good morning," Fuller called out without being able to see the new visitor's face.

"Good morning," came the response. Fuller could tell it was a man, but could not see him from where he was standing at the counter.

"Let me know if you need help with anything," Fuller said.

"Will do," the man replied.

Fuller went back to reviewing his inventory sheet as the man walked about the store. When he came into Fuller's view as he walked down one of the aisles near the register, Fuller did not recognize his face. Fuller's new customer had a shaved head, and a clean-shaven face. He wore a brown corduroy jacket and jeans. Fuller nodded at the man.

After a few minutes, the man in the corduroy jacket came up to the register with a box of lures, a compass, and a knife that had a two-inch blade.

"Anything else you need this morning?" Fuller said.

The customer shook his head. Fuller looked into the man's eyes. They looked black, as though the pupil had engulfed the iris.

"Nope. This is all."

Fuller rang up the items and placed them in a bag on the counter.

"I don't recognize you," Fuller said. "And while I don't know everyone in this town, it isn't that big. I have to ask, are you new around here?"

"Yes, I am," the man said, his voice was very deep. "I'm renting a small cabin up the road. Not sure how long I'll stay."

The man leaned forward to pick up his bag of items, and as he did so, a necklace dangled out of his jacket, which was not zipped all the way to the top. The necklace was silver with a red heart pendant at the end of it.

"Well, I'll be seeing you around, Jack," the man with black eyes said.

Fuller's face turned white when he saw the necklace. He did not think it could be true. His eyes must have been deceiving him.

"How did you know my name?" Fuller whispered.

"It's written on the front door of the shop," the man said. "It says 'Jack Fuller – Owner' right below the store hours. I just figured that would be you."

Fuller nodded cautiously.

"That is me," Fuller said.

"All right, then," the man said as he turned and headed for the door. "I'll be seeing you around, Jack. Happy Halloween."

Fuller did not respond. He was frozen behind the counter. He thought of Vanguard, Alicia Martin, Josh Martin and Houston

West. He thought of the dark demon in Orchard Park, and the necklace it had worn. He thought of Joan, and her wearing the same necklace. He was sure that this man who bought lures, a compass, and a knife had been wearing the same necklace.

Fuller felt a familiar feeling creeping up from his belly.

"It's here," he whispered.

An hour later, Larry Wixbaum knocked on the door of Harry's Bait and Tackle Shop. The hours on the door said the store was supposed to be open, but the "closed" sign hung in the window. A handwritten note was below the sign that Larry thought could not be true.

"Closed for Halloween Weekend," the note read.

"C'mon, Jack," Larry said as he banged on the door. "Who closes for Halloween? Open up."

Larry knocked on the door and looked through the windows for twenty minutes in the hope of buying some new fishing lines. No one came to the door.

Jack Fuller heard Larry's calls from his seat inside the storeroom. Fuller had locked himself in there after the man in the corduroy jacket had left. His feeling of despair had grown in the last hour. Fuller had a gun in one hand, which Fuller had inherited with the store, and the biggest knife he sold in the shop in the other. Fuller knew neither weapon would be of much use if the dark force was back in his life. Still, he felt a little more in control with the weapons in his hands.

Fuller stayed in the storeroom for twenty minutes after Larry Wixbaum's last knock. Then he scurried out of the bait and tackle shop, and ran back to his cabin. Fuller thought he should stay in his small cabin until Halloween passed, thinking if he could survive until November 1 that everything would return to normal. Fuller stayed awake all night pacing in his small living room, and periodically looking out the window for any sign of Barnstead's newest vacationer.

Fuller did not want to sleep for fear of his nightmares returning. Eventually, in the afternoon of Halloween, Fuller's eyes became too heavy to keep open. Sleep swallowed him quickly. His dream brought him back to Orchard Park. A familiar voice echoed down from above.

Come find me, Jack. Come find me again.

A knock at the door of his cabin roused Fuller from his afternoon slumber. He noticed the sun was nearly set. The knock came again, with more force than before. Fuller sat up and reached for his gun when the knock came a third time. Fuller had no desire to go to the door. If the dark force was on the other side, it would have to come in and get him. Fuller would not welcome it back into his life.

There were no more knocks after the third. Fuller stood, and began to pace the room once more.

Come find me, Jack. Come find me again, echoed through his head.

Acknowledgments

I would like to thank my parents for their support in my pursuit of this dream. I would like to especially thank my mother for lending her eyes and time to edit this story, and allowing me to bounce ideas off of her.

Hannah, there is no way I would have finished writing this had you not come into my life and pushed me to keep working on it.

My extended family – if your last name is Juettner, Hopkinson, LaRose, Reinke, Shadyac or Stakulis, you have some way, somehow steered me toward creative writing and storytelling. For that, I thank you.

Collin and Alyssa, thank you for a cover that was beyond anything I could dream. I loved it from the moment I saw it.

Lastly, Professor Nicky Beer, without your class at Mizzou in the fall of 2005, I never would have had this idea. Without your suggestion, this would have remained a poem.

About the Author

John Juettner was born and raised in the Northwest Suburbs of Chicago. He graduated from the University of Missouri with a Bachelor's of Journalism. John began his writing career covering prep and collegiate athletics in Chicago's Northwest Suburbs and Mid-Missouri.

The Mother Who Loved Halloween is his first novel.

Twitter: @johnjuettner
Facebook: facebook.com/johnjuettnerauthor

www.johnjuettner.com

Made in the USA
Charleston, SC
28 November 2014